M000029576

SEDUCTION
OF A
PSYCHOPOMP

Erogenous Hand Holding and Other Ways to Tame Your Reaper

ELSIE WINTERS

SEDUCTION OF A PSYCHOPOMP

Copyright © 2023 by Elsie Winters.

All rights reserved. Printed in the United States of America. No part of this book may be used or reproduced in any manner whatsoever without written permission except in the case of brief quotations in critical articles or reviews.

This book is a work of fiction. Names, characters, businesses, organizations, places, events and incidents either are the product of the author's imagination or are used fictitiously. Any resemblance to actual persons, living or dead, events, or locales is entirely coincidental.

For information contact: https://www.elsiewinters.com

ASIN: B0B4PX7ZDC

ISBN: 978-1-7375355-2-2

Cover illustration by Amira Naval | navalamira@gmail.com

Editing services provided by Wolffe-Stoirm Publishing

For my husband—my own personal Grim.

Contents

Chapter 1

Grim

THERE'S NO SUCH THING as a real immortal.

At least, not in the way that most people assume. Those of us that live longer than memory—longer than myth—would eventually be called home to the Creator, whether by his own design or the heat death of the universe. The immense boredom of wandering the planet, even among the various planes of existence, would be too much for any of us to bear for an actual eternity.

That was what I tried to remind myself of as I stood on the wet pavement in front of a single-story craftsman house in a quiet neighborhood in North Seattle. Death—the end of one's corporeal form—eventually came for us all, in one way or another. I didn't know the name of the man who owned the house, had never met him, but as I climbed his steps and passed through the locked front door, I watched the moments he held dearest in my mind's eye. It was never the grand events that these souls broadcasted out into the universe as they separated from their mortal bodies. Not the weddings or the graduations, though occasionally the birth of a child made its way in. It was the quiet moments—the man's wife handing him a perfect cup of tea, an afternoon nap on the couch with his favorite cat, his daughter's giggles as he pushed her on a swing, the scent of the perfume that his mother had favored when he was young.

I did not know him, but in that moment, I *loved* him. Just as I loved thousands of souls that I had escorted safely into the afterlife over the years. I never knew their names, didn't know where they came from, or where they were going, but I knew them for a few brief moments. Knew the shape of their soul and who they were at their core. Saw them in their final moments and bore the duty of protecting them on their steps to the other side.

The tug of his soul pulled me through the darkened front room of the house. If I'd possessed the ability to broaden my focus, I would have noticed the favorite cat perched on the arm of the sofa, watching me as I crossed the room in silence. Or the progression of family photos that showed children becoming adults and having children of their own spanning the length of the hallway. Or the soft, even breaths from the man's wife, still sleeping peacefully beside his now unoccupied body, unaware her beloved was with her no more. But his soul called to mine, and everything else was unimportant.

I stopped at the end of their bed, one foot in the natural world and one foot in the ether. His spirit hovered directly above where he had slept, his presence illuminated by a faint white glimmer, invisible to anyone who couldn't see into the spirit realm. It's common for people who don't realize they're dead to remain in the same spot they died in, perhaps even going about the same tasks they were performing when they passed. A faint sense of relief stole through me to find that he had not gone wandering. He was still safe.

Well, as safe as a dead man could be, in any case.

My magic was already thrumming through me, wrapping my body in a cloak of shadows to keep me hidden from every-thing—except for the occasional house cat—and allowing me to step through physical objects. I drew more magic into myself and reached into the darkness around me to pull my lantern staff from the shadows, producing the nine-foot rod with prac-ticed efficiency. It was a good weapon, one I could morph into any number of useful objects, but for now I simply required its light. I planted the end of the staff on the floor and pushed my magic into it, lighting the lantern with a soft glow that mimicked the glimmer and swirl of the man's spirit. Noticing me for the first time, his essence rose higher and drifted toward me, everything in him focused on the light I held.

"Come with me," I instructed.

IT WAS STILL DARK when I returned to my apartment that morning. The air was cool and damp, with a hint of chill that signaled the end of summer as I made my way back to my one-room apartment. This unit was considerably smaller than the one I'd shared with some friends a few years ago, but after they'd moved on, I'd downsized rather than find new roommates. It was comfortable, quiet, and centrally located in the Seattle neighborhood I'd been assigned to. It also drove my mother to drink. She couldn't stand the thought of me living out here in the Void, the human world where there was no magic. I didn't mind it.

There were other assignments that reapers could take. We were often placed as guardians within the Boundlands, the magical realm that I came from. But the strongest, most powerful reapers were needed to collect souls within the Void. This place was considered one of the more dangerous for an unprotected soul, and there was something about attending to someone in their final moments here, protecting them as they made their last journey home, that engaged a primal part of me. When the request had been made, I had accepted without question, much to my mother's displeasure.

I paused in front of the door to my home, noting the familiar feel of my sister's magic, before turning the knob to enter. "Yelena," I said, by way of greeting.

"Victor," she returned, greeting me with the name that only my family or those who knew them ever really bothered to use. I had many names, and that she had chosen "Victor" over the diminutive "Vitya" spoke volumes about her mood.

Yelena was daintily perched on my couch, reading one of my books in the dark. Since neither of us needed much light to be able to see, I didn't bother to turn it on, moving to the kitchenette instead. "Cabernet?" I offered.

"Not for me, thanks. You have a very strange relationship with your friends."

I glanced up from pouring myself a glass of wine to find her gesturing at a photo that hung on my living room wall, not bothering to look up from the history of elvish languages she'd pilfered from my shelves. I lifted my gaze to the object of her curiosity—a large, framed photo of me holding my friend Levi in a bridal carry. Redecorating my space with odd objects was a common amusement for him, but he'd raised the stakes on the financial cost of his pranks in recent years. After I'd moved in here, he'd launched himself into my arms one day and convinced our other former roommate, Jordan, to snap a photograph, then had the thing blown up and framed. I came home one evening to find it hanging on my wall.

I had never been in the habit of locking doors since my entire family shared my ability to walk through walls. My sister Yelena, in particular, has no respect for any form of physical barriers, and so I'd never bothered. It was something Levi found great delight in, often sneaking in to place objects he found humorous in my space. Yelena had never seen the appeal of befriending a mortal, and most mortals found our presence somewhat disturbing anyway, so she had no real impetus to understand.

I leaned against the kitchen island as I took a sip of my drink and ignored her remark. "Why are you here, Yelena?"

"Grandmother wants to see you," she said, finally snapping the book shut before standing to replace it on my shelf.

I considered her words, watching my sister as she scanned the spines of my other books. Our grandmother was the functioning matriarch who doled out assignments within our little section of the family; this wasn't a social call. Spectral messengers didn't travel here in the Void, but she could have sent a hired runner to find me—cell phone technology was too 'new' for her to even consider utilizing it. But she wouldn't have sent my sister for me at—I checked the clock—four in the morning.

"Why are *you* here?" I repeated quietly, stressing the part she hadn't answered.

Yelena straightened from my bookshelf, flipping her chin-length dark hair behind her ear and glaring at me as she crossed her arms defensively in front of herself. "I'm making sure you don't go to this meeting without me."

I took another sip of wine before thinking better of it and draining the glass. "You know what it's about," I surmised.

"I have my suspicions." She watched me carefully as I set my empty glass on the counter. So whatever it was, she wasn't happy about it. Yelena had always been protective of me, even though we didn't have a typical sibling relationship. With age gaps as large as my family had, I didn't think anything was truly typical in our family dynamics. She'd been over four hundred years old by the time I was born and had never really seemed to know whether what she felt toward me was maternal or sibling rivalry. Stubborn as she was, I had no desire to get between her and our grandmother.

We might as well get it over with. I raised my eyebrow at her, and she stepped back to make space in my living room. My magic rose as I approached her, pulling shadows around me and reaching into them to draw out my staff, the column solidifying in my grip instantly. I thumped the end against the floor, lighting the lantern that hung from the crook at the top with its soft, flickering glow, and simultaneously ripping a hole in the veil of reality.

Most magical people who could survive traveling between the Boundlands and the Void used large, permanent Gates that connected specific cities in the two dimensions. Since reapers could make our own portals both into the Underworld and out of it, we used it as a midway point to step between wherever in the various realms we wanted.

The portal settled in front of us in a swirl of purple and blue light, opening to reveal the gently sloping bank of the

Mahajarem—the celestial river that carries souls and spirits of all kinds between the lands of the living and the dead. I held my hand out to my sister, gesturing her ahead of me, and waited for her to pass through before following behind.

Chapter 2

Grim

IT WAS SNOWING WHEN we exited the portal into the southern courtyard of my family's estate in the Boundlands, and I let my staff dissipate along with the portal behind us. Snow wasn't unexpected this time of year, as the castle had been built into the craggy slope of a northerly mountain, but the chill felt unnaturally sharp tonight. Loud clanging from an outer bailey rang through the night air as we made our way to the main keep, indicating there was a sparring match in progress even though the sun wasn't up yet. Someone was restless. My sister 'tsked' at the noise but held the door open for me with only a glare toward the bailey.

The smell of my childhood home greeted me—cold stone and warm bread—and I felt some of the tension I always carried in my shoulders loosen as I stepped inside. The familiar halls of the keep were open and vaulted. They had been updated to the Renaissance-Gothic style that had been in favor during my mother's youth, but even the original castle had been built large enough to be comfortable for someone my size. My sister was considerably smaller than me—though she was tall for a woman at just over six feet—but even she looked perfectly suited to the space as she walked beside me. At just over seven feet tall myself, I was always relieved to return to the places in the Boundlands that were sized appropriately... whether they were meant for other reapers, orcs, ogres, or giants. Humans in the Void built structures that seemed so small, comparatively.

Yelena led me past the sculpted bust of an ancient elvish

ruler whom my great-grandfather had been friendly with to a servant's staircase tucked away in the back of the keep, likely trying to dodge small talk with anyone who might be up. She swept up the stairs ahead of me, shoulders back and head held high as she turned into an upper hallway and knocked on the door to our grandmother's study. I turned a questioning look on my sister as we waited to be granted permission to enter, but she ignored me, looking for all the world as though she were preparing to march into battle. Maybe she was.

"Come."

Yelena pushed the heavy door open and paced into the study without a backward glance. Grandmother Zdenka was seated at her oversized wooden desk, writing with an old-fashioned quill in one of her ledgers, the space lit only by candlelight. I'd provided her with numerous modern pens, but she always said she preferred the feeling of a well-made quill tip as it scrawled across the page. Now, as I watched her cap the pot of ink and replace her quill in its holder, the image was charming enough to make me regret my prodding. Let her enjoy her old things.

My grandmother wasn't the soft, round, wrinkled woman that most people called to mind when they thought of "grandma". She was sharp angles with an ageless grace, a tall woman with the same raven-dark hair that she'd passed down to all her grandchildren, currently worn in a low twist at the nape of her neck. Her skin was smooth and unblemished, and to glance at her you might be forgiven for assuming she was perhaps close to my own age—somewhere in her early thirties, maybe a few years older or younger. But once you looked into her eyes there was no mistaking the millennia of wisdom she carried. Those same eyes fixed us with a familiar intensity as we entered her study.

Low burning coals in the fireplace told me she'd been in here for hours and, despite the chill in the air that her thick curtains hadn't managed to keep out, hadn't bothered to stoke the fire by adding more wood. She had servants to do such things for her, of course, but only the cooks would be awake at this hour. She was perfectly capable, but she was often preoccupied with her work.

"Well, this is a surprise," she said, lacing her fingers together as we took our places in front of her desk.

A spike of frustration flared inside me at her words. She hadn't asked for my presence as Yelena had said, and we were here wasting her time. "Forgive us. I was under the impression that you wanted to see me," I murmured, carefully trying to avoid directly implicating my sister in this breach of etiquette but knowing my grandmother would probably read between the lines anyway. I gave a small bow and leaned over to take my stubborn sister by the elbow, ready to haul her bodily from the room with me.

"Stay," my grandmother said, stilling my movements.

The look Yelena sent me was triumphant as I snatched my hand back, and the scowl I sent her only served to please her more. I was going to throttle her.

"I do want to talk to you. Though, I was waiting for a more appropriate hour to send for you." She turned a wry look on my sister, who stood silent and unbothered. As reapers, we didn't sleep much—a few minutes here and there—but manners kept us from straying too far from a normal daylight schedule, wanting to respect mainstream society's quiet hours and nocturnal habits.

I lifted my gaze back to my grandmother to find her giving me a considering look.

"I have a... proposal of sorts for you, Victor." The wryness in her expression returned and a niggling thread of anxiety wormed its way into my chest. I waited silently for her to continue as she studied me for another moment, before purposefully shifting her posture and directing her full attention to me—making it clear that my sister was not a part of the conversation. "Or perhaps a new assignment, if you're not amenable. But I would like for you to marry."

My heart rate sped up at her blunt words. I'd always expected that my family would arrange a marriage for me. It was the custom of our people. We lived so long that the choice to bind yourself permanently to another wasn't something to take lightly, and I'd heard the older generations scoff that it wasn't something they would want to leave to something so foolish as *feelings*. I knew this, but I hadn't considered that it would happen this soon.

"No," my sister interjected, her voice calm and resolute. "Absolutely not." The racing of my heart only increased with her refusal. I didn't care to be caught between the two most headstrong people in my family.

My grandmother continued as if she hadn't been interrupted, and I had to strain to hear her over the pounding of my heart. "If you're not willing to do so, then I would like for you to, at the very least, retire your position in the Void and take on guardianship of the girl while she seeks treatment for her illness here in the Boundlands."

"He's a child!" my sister interjected again, the calmness slipping from her voice.

I slid my gaze to my sister without turning my head, unimpressed with her appraisal of me. She might have been more than 400 years older than me, but that didn't mean she needed to call me a child.

Grandmother pressed her lips into an unhappy line, finally giving my sister her attention. I couldn't imagine the quarrels they'd gotten into over the past 436 years, but no doubt they were many. "Does he look like a child to you, Yelena? I seem to recall that he's been besting you in the arena since he was fifteen years old. He's thirty-two now, has spent the past decade fighting monsters in the Void, and is perfectly capable of speaking for himself."

Yelena ignored the barb about her fighting prowess, though I knew she would try to take it out on me next time we sparred. "He only gets one chance to find a mate, and you would give it away! He has the rest of his life to find someone on his own! Someone he likes."

"Like has little to do with love, Yelena. The older we get, the more set in our ways we are, and the harder it is for us to intertwine ourselves with another. You didn't want a marriage when one was offered to you, and I respected that. But I would like to give your brother a chance to make his own decision without you hovering about insisting he's somehow tied to your apron strings." My grandmother's patience with my sister's interruptions was wearing thin, and by the end of her reply her words were clipped and her tone short.

I swallowed thickly and tried to breathe past my fraying nerves. "What did you have in mind?" I asked my grandmother, hoping to keep the disagreement from escalating.

She studied my face again before answering, and I could practically feel my sister bristling beside me. "Queen Danica Morningstar of the Kingdom of the Rising Sun approached us about a possible arrangement for her granddaughter, Princess Celeste of the Dawn Court. Loathe though they are to see their precious children leave Faery, the princess is a special case. Her health is failing, and it seems no amount of treatment there is helping, so she's been placed in a magically induced stasis to buy her more time, though she doesn't have much. Since your magic would heal her, and she would provide you a nice wife, I think it could function as a lovely arrangement."

"That is preposterous!" Yelena practically shouted. "Why him? Ask Nikolai!"

To my sister's credit, my cousin Nikolai did seem like a better fit. He was 125 years old and had always seemed to draw the eye of the women around him.

My grandmother addressed my sister but never let her eyes stray from mine. "I believe Victor and Celeste would be better suited for one another. They're of a similar age, and I think it has potential to be a perfectly agreeable arrangement between our houses."

"Grandmother, mortals die all the time! Must we cry over every spent blossom that falls from the cherry tree?"

Grandmother's gaze snapped to my sister. "We do if it's our cherry tree that we've planted in our yard and tended carefully for many years."

"Then maybe we should take more care not to get attached to things that die," Yelena replied hotly.

I wondered at my grandmother's words. It wasn't uncommon for immortals to get emotionally attached to certain mortals, or even an entire family lineage. I thought of my friend Levi and his wife, Elara. From the first moment I saw her, I saw their life together. I saw their children, and their children's children, and I found I already loved these people who didn't even exist yet. Because they belonged to my dearest friend. I knew from the first moment I laid eyes on her that I would go to great lengths to care for these descendants of theirs, could easily imagine my future-self pulling strings and arranging marriages with my own descendants—if that's what it would take to ensure their well-being—simply because they were his. Therefore, I could not begrudge my grandmother her affection for this fae family, if that was what it was.

But my sister wasn't finished and sighed as she pinched the bridge of her nose. Her voice turned beseeching. "He gets one chance, Mama Zdenka. Even in an arrangement he brings a superior family line and immortality to the table. What does she bring?"

Our grandmother was unimpressed with Yelena's gentler tone. "As a princess of the Dawn Court she has a direct royal connection to the Kingdom of the Rising Sun and good genetics, Yelena," she explained as if my sister was particularly slow of mind.

"Obviously not, if she's dying," my sister snapped.

Grandmother merely shrugged, unconcerned, and waved her hand dismissively. "Victor's magic will resolve her of any pesky mortal afflictions. But she has a pretty face, and she'll make pretty babies for my favorite grandson." I nearly choked on my tongue. "She's a sweet girl and the pride of her grandmother."

"And this has nothing to do with the fact that Mom attended said grandmother when she began her reign," Yelena retorted sarcastically. *Ah, there it is.*

"Your disregard for the partiality of others smacks of hypocrisy, considering how jealously you guard your younger sibling," Grandmother replied.

I closed my eyes to block out the bickering, wishing I could close my ears as well, and then took a deep breath. This probably had less to do with my mother's attachment to the Queen of the Dawn Court and more to do with her and my grandmother scheming for a way to get me out of the Void, since the high fae were terribly vulnerable there, but either way, I'd always known that this day would come. I would never deign to shirk my duty to my family, to refuse what our matriarch thought best for us. I realized that the room had grown silent and opened my eyes to find my sister and grandmother staring daggers at each other, until they both slowly turned to pin *me* with those stares. I gave my grandmother my gaze and nodded.

"I am willing," I responded, resolving to be just that.

But what was I supposed to do with a wife?

Chapter 3

Grim

"I DO APPRECIATE YOUR personal sacrifice so that I might have a few days off work," my cousin said with a chuckle as he buckled his cloak about his shoulders. Nikolai never took anything seriously, especially if it had to do with me being thrust into a new situation. Rather, he seemed to find great joy in it, and I'd taken many lumps in the battle arena as a child while he found great amusement in "teaching me new things". At least... until I'd come into my magic and left him laughing face down in the dirt. *Small satisfactions...*

"Shut up, Nikolai," Yelena hissed under her breath. "I still don't understand why it's not *you*," she sneered at him as we stood in the southern courtyard of the castle two days after our meeting with our grandmother. Several members of my family would travel together to finalize negotiations with the Dawn Court, and the rest would attend the wedding. I was doing my best to ignore them as I waited for the elders to join us. "Why is she making the youngest marry this girl, if someone has to do it?" she grumbled at him accusingly. No one was *making* me do anything, but I wasn't going to debate it with her.

"Because she's saving the best-looking for last, dearest cousin," Nikolai responded with a teeth-baring smile as he ran his fingers through his hair with a playful flick. It was wasted on my sister, and he knew it, but that had never stopped him in the past. She was the only person he'd never managed to charm. He had always reminded me of Levi—charismatic, magnetic, quick with a sharp reply when warranted, though obviously he didn't have the underlying siren's magic that my friend carried. The thrall that Levi cast was a force my cousin could never compete with. They shared the same confidence and swagger, however, and it reminded me of the ache I felt that Levi couldn't join me on this trip.

I'd stood as best-man in his wedding, and he wasn't even allowed to *join me* at mine. The necessity of speed required us to take a portal through the Underworld instead of the Gate into Faery, and that wouldn't end well for my mortal friend. Not that the Gate would have made much of a difference. The high fae were generally unwelcoming of other mortals trespassing in their realm. Elara had promised they would throw us a party when we returned, but that wasn't what I wanted. I just wanted them to be able to witness our vows as I had theirs. Spoken words of promise imprinted on the souls of those held dearest to the speaker. Perhaps I was being too sentimental about it, but these people mattered to me. I was staring down the barrel of eternity and I wanted to share my special moments with my mortal friends. My family loved me, I knew, but as the youngest among a people who had lived for centuries among each other I'd never really felt as though I fit in entirely. Not the way I did with Levi.

"Why are you sulking?" Aleksei, my older brother, asked as he joined us in the courtyard, flecks of snow swirling about him as he moved. "Marriage is great fun. You'll see," he said with a slap on the back, which I didn't appreciate. This was part of why I liked living in the Void. Humans didn't try to talk to me. It was quiet there. No one touched me.

Nikolai barked a laugh at my brother. "Why are you wearing *greaves*, Aleksei? Do you plan to fight our way into Faery?" He took a mock fighting stance, earning an unimpressed sneer from Yelena.

My brother frowned at his leg armor and then back at Nikolai. "I don't like the feeling of underbrush grabbing at my legs, if you must know." My brother looked incredibly similar to me: tall, fair skinned, black hair, same facial shape. But where some would describe me as leanly muscled, my brother was filled out with bulky muscle and always carried a permanent five o'clock shadow.

Nikolai rolled his eyes and laughed. "You think the high fae don't have roads? We're just going to go bushwhacking through the woods to find the Court of Dawn?"

"*Holy Creator.* Shut *up*, all of you," my sister growled as my parents and grandmother exited the keep. "We can't enter at the roads anyway," she added with a grumble.

My mother shot a *look* at Yelena and Aleksei before scanning Nikolai and me with a practiced eye, her features softening as her gaze took us in. There was nothing soft about my father's gaze, though whether he was mentally listing all the ways we could embarrass him in front of the Dawn Court or calculating whatever new obligations and responsibilities he would bear to our expanding family, I couldn't say. Grandmother Zdenka wore a placid expression that could be mistaken for patience if you missed the sharpness in her eyes.

"Are we ready?" she asked, tucking a pair of gloves into her cloak, and not bothering to wait for a response. "Dmitri, if you would, please."

My father produced his staff mid step and planted it in the snow as he reached our group, opening a portal just beyond us to the Mahajarem. No boatman attended the river of souls just then, and we stepped through the opening into silence except for the slow-moving water below. Grandmother was the first one through, swiftly stepping to the side to make room for everyone on the sandy shore of the dimly lit cavern. The lights had no discernible point of origin, and they cast no shadow, which always gave the entire area a dreamlike appearance. My father was the last one to enter and allowed the purple-edged rift between the realms to close with a hasty snap. I ignored my own mild annoyance at the reverberation it caused in my chest. This was how he always operated. He immediately opened a new portal a small distance to our right, and my grandmother stepped through into Faery before it had even settled.

I followed through behind my mother, entering a large meadow with a wary glance at the melting remnants of wet snow, watching for anything that might be a danger to her. It was a pointless endeavor in her case. My mother could fully handle herself, but the need to ensure the safety of those around us was deeply ingrained in our psyche.

A thin layer of morning fog blanketed the meadow and weak beams of light filtered through the white-barked trees at the far edges of it, back-lighting the party of fae that waited to greet us. To one side, a smudge of mountains the color of bruises stretched low across the sky, and to the other there was nothing but newly budding forest as far as the eye could see. The sun's position behind the trees ahead told me it was currently a similar time as it had been in the Boundlands, but that didn't mean the passage of time would remain relative.

Humans mistakenly refer to the Boundlands as Faery, but that's because they don't know any better. The high fae had left the Boundlands many thousands of years ago and had taken Faery with them. This place was *real* but not *natural*. Time passed differently here, as Faery didn't align properly with any of the natural realms. Case in point: the budding trees signaled that it was spring here, but it was early autumn in both the Void and the Boundlands. There was no way to know how *much* time had passed until you left. One could spend a handful of days here and return to their homeland to find that a year had passed or merely a few minutes.

I shrugged my shoulders uncomfortably, trying to shrug off thoughts of my friends back in the Boundlands. It didn't matter how much time passed when you were immortal and everyone you cared about was too. But there was a small mortal child I cared about deeply back in the Boundlands, and the thought of returning to find him half grown into a man already made me feel strangely grief-stricken in a way I didn't understand.

The party waiting in the trees—lithely built high fae in full ceremonial armor, shining like glass with an iridescent sheen—rode forward on their mounts to greet us. The man at the front was the most heavily muscled, though still lean compared to most other races, with dark brown skin and tightly bound locs, and the soft purple eyes that marked his people as high fae gleamed with bright intelligence. The rest of the group bore the same willowy builds, pointed ears, and purple eyes, though they displayed a myriad of skin tones. Everything from light to dark and a few with deep greens and pale lavenders, but this was more telling of their momentary mood rather than any hint at ancestry, as they had the ability to shape shift at will. Their customs dictated that they keep their "fae" forms as a courtesy to outsiders, but among themselves they regularly morphed between any number of forms throughout the day.

"General Araton," my grandmother greeted the leader as he brought his mount toward us. They rode tall beasts called irin, which were built like a giant long-legged fox with white fur, a sloping, shaggy deer's head with branching antlers dotted with leaves and tiny petalled flowers, and a long, fluffy tail. His irin's eyes were intelligent as it eyed us coolly. Irin, much like the unicorns, would only deign to be ridden by the high fae.

"My Lady *Veardur*," the general greeted in return, using the high fae word for my people—spirit guardians—giving a respectful bow from the back of his mount.

"Does the queen think that we do not know the way?" my grandmother asked mildly as she pulled her gloves from her cloak and began to tug them on. The shadows around her feet swelled and darkened as she called on her magic to create her own mount, the rest of us immediately following suit. Our magic forced us upward in a fluid motion as the shadows grew legs and withers and necks, quickly solidifying beneath us into the dark shapes of well-formed horses. Like my staff, the shadow mounts felt solid to the touch but were disconcertingly transparent and wraith-like to others observing them. The fae took it as a matter of course, but their irin spooked and pranced in place.

"Providing the *Veardur* an escort to the palace is my honor," General Araton responded deftly to my grandmother. "And were I to shirk this honor, my beloved queen would have my head."

"I've never known her Highness to be one for taking heads," she muttered, ignoring the unhappy look my mother sent her way.

"There is a first time for everything, my Lady," he answered wryly.

My grandmother eyed him with pursed lips before giving an infinitesimal nod for him to proceed. If I hadn't known her as well as I did I might have thought I caught the briefest flicker of an eye roll.

The general led the way out, flanked by two sharp-eyed female soldiers while my family filed in behind, squeezing between trees and underbrush as we left the quiet meadow. The forest floor here was undisturbed except by their irin's recent passage and our horse's hoofs sank into the soggy ground of the old growth forest, something the irin seemed to have no trouble with as I watched their paws spread out to evenly distribute their weight as they walked. Though Aleksei was in front of us, he still managed to notice when Nikolai paused beside me to pick a bramble loose from his trousers, flashing him a childish grin.

It wasn't long before our party emptied out onto a hard-packed path. The original meeting point had been selected to be close enough to civilization while still being respectful of the fae's discomfort with having portals opened within their lands. Though reapers, or *Veardur*, as they called us, were generally welcomed and permitted unhindered passage in every land, they still disliked the idea of our portals opening and closing indiscriminately within their kingdoms.

The small path wasn't wide enough for many animals abreast, especially considering the irin's wariness of us and our mounts, but the fae still managed to slip in at the edges of our little party, as well as several more in front and behind. The dichotomy between our peoples was not lost on me; my dark-clad, shadow-mounted, taller family with exceptionally pale skin and our heavy cloaks, surrounded by the small, lean, brightly colored fae in their rainbow of skin tones and shimmering armor on the backs of pristinely groomed white mounts. I wondered if the visual separation between my wife and I would be as pronounced. Would it bother her?

"Are they... guarding us?" Nikolai interrupted my thoughts with a whisper, leaning out of his saddle toward me in an annoyingly conspicuous way.

"They can hear you, *idiot*," my sister hissed at him from behind us.

It did appear that the fae were guarding us, stationed around us and riding with a hand on their sword pommels, constantly scanning the surrounding woodlands for threats. The idea was amusing—that my family would need protection from marauding bandits or wild beasts by mere mortals—but I found myself charmed by this general and his commitment to his queen's request. I supposed it did explain my grandmother's bristling response. She could eat this general and his soldiers for breakfast and no doubt found the entire encounter condescending.

"We can go faster, if your animals can handle it," my father muttered quietly to one of the soldiers behind us. The general must have heard him, because he signaled with a hand and all the irin picked up their pace, stretching their long legs to cut across the ground more quickly. It wasn't much longer before our path connected with a major thoroughfare and we could pick up even more speed. I could practically hear my grandmother's teeth grinding with the need to go faster every time we passed through a village instead of going around, slowing to a painful crawl to maneuver around pedestrians and hawkers who stopped to stare. Even when we found flat, open roads in the countryside, we were hampered by the relatively slower top speeds of the irin and the soldier's need to rest them every few hours due to the maintained pace. It was just before midday when we crested a rise and finally caught our first glimpse of the Dawn Court's Morning Palace in the distance, and it was then that I realized my stomach was twisting itself in knots.

This wasn't the Palace of the Rising Sun, where the queen

resided most of the time, but it was still notable in its own right. Perched on the edge of a river, its spiralling white towers jutted into the sky, built of glittering stone selected specifically for its ability to catch and refract the sunlight into its multitude of hues. Draping vines climbed the sides of the towers and cascaded from the outer staircases and balconies, further softening the tumbled-stone exterior. White statues carved of the same stone soon began to dot the left of the roadside as we grew closer, men and women of some renown in these people's history, set to watch the sun breach the horizon each day for eons. I studied their weathered faces as we passed them, cold, arrogantly poised figures with delicate features currently washed out by the harsh angle of the midday sunlight. Were these ancestors of the woman I was selected to wed? Or leaders or war heroes of some kind that she'd been told stories of throughout her childhood? I glanced over my shoulder to see if my family had any noticeable reactions to any of them. It was entirely possible they'd even personally known them. But they only stared straight ahead toward our destination, faces impassive and unimpressed by the ancient carvings.

As we neared the front gates, the sound of the rushing river behind the palace finally grew loud enough to be heard over the clatter of our horses' hooves on the cobblestones, followed by the clanging of the heavy metal gates being hoisted open and the shouts of soldiers and stable hands. After several hours of listening to nothing but the rhythmic sounds of our mounts or an occasional remark by our escorts, the din was nearly deafening.

Once we were in the courtyard, my grandmother waved away a young wide-eyed stable boy who came to take her horse, releasing her magic and allowing her mount to dissipate so that it deposited her neatly on the ground. His mouth dropped open as the rest of us allowed our own mounts to evaporate in the wind, until he finally noticed the stable master yelling for him to take one of the irin from the soldiers. A swarm of palace staff ushered my family inside, up the massive stone steps and through the greeting rooms. A great hall was being prepared for us for the midday meal—apparently, we'd made better time than expected—and so we were welcomed into an enormous solarium by the royal family instead. Bright sunlight streamed through ornate windows larger than most houses, and paved pathways meandered through the perfectly manicured indoor garden full of tropical flowers that could never have grown in this kingdom's climate otherwise.

I kept to the edge of the cheerful gathering, watching the happy reunions and pleasant greetings, disturbed by the cacophony of voices and bustling servers. Trays of appetizers were offered as refreshments to our party, but I refused them because the nervous feeling in my gut hadn't abated at all. The room was very bright, and I pulled my magic around myself as I drifted farther from the group, seeking the dimmer solitude under one of the sprawling trees, hoping the light-bending properties of my shadow cloak would keep me from having to talk with anyone who didn't know to look for me.

I felt my cheeks heat when that was how my grandmother found me, seated on an ornately carved bench, watching the group's interactions from within a cocoon of my own shadows. Like I'd done when I was a child. But she didn't comment on it at all, just sat down beside me and watched with me as my family was pulled into further negotiations with the bride's family. I steeled myself, waiting for her to insist that I introduce myself to my future in-laws.

But that wasn't what she said. "I don't know why they're bothering. I've already worked everything out with Queen Danica," she muttered. "I wouldn't be surprised if your sister demands a bevy of goats in exchange for your hand."

I looked at her out of the side of my eye, but she just continued grumbling.

"Since the queen isn't in attendance yet, nothing about the arrangement can be changed anyway. Yearly visits this, weekly stipends that. What do they think we are? Savages?" She huffed, clearly as over the pleasantries and chit-chat as I was. "Aren't you hungry?" she asked me abruptly.

I shook my head slightly, too nauseated to consider eating.

"What do you want?" she asked quietly, matter-of-factly, her piercing eyes raising to mine as she studied me intently.

"I want to meet her."

Chapter 4

Grim

I<small>T HAD BEEN A</small> momentary, ridiculous hope that I might escape with no introductions at all, but at least my grandmother kept it to a bare minimum before pressing a cup of hot, honeyed tea into my hands, saying, "Drink this. It will settle your stomach." It did not.

The blood rushing in my ears made it difficult to hear the nattering, one-sided conversation kept up by the young fae girl with wispy blonde curls tasked with escorting the two of us to the royal family's residential wing. She wasn't as experienced with holding on to a single form, and shimmering, ethereal wings flickered in and out of existence behind her as she led us down halls filled with antiques and up stone stairs covered in the plushest carpet. The girl paused to knock at a polished wooden door, opening it wide when we were called to enter. There, on a massive four-poster bed laden with heavy blankets, lay my wife. Perhaps "betrothed" was the correct title, as we hadn't performed the ceremony yet, but to me it didn't matter. She would be mine, and so she already was.

I didn't see the people moving hectically about the room, rushing to put away the shimmering gown that hung in the corner, preparing poultices on the sideboard, or shooting us uncomfortable looks as they tucked her bed linens around the mattress. My eyes found the small woman with blonde hair and an unhealthy, grayish cast to her fair skin and stayed there as I took in her broken form. She was horribly ill. The circles under her closed eyes were sunken in a way that told me dehydration had been her companion for a very long time, and her cheeks were gaunt and hollowed. Her wings, a feature that every other adult fae had taken pains to hide from us outsiders, were prominently on display, crumpled things tucked beneath her as she lay resting on the bed. Small, dainty antlers arched from her brow to hold back her hair—another feature that healthy fae would never show to a non-fae. Truth be told, this sickly creature looked closer to death than many of the bodies I'd collected souls from. I couldn't imagine her suffering.

It wasn't until the servants began to trickle out, squeezing past us through the door of the antechamber in an effort to flee the awkwardness of our first meeting, that I became aware of others in the room. I was at once overwhelmed by the bustling movement and—as I lifted my gaze to take in the fierce woman with fire in her violet eyes who must have been her mother, leaning over the woman with a damp cloth to wipe her brow, looking every bit the part of a lioness protecting her cub from intruders—I was filled with regret at interrupting what felt like a private moment. My grandmother sensed my hesitation and took my hand, making it so I couldn't retreat. Though I towered over her, I was immediately five years old again, holding my grandmother's hand and trusting that she knew how best to confront every difficult situation. Perhaps I'd never truly grown out of that.

She towed me gently along with her as she stepped into the room to greet my future mother-in-law. Arresting though the crown princess was, it was her daughter that drew my attention, my gaze drifting back to her small form as though magnetized. It was a strange feeling, being this close to someone who—for all intents and purposes—really should be dead, and *not* seeing their core memories and inner psyche playing out on a loop in my mind. I couldn't see any of her past at all, and I was surprised at how much that disappointed me. Not that I wanted her to be dying, but I wanted to *know* her.

I focused my magic, poking tenderly at her spirit with little tendrils of my power. No hint of her past or her inner thoughts, and I only caught the vaguest glimpses of our future—hints of things that might be, indistinct impressions, maybe that seemed more like an unformed dream than anything coherent. This wasn't entirely surprising. I could often see threads of people's futures, though the closer I am to someone the easier it is to follow those threads. Because of my friendship with Levi, I'd known the moment I saw Elara that she was meant for him, and the image of their child, Lysander, had flickered into existence almost instantly at his conception, the shy boy clearly detailed in my mind, but the man he would someday become was fuzzy at the edges. I'd found myself already strangely possessive of the child, even before his mother had known she was pregnant. People passing on the street were much more difficult to see, the little choices that they made spider-webbing out into dozens of possible futures that may or may not happen.

Torn between the need to know her and the embarrassment of feeling like I was invading her privacy, I retracted my magic and let it dissipate.

"Don't worry, she's much prettier when she's not sick," the little fae girl said, standing at the foot of the bed and turning to me with the most innocent expression on her tiny face.

I blinked at her in horror, the heaviness of her words feeling as though they would crush my chest. As if this woman's prettiness or lack thereof dictated her value. As if I were a horse trader come to check the teeth of some broodmare to see if she was worth purchasing.

My grandmother squeezed my hand where she held it, and I flinched as her words came back to me. *"She has a pretty face, and she'll make pretty babies for my favorite grandson."*

"That's quite enough, Roxana," the older woman's voice was an icy wind in the dead of winter.

"I'm just trying to help!" the child protested indignantly.

"Go join the luncheon, please." The woman's tone made it clear that it wasn't a suggestion, and Roxana flounced out of the room with an angry huff.

The woman—Crown Princess Aurora, my memory finally supplied—cast us a long-suffering look before muttering, "Please pardon my niece. I'm not sure why they sent a foolish child to escort you here."

Because the rest of them are all bound up in debating what they think the ground rules of my marriage should be, I thought to myself, my eyes drifting back to Celeste where she lay on the bed. She looked so very small.

"Children often say foolish things, Princess. Your daughter is still strikingly beautiful, dear one," my grandmother assured her quietly, releasing my hand and approaching the bed. "Even death could not strip her of that."

I grimaced at that. Did it matter if the face you left behind held to some standard of beauty when you died? It brought to mind the image of a trampled flower, its petals crushed and stem ruined. It still had a form of beauty in that you could tell that it had once been a beautiful thing, but what stands out after its destruction is the loss. The tragedy of something so delicate and ephemeral destroyed beyond repair, pulled ever further from beauty by the mechanism of decay.

Her mother frowned, and I assumed her thoughts ran parallel to mine, until she said, "Beauty or no, I've long feared that death would steal her away from me." She took a deep breath and released it, passing the damp cloth over her daughter's forehead and smoothing down her hair with it. "Now it seems that you will anyway." Bitterness and exhaustion leaked through her words.

A knock at the door required her attention and every ounce of tiredness and pain instantly disappeared from her expression, her features a perfect mask of strength and patience. "Yes, tell them I'm coming," she told the servant. She sighed again as the young man left, the mask falling away and weariness creeping back in. "Forgive me, dear *Veardur*, and welcome to our home. I'm afraid I must attend to another problem. I trust that my Celeste is safe with you as a chaperone," she said to my grandmother, casting me a glance that was so fast I might have imagined it before departing the room at my grandmother's nod.

"Chaperone, pah," Grandmother said once she was gone, as she made her way around the bed to take a chair where Princess Aurora had been standing. "If I didn't trust you alone with the girl, I wouldn't have arranged for you to marry her." She lifted a hand to Celeste's forehead, frowned, and then dipped her fingers into the water on the bedside table to test its temperature.

I drifted closer to watch her work, carefully observing everything she did. Would I need to do this for Celeste after we were married?

She dipped the cloth into the bowl of water again and carefully wrung it out before dabbing with breathtaking familiarity at the girl's face. I supposed when you've been around dying people for a millennium, one sickbed is much like any other. Though one would think that I might feel the same, having witnessed more sickbeds, mortal injuries, and private moments in my relatively short lifetime than most people did in their entire lives, that was somehow different. I *knew* those people because they showed themselves to me. They showed those of us who could see it every corner of their souls in their last moments, and in knowing them, I loved them. But this woman, Celeste, was a complete stranger to me. I didn't know her favorite recollections, or the people who formed her earliest memories, or the shape of her smile when she was pleased. I felt bereft.

"Tell me what you're thinking, Victor," my grandmother uttered quietly.

I shoved aside my most pressing thoughts, since *"I don't know her"* was a silly thing to admit to feeling uncomfortable about in this situation, and stated another simmering concern instead. "It seems a great cruelty."

"What does?" she asked, pausing with the cloth halfway back to the bowl as she turned to study me with a startled expression.

I let my gaze fall to the frail woman's form, considering the magical stasis her doctors had placed her in to keep her from dying, though she was clearly right at the cusp. It took me a moment to find the right words. "To drag her back into the land of the living when she's already so far gone." Wouldn't it be simpler—*kinder*—to allow the natural progression of things?

"Hm," was my grandmother's only response as she turned back to whatever it was that she was doing. Neither of us spoke as she smoothed Celeste's hair behind her small antlers and then wrapped her hands briefly around another bowl next to the first, I assumed to feel the temperature again, this one full of brown colored liquid, and sniffed at it. She found a spoon on the side table, dipped it into the liquid—apparently a broth—and raised the tiniest amount to press gently against Celeste's lips. I watched with rapt attention, noting the way she held the spoon, the way she only allowed a drop at a time to enter the unconscious woman's mouth, waiting until she swallowed to add any more. "I know you're aware that sometimes babies, in the natural process of birth, get stuck in the birth canal."

My gaze snapped back to her face, though she was still focused on what she was doing.

Her voice was soft as she continued. "And these days, when they are stuck so tight they cannot pass through—when coaxing, position changes, forceps, and even magic have failed—the mother is subjected to a cesarean section and the baby—sometimes rather forcefully—is backed out of the canal by the surgeon's hands." Grandmother replaced the spoon in the bowl and used a dry cloth to dab at Celeste's mouth. "If she was ready to give up, I might agree with you," she told me. "But this girl wants to live." She frowned thoughtfully at Celeste for a moment and then tried again with the spoon. "In her anxiety and weariness, Her Highness claims that we are Death, stealing her daughter away from her after all. But of course, we are not. That is her emotions talking. We are the surgeon's hands this time, cheating death. I think we can cheat death once every few hundred years."

"As a treat," I murmured.

She flicked the briefest glance at me with a wry little grin, there and gone. "As a treat," she agreed. But then she sighed, and her tone took on a more somber note as she continued. "But just like the surgeon prying an infant out of a birth canal backward, this will be a very difficult thing. Painful." She looked at me again to see if I was paying attention, but she needn't have. I was hanging on her every word. She abandoned the spoon to the bowl of broth and turned to face me fully, gently reaching down to take Celeste's hand in her own. "The Handfasting, of course, is a painful thing for both of you." She turned the small woman's hand over and studied her palm and the veins of her arm for a beat, before simply sliding her hand against her palm and holding it in a comforting way. "Just like birth, again, the pain is a necessary part of the process, I'm afraid. But the girl..." She paused to look at her face. "She will need time to heal from this, and it will be very difficult for her."

"How will she even be able to make it through the ceremony?" I asked doubtfully. She looked as though she might breathe her last right here if it weren't for the magical stasis they had placed her in.

"They have an alchemist on staff. I'm sure they will prop her up with any number of healing draughts to get her through the ritual." Healing potions were financially out of reach for most people, but I supposed it made sense that a royal family would have their very own alchemist. Especially with a child as ill as Celeste appeared to be. They were borderline miraculous in their abilities to repair injuries and minor illnesses, viral infections, that sort of thing. But their abilities didn't always stretch to genetic disorders or magical infections. My former roommate, Jordan, hadn't been able to be healed of his vampirism once he'd been infected, for instance. "How long the potion will last, I can't say, though. I've never kept track of such things." She turned that penetrating gaze on me once again as she held my future wife's hand. "You will need to take good care of her, Victor."

I nodded. Of course I would.

"She will not be immortal immediately, and though this disease will not continue for terribly much longer beyond the ritual itself, she will still be able to be killed for several years. Your only duty during that time is to protect her."

Chapter 5

Grim

"OH, NO NEED TO knock." The next day I heard my sister's voice through the door of my assigned guestroom a heartbeat before she opened it, knowing full well I wouldn't have locked it. She held it open for a train of wide-eyed servants as they carried in covered dishes of food and armfuls of clothing. My cousin Nikolai traipsed in behind them and then flounced onto the velvet settee in the corner, watching as the servants descended on the room like a swarm of bees, straightening the bed where I'd lain for a grand total of five minutes, depositing the food trays and explaining the breakfast options, and finally encouraging me to stand from the armchair I was occupying so that the seamstress could hastily double check the final fit of my wedding attire. The entire affair took less than a minute in total and then they were gone again, flitting off to the next urgent matter, leaving me alone with my family.

My sister frowned at their abrupt departure. "These people act like they think we're going to open a portal to the underworld right beneath their feet," she muttered as she closed the door.

"You must admit, you've done it before," Nikolai stated mildly as he pilfered a wedge of fruit from my meal. I wasn't hungry anyway.

"Only to you." She breezed over to the armoire and opened it, inspecting the clothing the fae had provided for me.

"Because I'm the only person you can't beat in the training yard without cheating."

I picked up the ancient tome I'd been reading before they came in, an attempt to distract myself from my nerves, and endeavored to ignore them.

"Eh, I can't beat Vitya anymore either," she admitted, using the family's nickname for me. "But then I heard you can't either," she smirked at him. "Perhaps you should try cheating, Kolya. I hear it's very effective. Oh, these suits are *stunning*."

"What are you reading anyway?" my cousin asked, tipping my book up with a finger. He dropped it and huffed. "I can't even read that." It was a treatise on lingual drift in the high fae languages from before they had written history.

Yelena turned a disgusted look on him, and I had half a mind to open a portal to the underworld right there beneath both of them, but my mother chose that moment to walk into the room.

"Dearest Mila, thank heavens, you're just in time to save me from your daughter ranting at me for not being able to read a dead language," Nikolai said by way of greeting.

"The book is *about* a dead language," Yelena howled at him. "It's *written* in perfectly serviceable modern *Talac* which is still spoken *today* in Faery."

In Nikolai's defense, *Talac* wasn't spoken in any of the regions he'd ever been assigned to collect from, so he really had no true need to learn it. As a point to my sister, however, our kind had an affinity for languages. They were a fundamental connection between peoples and cultures, and as such they were integral for our work in interacting with the dying in a way that provided dignity and a sense of safety for those in our care. To say picking up new languages came naturally to us would be a massive understatement. It took a special kind of laziness for one of our kind to make it to the age that Nikolai had and not be able to read a single word of one of the currently utilized languages. Even if Faery wasn't a realm that he spent much time in.

My mother ignored their dramatics. "What are you two doing in here this early? Kolya, don't you have your own breakfast to eat?" She swatted at his hand as he snuck his fifth slice of fruit. "Vitya, darling you must eat something. It will be a long day."

"And a long night, if you know what I mean," Nikolai said with a laugh.

I lifted my gaze to my cousin and stared at him with open contempt. I loved my family, but I began amassing my magic to remove this one in particular from my assigned room by force. My mother hissed at him. "You haven't seen the state she's in, but that sweet child is in no shape for such things, so don't even joke." She flashed me a warning look that made me release my magic. "They're going to wake the poor dear this morning, and I can't imagine how difficult this day is going to be for her. You're always a gentleman, Vitya. Please keep in mind her state of health."

My jaw dropped open at the implication, but she ignored my reaction entirely.

"Now, I just stopped by to bring you this," she said as she approached me, holding out a small, decorative box. I took it from her gingerly, lifting the hinged lid to see the heirloom nestled in white satin inside. It was called the Twilight Star—a ten carat, emerald cut, blue diamond mounted on a gold cord necklace. The stone itself had been gifted to our family by a fae emperor three millennia ago, and my mother had retrieved it from one of our vaults at my grandmother's direction.

"Thank you. It's perfect," I told her sincerely.

"Well. I think it fitting that it be worn by the people it came from. I only wish we'd had time to have it mounted in something with more personal meaning," she demurred. "She can, of course, have it remounted however she sees fit." She gazed at the piece with admiration before smiling at me happily, all unnecessary admonishments forgotten. "Your father and I will have other gifts for her of course, but that one will be from you. Now, since you're here, Lena," she said, turning toward my sister as she moved to leave the room, "they're set to do bridal party hair just after noon. Kolya, you'll have to do your own hair," she told him with a teasing glint, giving my cousin an affectionate pat on the cheek as she passed him. "I will check on everyone later."

"I can't believe you're going to be the Best Man," Nikolai grumbled at my sister as soon as the door clicked shut. He grabbed another slice of fruit from my tray, and my sister launched a thick tendril of shadow magic at him, knocking the food from his hand before he could react.

"I'm his Best Man because I actually care about him," she retorted, taking the tray of food away from him and setting it on the bed next to me. "Stop eating all his food."

Nikolai stared forlornly at the slice of fruit on the floor. "It's not like he's eating it, and now look at what you've done. Now none of us can eat it." He flopped back on the couch. "You're not even a *man*," he groused, returning to his earlier complaint.

"You're certainly not the best," she retorted, returning to the wardrobe and straightening the clothes she'd been looking at before closing the door.

Nikolai burst out laughing, and Yelena turned to smile at him. "You know the only reason I'm the Best Man is because his little mortal friends aren't here," she conceded.

I glowered at her.

Nikolai waved his hand in the air at me. "Where is Aleksei? Shouldn't he be in here fighting for his right to lord Best Man Status over the rest of us? I've got jittery energy to burn. Do you think the high fae would mind if we took a spin in the training yard? We could battle each other for the position of Best Man!"

Yelena answered for me, knowing I had no idea where anyone was. Nor did I care, as long as they weren't in *here*. "Aleksei's wife arrived this morning with the rest of our families. He clearly cares about her more than us."

I sighed quietly. This wedding ceremony couldn't come fast enough.

THE GREAT HALL WAS cavernous, at least four stories high at its peak. Weak sunlight streamed in through the equally tall stained-glass windows behind where I stood on the dais, though not nearly as much sunlight as there would have been during their traditional morning weddings in this room. It was built facing east to catch the early morning rays, but tonight, in an effort to illuminate the darkening space, candles and fae lights cast a soft glow from their perches on the numerous balconies lining the two side walls. The timing of the evening ceremony was a display of graciousness from our hosts, a silent effort to honor the traditions of my people instead of their own. Our vows were usually given at dusk in a very small, brief ritual.

The aisle itself was relatively short, and the balconies empty—other than their lighted occupants—and while they were packed, the benches held far fewer guests than a standard royal high fae wedding would host. Their usual weddings were generally political affairs, celebrations of alliances between often warring kingdoms that lasted nearly a week in total. Multiple feasts, royal progressions through cities in both kingdoms, tournament battles, and grandiose shows of opulence. While a ceremony of this size was far larger than I would have chosen for myself, it was both a display of compromise on the fae's behalf and a testament to how quickly this marriage had been arranged. I hoped Celeste wouldn't be too disappointed in what she would surely see as a lack of ceremony for a day she might have looked forward to for years. My heart sank at the thought as I scanned the room.

The fae in the audience wore a veritable riot of colors. Every hue of the rainbow was represented in gossamer, flowing, hand-painted fabrics, and the fashions here aspired to emulate natural things like butterfly wings and flower petals. The wedding party's attire, both my sister behind me and Celeste's sister on the other side of the dais, and including my own suit, was jet black with a subtle iridescent shimmer—a choice that had clearly been another deliberate concession. A nod to our shadow magic and tendency toward darker or neutral clothing, but they hadn't been able to resist the *hint* of flair. My family sat together wearing their traditional dark, formal clothing. No, this surely wasn't what she would have expected of her wedding day.

Low notes drifted in from a stringed instrument, saving me from my spiraling thoughts. My grandmother took her cue to step up beside me. She was both our officiant and the obvious choice to perform the necessary ritual. Nervous butterflies erupted in my chest at the thought, an anxious reaction I was recently becoming well-acquainted with. I took a deep breath and released it slowly, only to have my lungs revolt as the doors at the end of the aisle opened wide. Every person in the room shuffled around in their seats to stare at Celeste where she stood in the open doorway. No one stood with her, the custom of being "given away" not one that was practiced here. The bride was to walk down the aisle of her own accord, proof that she came willingly and without coercion. I hoped.

My eyes immediately locked with hers, my heart exploding into a sprint in my chest. It was the first time I'd seen her eyes open, and I was struck by how the flickering candlelight shone in their lavender depths. She looked... better. Miraculously. Shockingly. Like maybe she wasn't even the same person I'd watched in her sickbed only yesterday. Her wings and her antlers were gone, carefully tucked away wherever it was fae kept the body parts they weren't using at the moment. Her skin was radiant and glowing, every trace of dehydration gone. Her wavy blonde hair was gathered artfully behind her head, the front strands twisted back so that they cradled the golden diadem that sat above her brow.

And her dress... My brain stopped functioning for a full two seconds while I processed it. A shimmering black gauze with a plunging neckline that ended just above her waist. I had to force myself to breathe. Thin ribbon straps held her gown on her shoulders and were connected to two long swathes of tulle that fell behind her in a cape. The translucent fabric of her bodice was gathered at her waist and fell in layers of cloud-like tulle around her feet. Radiant sun motifs were embroidered in gold-colored thread over the outer layer of the entire garment.

"Wow," I heard my sister whisper from where she stood behind me.

At a standstill, Celeste looked like the confident queen she would have been raised to be, ready to greet her court. But I noticed her hands begin to tremble as she clutched them in front of herself, and as she took her first step, she seemed a little unsteady. My grandmother's words from yesterday came back to me. *I'm sure they will prop her up with any number of healing draughts to get her through the ritual.* Her expression showed a flicker of uncertainty, and now that I was looking for it, I saw that her cheeks were still gaunt, her frame still unnaturally thin, even for a fae.

She broke eye contact with me, and her gaze darted through the crowd of upturned faces. As I watched, her expression flickered between cautiously hopeful to resigned to disappointed to... hurt? She lowered her eyes, trying to continue her furtive search of celebrants, obviously unable to find whatever, or whoever, she was searching for. Her steps were hesitant and slow, her breaths rapid. When she raised her eyes again, they were red-rimmed and poignant.

My heart was pounding as her eyes finally flashed to me and she gave me a watery smile. Her next step was an unsteady, faltering movement, and my hand twitched toward her involuntarily. By her own traditions she was supposed to walk the aisle by herself, but every precarious step had me nearly leaving my place to ensure she didn't fall in front of all these people. By the time she reached the dais, I was unable to stop myself from reaching down to help her up the final two steps to the platform. A single tear fell from her eyes as she climbed the steps, its track leaving a mark down her cheek. My heart shattered into a thousand pieces.

She was *clearly* upset about the wedding—or marrying me. I hadn't even thought of how trapped she might feel: marry an unknown reaper or die. I couldn't breathe. Maybe she hadn't even been aware she was to marry me until they'd woken her up this morning and she was still in shock at the idea. Maybe she didn't want this at all. I had to know.

I bent close to her, keenly aware of the hundreds of eyes staring at us from the dozens of benches behind me, and spoke as quietly as I could. She shivered as my lips brushed the shell of her ear. "Is this what you want?"

Her expression was startled and horribly embarrassed, but she didn't respond, simply stared at me in confusion.

I tried again, quiet as a breath. "You don't have to do this," I told her sincerely. "You can walk away right now if this isn't what you want." The thought that she might be standing here holding my hand unwillingly made my stomach churn.

But she tightened her fingers briefly on mine and her voice was quick this time as comprehension dawned. "No, I want this. Thank you." Her whisper was strained, as if she hadn't used her voice in a very long time. She flashed me a consolatory but still watery smile. I didn't feel consoled.

Perhaps it wasn't the marriage that she found objectionable, but the wedding ceremony itself. I glanced at the crowd. To any fae with knowledge of royal customs it would be obvious that this was a rushed affair. Maybe there were people she'd wanted to be here who couldn't make it in time. Or maybe she'd dreamed of the entire elaborate week-long ceremony, something she clearly wouldn't be able to withstand in her current health, even if her family had managed to cobble it together in time. Or her dress... I'd never seen a garment that stole my breath the way this had. Now that she stood next to me, I could see that the back was open all the way down to the curve of her rump and the cape stretched behind her in two separate strips, gathered at the tops and spreading out as they trailed below. But it was black, and maybe she had wanted something more colorful like the rest of her people.

I couldn't change today, but I could give her whatever celebration she wanted once she was well.

She squeezed my hand again, and I found her to be a little more composed, her smile a little more encouraging, even if it didn't reach her eyes. She turned toward my grandmother, so I followed her lead, hoping that she knew what she was doing.

Maybe... maybe she just didn't feel well. She didn't release my hand, so I continued to hold it, grateful for this small connection to her in the face of her uncertainty.

My grandmother silently studied both of our faces before coming to some satisfactory conclusion and reaching to take each of our free hands. She spoke a blessing over us in one of our old languages, and then switched to the predominant language of the fae, delivering an opening to the ceremony and a bid to the Creator for his approval of our joining. And then, raising her voice so that even those in the farthest reaches of the room could hear her, began the opening words of the ritual, modified slightly with brief explanations for our hosts. "The *souls* of all men, both mortal and immortal, are everlasting. They are a spark within us that does not grow old or wear out. They cannot be killed and do not fade away. They *persist* forever. So too, is the blood of my people, whom you call *Veardur*. Long ago when the ancients first walked the earth, we were set apart by the Creator in service of the souls of his beloved mortals, our lives for his purpose. As a benevolent concession for this submission to his desire, he acknowledged that a life of immortality presents a problem in selecting a mate. In response, he granted us a gift. Each of us carries in our blood the power to secure for ourselves a *single* helpmate, someone to walk beside us in our eternal duty, to make that which was mortal, immortal through our living vows. Through the gift of our blood this night, Princess Celeste will join us in supporting Victor in his duty to all mankind."

She paused to take a breath before addressing my companion, her voice still raised to carry throughout the room. "Her Royal Highness Celeste Morningstar, Princess of the Dawn Court, Daughter of Her Excellency Crown Princess Aurora of the House of First Light, Granddaughter of Her Majesty Queen Danica of the Kingdom of the Rising Sun, do you know who this is?" she asked, gesturing to me.

"Yes," Celeste answered, her voice still hoarse. "He is Victor of House Molchanov." The first time I'd heard my name on her lips.

"And do you take him to be your husband?"

"I do." Her voice was still rough, but those two words possessed a confidence that loosened my lungs just the tiniest amount. Every muscle in my body was still strung as taut as a bowstring.

My grandmother looked to me. *"Veardur,* Victor of House Molchanov, son of Dmitri, son of Ratimir, son of Kallistrat, son of Malkh, do you know who this is?"

I swallowed thickly before answering. "Yes. She is Celeste of House Morningstar."

My grandmother's face took on a pleased softness that I was unused to seeing on her person. "And do you take her to be your wife?" she asked, with the smallest hint of a smile.

"I do," I answered as clearly as I could.

Grandmother nodded once, releasing our hands and stepping back to allow us to speak our own words if we wished. I took Celeste's other hand in mine, holding both of them and facing her in front of the crowd. She took a bracing breath and raised her eyes to mine.

"I, Celeste, vow to you, Victor, to turn my face to you every morning just as the sun turns to us, to go where you go, to take your people as my own, and to support you as your wife, 'til d—" She faltered for half a beat, clearly about to speak her people's traditional, "'til death do us part" before catching herself. "Forevermore," she finished instead, the word sounding breathy and uncertain.

I spoke the words of my own people, hoping they were enough. "I, Victor, grant you, Celeste, my shelter, my protection, my service, my immortality, and my commitment to be yours in my entirety, from now into eternity." In whatever way she wanted, be that as a friend or a husband. Whatever pleased her and made her feel safe.

I released her left hand, reaching behind me to take my wedding gift from my sister, and noticed immediately that Celeste leaned more of her weight on me where she held my left hand in her right. I abandoned my attempt for the box, stepping closer to Celeste so that I could brace her up without being noticed as easily.

"Open it, Lena," I murmured to her.

And bless her, she did, opening the box and retrieving the necklace for me so that I could hang the Twilight Star around Celeste's neck with only one hand. Several people in the audience gasped as I held it aloft, but I couldn't tell from where because I was trying to focus. I was careful, so careful, not to disturb her hair or pointed ear tips as I looped the golden chain around her head and settled the stone below her collarbone. The blue diamond gleamed even more brightly than the wearer's eyes.

She gave a shallow curtsy, gripping my fingers even more tightly as she did, and then reached to accept something from her sister. It was a thin golden diadem, a match for the one she currently wore, and I bowed to accept her placement of the circlet on my head. When I rose, she seemed a little more at ease, admiring the diadem she'd placed on me and watching my face for my reaction.

"Thank you," I murmured with a shallow bow. I didn't miss the way her left hand wandered up to touch the Twilight Star where it hung on her chest, and I couldn't help the hint of a smile that formed at the sight of her timid show of appreciation. I could shower her with any number of gifts if they were something that brought her joy.

I glanced up when my grandmother turned away to the large stone altar behind her to prepare the knife and binding cloth. I removed my outer jacket and handed it to my sister as swiftly as I could, careful to make sure that Celeste was able to remain standing on her own while I did. My sister was kind enough to step forward and cuff up the sleeve of my left arm for me, since that would leave Celeste without support for longer.

"Does it hurt?" Celeste whispered to me when Yelena had taken her place again.

I looked down at her small face, watching her luminous eyes as she watched my grandmother's preparations. "Yes," I answered her honestly. It would be even more painful for her than it would be for me, as my magic worked its way through her body and fought off the illness that wracked her. "Don't look when she cuts you," I warned her. I was prepared to catch her if she fainted, but it would be a difficult task while our arms were bound.

Grandmother turned back to us, knife in one upturned hand and the long, gold-colored strip of linen in the other, and nodded to me. I took hold of my magic, just enough to be able to control the shadows or create a portal, and saw the cloak of shadows begin stretching down toward the floor from my shoulders. She twitched the fingers of her hand closest to me upward, a sign that she wanted more, and then did it again, and again as I continued to draw in more power. I held more magic in that moment than I'd ever held in my life, feeling power beginning to rend out of me in streams of swirling darkness that made the candles around us flicker wildly. My cloak stretched down past the steps of the dais and out into the aisle, the edges of it roiling and turbulent, unable to settle into place. In the back of my mind, I heard loud gasps echoing throughout the chamber from the fae side of the room, but they seemed very distant from within my storm of magic. Reality seemed to fade in and out of existence around me as it overlapped with the spirit world.

My grandmother gave the slightest nod to tell me it was enough and reached for my exposed left arm, taking my wrist gently in the hand that held the cloth. My gaze darted to Celeste to find her staring at me with open fear. No, not just at me—at my eyes. I closed them briefly, remembering suddenly that she had probably never seen a reaper hold any large quantity of magic and wouldn't have expected the white haze that covered over our eyes when we did.

"It's still me," I whispered to her gently.

She heaved a shuddering breath and seemed to come back to herself, remembering the audience and swallowing down her fear.

I waited a few more seconds for her to regain her composure and then looked to my grandmother, who stood patiently with my wrist in her hand, and nodded for her to continue.

She placed the tip of the knife against my inner forearm and sliced downward, heedless of the veins and tissue as she cut, knowing I could heal myself before I bled out. She spoke as she cut, and pain lanced through me as I refused to allow my body to knit itself back together. "With this gift of blood, you gain an equal partner to walk with as you step into the dark unknown of endless ages." Blood welled up and dripped onto the carpet in front of me.

Celeste's breaths came faster.

I reached under her exposed arm with my cut one to allow her to lean against me, then reached across with my right hand to touch her jaw, pulling her face toward mine. "Don't look," I reminded her, willing her to look at me while she trembled and shook with pain. I supported her weight as she flinched involuntarily in her body's attempt to pull away from the pain of the knife cutting her flesh.

"With his blood you are welcomed into the gift and the duty of our people: immortality and the service of the mortal world."

I felt the cloth loop under our arms and knew the pain was about to become infinitely worse for her. "Forgive me," I whispered to Celeste as my grandmother turned our arms and pressed our open wounds together to allow the blood to mix. I took her right hand into my left and laced our fingers together tightly.

"May it strengthen your body and fortify your soul as you stand with your helpmate against the ravages of time. And when the worlds around you change so as to become unrecognizable, may you always turn within to find each other, a familiarity, and a comfort within the divine spark of your own souls, knit together in this moment and bound as one forevermore."

I didn't even wait for my grandmother to finish knotting the cloth around our arms, the symbolism less important to me than sparing Celeste even one unnecessary second of pain. I poured my energy and power through the opening in my arm into her, doing my best to throttle the flow at first so as not to overwhelm her, and finally releasing a torrent into her open veins. The shadows around me whipped and flailed, and wind howled loudly in the front of the room. My cloak was like a living thing, thrashing about as if being buffeted by a hurricane.

Celeste collapsed against me, and I stooped to hold her up while struggling to direct the final magic she needed into her, threading it through her veins, and binding her soul in it. Her sister rushed forward to take her other arm, and my grandmother gripped her waist with one hand and supported her limp neck with the other.

My task complete, I called my magic back into my body, sealed the wound in my arm, and released the excess power I held back into the ether. Every light in the room had been blown out, the sun was set, and the audience sat tensely in the sudden silence and complete darkness. Celeste immediately began to rouse, blinking in confusion at the lack of light and three people supporting her weight. My grandmother stepped back as she gained her footing again, and her sister released her with obvious reluctance.

Hesitantly, the fae began to extend their magic to the fae lights in the balconies, relighting them each slowly, one by one. The resulting glow was much softer than when the candles had been lit, lending a cozier atmosphere to the oversized room. Everyone, including the reapers, seemed frozen in their seats.

"You may kiss the bride," my grandmother whispered into the silence.

Chapter 6

Grim

I SHOT MY GRANDMOTHER a dark look. I wasn't going to kiss a woman just coming out of unconsciousness, no matter if she was technically my wife or not.

But Celeste—either simply used to doing as she was told, or one for following rote tradition regardless of context—raised her face to mine, even in her woozy state, and presented herself for a kiss. Tradition could be damned as far as I was concerned, but I wouldn't embarrass her by denying her a kiss she *appeared* to be seeking in front of a crowd.

I gritted my teeth and leaned down to brush my lips against hers in the most chaste kiss one could manage while cradling her against my side with our arms still tied between us. The fae half of the audience erupted into raucous cheers. "Remove the binds, please," I whispered to my grandmother, but she was already working on sliding the cloth over our hands to preserve the unity of the knot.

"Take her to the private drawing room on the back left," she instructed quickly as she tucked the cloth around Celeste's arm to keep it from dripping everywhere.

Celeste was practically zombie-like in her movements, probably in shock, and proceeded to try to step down from the dais. She missed the first step and never got the chance to connect with the ground because I scooped her up as gently as I could and cradled her small form against my chest. She was far too light in my arms, and the tears that leaked down her face and onto my shirt made my heart lodge in my throat. The fae continued to whistle and cheer as I carried her out, but I didn't even notice, as focused as I was on the woman I held. The vestibule had several doors, but the one my grandmother indicated had a servant waiting next to it with a stack of cloths and a bowl of steaming water. I stopped to open the door—remembering at the last moment that I couldn't simply pass through it with Celeste in my arms—but my grandmother's hand was there already, reaching around me to turn the knob.

"Set her on the desk," she told me as she took the supplies from the waiting servant.

I frowned at the hard surface of the writing desk and found myself reluctant to set her down. What if she tipped over? But my grandmother eyed me expectantly, so I did as I was told, acknowledging that it would probably be easier for her to work on Celeste without my arms in the way. I sat her on the desk as carefully as I could and held my hands out, ready to catch her, long enough to make sure she was stable. She wobbled but stayed upright—at least for the moment. I was ready to catch her at the first sign of trouble.

My grandmother set the bowl of water next to her and dunked a cloth from the stack she set next to it, wringing it out and handing it to me. "Wipe your arm," she told me as she soaked another one to use on Celeste and took a seat in a hard-backed chair in front of her. "Let your wings out, girl," she muttered as she focused on wiping the blood from the sides of Celeste's arm, staying clear of the incision at first. "There's no one here to judge you, and there's no sense in wasting the energy on it when you need it to heal."

Celeste's body gave a mighty shudder, and suddenly her wings were at her back again. Soft, ivory-colored feathered-things, tipped in pale pink. Even the tiny antlers that appeared at her brow were ivory and pink. She looked like the images humans had always painted of angels. An amusing thought, considering real angels looked *nothing* like this. She was panting hard with the effort of shifting, or maybe finally allowing herself to react to the pain, and as her breathing began to even out her weeping began in earnest. Tears poured down her face as my grandmother began to dab at the wound she had created.

"Oh, sweet child." My grandmother placed the rag back in the bowl of water, turning it red with our mingled blood. She sat back and looked at Celeste, taking both of her hands in each of her own, and frowned. "Dear one, I do believe you're done being paraded about for the evening." She squeezed her hands gently, patted her shoulder, and then stood and turned to me. "This one needs to be in bed. Finish cleaning her wound for me and bind it tightly. The magic you gave her and whatever healing draughts are left in her system will help it to heal faster, but binding it will stop the bleeding and help ease the pain. Her draughts appear to be wearing off already, so I'm going to go talk to our hosts and see if they have any more, or if it's possible for her to be excused from the dinner. This is just too much." She took my hand and gave it an affectionate squeeze, and then exited swiftly, leaving me alone with Celeste.

My wife.

I fingered the bloodstained cloth in my hand from where I'd started to clean my arm, and set it next to the bowl, taking up a new one and slowly lowering myself into the seat in front of her. "May I clean your wound?" I asked quietly, watching for her reaction to my closeness.

She blinked at me in confusion and then nodded, and I noticed her wings quivering slightly with her efforts to stem the flow of her tears, her lungs hitching repeatedly. Had I thought my heart had shattered into a thousand pieces before? Now it was in a million.

I took her arm in my hands and, as gently as I could, began to wipe the blood away. Around her wound the scarification of the binding mark was already beginning to form—light pink raised patterns of swirls and bands that would darken with shadowed pigment over time. There was something deep within me that responded to the sight of the marks, even as faint as they were. It was a visible mark that my magic was within her, bone deep, and in a very primal way she *belonged* with me. She quieted as I worked at cleansing and rinsing and wringing and dabbing until finally all the blood was gone from her skin. My grandmother still hadn't returned. I found soft medical gauze and strips of cloth at the bottom of the stack and pressed the gauze firmly against the wound, directing her to hold it for me as I prepared the over wrap. The cut was barely oozing now, but I wrapped it tightly and tied it off.

"What about yours?" she asked when I finished.

I lifted my arm to inspect the mess of drying blood and dipped the cloth back into the water. Giving my skin a half a dozen rough swipes removed the bulk of the blood. She gaped at the mark that had already solidified on my own arm; dark swirls and bands that mirrored what her own would look like. The shadow magic was already embedded deeply in my skin and the only thing that remained of the wound was a pink stripe that would be gone by tomorrow. I wished she could heal from this as quickly as I could, but it would be a long time before my magic had settled that deeply into her cells.

There was an odd blankness behind her eyes as I finished cleaning myself, perhaps numbness or tiredness. I didn't know, and the not knowing concerned me. I replaced the cloth in the bowl again and considered her expression. The blankness was even more upsetting than the weeping. "What's wrong?" I asked her as quietly as I could, as I could hear my grandmother's footsteps coming nearer.

"I don't want to be here anymore," she answered in her hoarse whisper, but I didn't know what that meant. Here in this room? Here with me? Here in the castle? Or Faery? Silent tears began to leak from her eyes again as my grandmother knocked. I stood warily, unsure of what to do or how to respond to her statement, and stepped to the door.

I opened it to find my grandmother a few steps away, leaning against the wall with her arms crossed, so I joined her in the outer vestibule and pulled the door shut behind me. She heaved a heavy breath and released it slowly, clearly frustrated, and then paused to listen. Satisfied that no one was within hearing distance she finally spoke. "The royal family is adamant that she joins the reception. It is, after all, her wedding reception," she admitted with a sigh, "and would reflect poorly on them if she didn't attend."

I frowned, glancing toward where Celeste sat even though I couldn't see her, picturing her tear-stained face.

"I know," Grandmother said, responding to my unspoken concern. "Having her pass out during the reception would also reflect poorly on them," she grumbled. "I explained very clearly that the ritual was quite painful for her and she's incredibly tired now. The magic you gave her will take time to heal her. But they wouldn't hear it, insisting that, now that she has your magic, she should be fine. Even her mother was horrified at the thought of her not attending, regardless of the toll it will take on her, which surprised me given her behavior yesterday. I'll never understand the other races' need for such pageantry surrounding the taking of a wife, but I accepted long ago that it isn't worth fighting what I cannot change and I cannot change ten thousand years of cultural norms. She's a princess, and since she isn't useful for securing an alliance or better trade relations through her marriage, the queen's advisors seem determined to gain prestige by showing off to all and sundry that she's marrying a *holy Veardur*." She pursed her lips disdainfully, but it was her eyes that hid flames of silent wrath. "They said they're expecting her to receive all the heads of state at this dinner while 'displaying the dignity befitting her position'," she finished with an irritated hand flick. "They think suffering through one dinner is the least she can do for her kingdom. I suppose it's just one dinner, but we should try to keep it as brief as possible for her. Give her some time to compose herself before you bring her down and please try to ensure she's tidied up. I will hold them off for as long as I can." She stood up on her toes to kiss my cheek, so I leaned down to make it easier for her. "Support her weight where you can, and I'll try to run interference. We'll get through this."

It was an attestation of my grandmother's devotion to propriety and social obligations that she assumed we should abide by these demands of our presence we found undesirable. Not only had I no such devotion, but I felt something happen inside of me as my grandmother walked away—a shift in my thinking that I found difficult to explain.

For my entire life I had embodied the essence of the dutiful reaper so as to be better able to do my job. From the time that I was a very young child, much of my time had been spent learning the languages and customs of the other races and their cultures. Once I reached middle grade, I was enrolled in public schooling so that I would have a more complete understanding of the peoples we lived among. Every afternoon and weekend that was not spent learning weaponry and magical combat skills was spent with tutors of various backgrounds, learning about their histories and traditions. It was impressed upon me in countless ways how traditions and culture are bound up in who a person is, how they see themselves, how they interact with the world around them. Respect for people and who they are is of utmost importance in the collection of the dead.

My priorities up until this point in time had been my family and closest friends—which are just another type of family—and my duty as a reaper. Normally, I wouldn't have hesitated to do as I was told by my family. It wouldn't have crossed my mind to do anything other than comply graciously, to support Celeste as she bore the duty of attending our wedding reception, and honor my people by getting through the evening respectfully and silently, meeting every curtsy with a dignified bow and a quiet nod. But my very short list of priorities now included a new addition, and everything that had belonged there previously had by necessity shifted down one place to make room for her. The fae had *given* me this woman as my wife, and what *she wanted* mattered far more to me than what *they wanted*, or even what my family expected of me. Culture and tradition were very weighty things indeed when I was collecting the dead... But I was not currently tasked with collecting the dead.

I turned the knob behind me and stepped back into the drawing room, noting the way Celeste was slumped sideways across the desk with her head on her uninjured arm. Her eyes were closed but her breathing wasn't even, so I didn't think she was asleep. "Celeste?"

Her eyes opened slowly, pinning me with that dull, exhausted look, and I made up my mind.

"Do you want to go to the wedding feast?" I asked her first, not wanting to choose for her.

She shook her head slightly, sadness washing over her features again.

I nodded and weighed our options. "What do you want to do?"

"I don't know," she whispered sadly. "I just don't want to be here anymore." The tears welled up in her eyes again and began to leak out the sides.

"Do you want to leave here?" I asked, wanting to be absolutely sure of her desires before I did something drastic.

She gave a humorless laugh, as if the idea were impossible. We had two more days with her family while we worked out the final details of our arrangement, where they would try to have a say in where we lived and how she spent her time with me and what they felt she owed her kingdom. "Desperately," she said softly, forlornly.

I stepped up to the desk and then hesitated. "May I carry you?"

She blinked at me. "To the dinner?" She lifted her hand toward me with a confused expression and tried to sit up.

I stooped forward and gathered her against me, taking care to gently fold her wings for her as I held her in my arms. I seized enough magic to pull the shadows around us and carried her to the door, opening it quietly. Walking as softly as I could, I made my way down the vestibule and listened for anyone else that might be around before stepping into the hallway. Wrapped in shadows, we only needed to avoid the other reapers, for the fae's eyes would slide right past me.

I hadn't been to her bedroom from this part of the castle, and the trek would have been much easier if I could have just walked in that direction and simply passed through the walls with my magic, but I didn't have too much trouble finding my way there. We passed a multitude of servants in the hallways, but everyone else was presumably already at the reception dinner, and the servants never even turned their heads. I sat her on the bed.

"What are we doing?" she asked.

"Leaving." I eyed the trunks stacked in the corner, having been prepared by staff already for her upcoming departure. My family would have to bring those later. I opened her armoire and found only dresses for the next two days—delicate ceremonial dresses much like the wedding dress she wore now.

"We can't just—" she broke off as I paced to the trunks and flipped the top one open. Here were sturdier garments and shoes. I would buy her whatever she wanted in the Boundlands, but the fashions were different there. If this was what she felt comfortable in, she would have a much harder time finding anything like it outside of Faery.

I lifted several outfits out and a pair of shoes along with a small bag of what appeared to be undergarments and set them on the bed. "Do you have a cloak?"

She indicated another trunk.

"Saddle bags?" I asked as I hauled open the second trunk and pulled out a heavy green velvet cloak. I glanced at her when she didn't respond, only to find her staring at me in wide-eyed confusion again. That was fine, better confusion than blank looks or tears. "Put this on," I said as I handed the cloak to her before rummaging through the second trunk and finding a canvas sack with buckles. This would do. I stuffed her clothing inside it and glanced around the room again. "Is there anything else you want to bring?"

She opened her mouth and closed it several times before blinking and looking around the room in thought. Her eyes locked on a table in the corner with some small boxes, and she started to lower herself off the bed.

I gave her my hand and helped her down, pausing to fasten her cloak around her shoulders before helping her to the table.

She opened several, looking over their contents briefly before finding what she wanted; a tiny box full of little, carved trinkets and charms that she closed back up and held to her chest, looking at me as if she didn't know if this was what I meant. I wondered what special value they held to her and wished I could take the time to study each one, but instead I helped her back to the bed and held the sack open for her to place her box in. "May I?" I asked, reaching for her diadem. The irony of me removing the "halo" from this woman who very much resembled the modern interpretation of an angel before stealing her away was not lost on me. I lifted the circlet from her brow and tucked it into her bag, before removing my own to include as well and buckling the bag shut. I shouldered the bag and lifted Celeste again, tucking her cloak around her. It might not be enough. I snagged the blanket off of her bed and wrapped that around her too.

"Can you shift into anything small enough to fit through the castle gates?" I asked her.

She just looked at me with a bewildered expression.

What a pain it must be to be trapped in a corporeal form all the time. "No matter." If I couldn't carry her through the walls, and getting out through the castle gate was off the table, the next best option was through the maze of servant's passageways and down over the wall. I carried her out into the hallway and lifted the decorative tapestries that lined the wall until I found one of the small doors. It was clear from her expression that Celeste hadn't spent much time wandering these darkened corridors or their narrow stairwells, but their purposes suited me just fine. There was no light here, except for the few servants carrying candles that I stepped aside to allow to pass, which only served to make my magic easier to gather. I followed the smell of cooking food, knowing that the kitchens would have doors open to the outside for extra ventilation.

"How do you see?" she whispered after the light from the second servant had faded away down the passage and we were swathed in darkness again.

I didn't answer her because I started to hear the noises from the bustling kitchen up ahead. Sticking to a pathway along an outer wall, I followed a man in uniform through the kitchen and out of the doors into the bailey. From there I spied more stairs up the wall and climbed them to stand by the ramparts. I paused next to the stable yard looking for the best way over the wall, and Celeste whispered, quiet as a breath, "I don't think the irin will let you ride them."

I headed down the parapet walkway, leaving the stable yard behind. "I don't need them."

Chapter 7

Grim

THE NUMBER OF ARCHERS I passed on the castle walls made it difficult to find a place to slip over. Not that I was concerned they might see me, and the noise of the rushing river behind the castle would probably cover soft noises, but I loathed the thought of drawing unwanted attention. I finally found a section of wall with no guard, and leaned over the edge to judge the distance to the ground—these outer walls only appeared about a story and a half high.

Celeste stiffened in my arms as I judged the distance down. "Do you want me to fly down?" she asked, her quiet voice pitching high with nerves.

Fly down? She could barely walk. She'd probably plummet like an injured dove. "No. Don't scream." I waited for her to nod and show me she understood, and then leapt from the ramparts to a stepped ledge a shorter distance below. From there the final story was an easy drop to the ground. Celeste gasped as I landed, and I froze. I held her tightly while I crouched, balancing on the balls of my feet and waiting to see if anyone had heard us.

"Sorry," she whispered when she felt my muscles relax, and clutched her blankets closer. "I didn't expect you to just *jump*."

"How far can your people see at night?" I asked when it became clear no alarm would be raised. I planned to make use of my shadow cloak the whole way out, but trying to tie a saddle bag on a wraith while simultaneously keeping Celeste from falling over *and* ensuring we stayed silent and hidden would be a bit more to juggle.

She peered around, her eyes shining in the moonlight from her cocoon of wrappings, before pointing tentatively to the road that led into the castle grounds. "With both of the moons shining like this I can see easily to the third monument from here."

Staying in the shadow of the castle wall was probably our best bet for mounting up then, even if it did make us more likely to be heard. I gathered more magic and summoned my horse, forming it complete with a saddle and buckles this time.

Celeste stiffened in my arms again but didn't speak.

"If I set you down next to the wall, can you lean on it to stay upright for a moment?" I asked in a breath against her ear.

She didn't answer, too focused on staring at the horse.

"Celeste?" I prompted again.

She nodded—too quickly to have actually assessed herself, in my opinion—so I lowered her to the ground carefully and then waited to be sure she had her footing before releasing her and turning to the horse.

"Why doesn't it move?" she whispered uneasily as I unslung the pack from my shoulder and began to buckle it behind the saddle.

I cast her a wary glance as I finished strapping it on.

She was staring at my mount.

"What do you mean?" I asked, confused. It moved just fine when I wanted it to. Right now, I didn't want it to.

The river was loud, but this still wasn't the best time to be talking. I double checked that her pack was secured and then gathered her up in my arms again. I tucked her cloak and the extra blanket around her before stepping into the stirrup and hauling her up into the saddle with me. A little more magic ensured we were properly shrouded in shadows and then it was time to set off toward the road. We'd stick to the soft ground beside the cobblestones until we were out of hearing range.

"It doesn't look around or twitch its ears or shake its bridle," she whispered.

"That's because it isn't real." Did she think I created flesh and blood animals out of nothing? A summoned wraith had no care of its surroundings, nor did it suffer from boredom or agitation.

I kept our mount to a walk, and as we passed the second monument that sat beside the road, I looked back to watch the castle. There was no movement among the towers that rose, gleaming and white, beneath the moonlit sky.

Celeste never looked back.

Once we passed the third statue I spurred the mount to a quicker pace, first at a slow trot and increasing to a full gallop. I wanted to be miles away before my family had a chance to come after me. They would know where I was headed, but I didn't plan to let them catch me before I got there. There was only one Gate from the Boundlands into Faery—the rest having been systematically destroyed in the many millennia since the Great Migration—an effort to keep outsiders from coming in and to have fewer points of entry to defend during a war. Now they only warred among themselves.

The original plan had been for Celeste to ride out of the Dawn Court in an irin-drawn carriage with a full accompaniment of my family and the general's soldiers for protection. It would have taken several days of travel to reach the Gate in such a slow-moving caravan. Even without the carriage, if my family were accompanied by irin at their top speeds, it would take two or more days if they made for the Gate. But since I had Celeste—if they didn't simply follow me—they wouldn't need the Gate anymore at all and would have a much shorter trip into the wilds to open a portal. And then there was the factor of whether they would rush to leave or stay to finish the arrangement with the Dawn Court. Perhaps they would stay in an effort to appease the queen after the impropriety of my departure.

I kept to the main road until I reached the first city and opted for a side road to keep from slowing down. Hours passed as I carried her, acutely aware of her soft, slight frame pressed against me, with nothing but the moons to guide us and the tall spires of trees to witness our passage. The occasional nighttime traveler braved the darkness and howling winds with a lantern hanging from their cart, but for the most part the roads were empty. I moved to the side for the few travelers we passed so as not to frighten them with the clatter of unseen hooves, cut wide around all the villages, and avoided the cities entirely.

Only someone on the brink of sheer exhaustion would have been able to fall asleep on the back of a sprinting horse, but Celeste did—curled up in my lap, her body limp in unconsciousness, her head resting against me. I kept my arms securely locked around her and was careful to keep her balanced across my legs to protect her from being jostled too much. I made sure to keep her cloak pulled down, to protect her face from getting chilled, and was grateful for its protection of her delicate looking wings against the buffeting winds.

We were outside of a county called Eryvale when I first spotted the glowing yellow eyes of ghouls lurking in the forest. They turned to watch us pass from their distant hiding places, but we were there and gone before they could do anything else. I quickly shifted Celeste's weight and summoned my scythe to have it ready, knowing that, where there were a few, there would be many. The high fae did a good job of keeping the numbers of these parasitic apparitions down in areas with denser fae populations, but they proliferated when left unchallenged by those with the old magic. From what I'd been told, ghouls and other specters had been all but wiped out within the Boundlands when the high fae had lived there, but now that they were gone, even the heavily populated areas sometimes had problems with things like fades and banshees wandering in. Every realm has its own fitful colonies of the vicious specters, but for some reason the high fae had always been the most vulnerable to their predation. Luckily for the high fae, the old magic they carried was the most effective way to repel them. At least, for a mortal.

Not even a league later I encountered a seething mass of specters right upon the dirt road. The apparitions were eagerly lying in wait for a lone traveler or two in this quiet region of the world, hoping for an easy meal. Someone who might not recognize they were there until it was too late. Since even the fae couldn't physically see them, they weren't expecting me to be ready for them as they reached out their long, spindly arms in an effort to drag me from my mount. A wide arc of my scythe lopped off two heads, their spectral forms vanishing before their heads even hit the ground. I looped my weapon around overhead and brought it down on a trio directly in front of us, slicing them in half before their dissipating spirits were trampled beneath my wraith. I swung again and again, spinning my scythe in deadly circles, heedless of the trees I rode through. My weapons could pass through them as easily as I could.

Though I hated to slow down, I turned off to chase down a few specters at the back of the group. I morphed my scythe into a spiked mace on a chain long enough to tag the remaining few from a distance and made sure they dropped before continuing on my way. My friend Jordan's ability to create a rolling wall of fire would have come in handy here.

It wasn't my job to purge the world of its scourge of these spiritual vermin, but at least I could leave it a little safer for the fae who lived here. I turned my mount back to the main road and considered the "angelic" fae asleep in my arms. I was grateful that she hadn't been awake to be frightened by the attack, but how deeply was it normal for one to sleep? She was still breathing normally, but her unconscious state began to make me a little more anxious.

I rode harder as I came across larger and larger groups of rogue wraiths, and eventually had to start picking and choosing the times when I struck out at the groups of wandering ghouls or banshees and when to leave them be. If they were close enough to the path to be within easy striking distance, I took them out at the knees, but I didn't go chasing any more down. I could spend days I didn't have here trying to wipe them out and still barely make a dent. The remaining Gate was purposefully situated within the most desolate badlands, and the further we got from civilization the more groups I came across.

I considered creating a pack of shadow hounds to keep pace with me as another line of defense, but that would cause me even more magical drain.

The wraith I rode was a spectacular conjuration. I didn't have to worry about it flagging or colicking or breaking its legs while I drove it for hours at top speeds through these darkened countryside roads littered with dips and valleys. The issue that arose was that my mount was essentially *me*. It was created and sustained by my magic, and combined with the use of my power for the binding ritual, I'd never used *this much magic* sustained over this amount of time before. The faster we rode, the more energy was pulled from me. Every conjuration had a price it required to be paid.

I rode through the entire night, killing any wraiths that came within reach. As the sky began to lighten, I finally decided to make use of the lessening darkness before it was gone. My path had taken me through the outer reaches of both the Kingdom of Falling Stars and the much smaller Midnight Kingdom, and I was now on the farthest-reaching borders of the aptly named Empire of Open Skies. I stopped briefly in an open field with no ghouls in sight and shook my muscles out, unused to spending so many hours in the saddle.

I gathered magic from the decreasing darkness and created a pack of shadow hounds—stockily built, heavily muscled dogs that easily resembled the slavering hellhounds of mythos. The seven large hounds spread out in a circle around my mount to keep watch for me while I focused my attention on my companion. The fae soldiers we'd traveled with on the way in had taken the opportunity to stretch their muscles each time they rested their mounts, and that had been a much shorter journey than what we'd just completed. Shouldn't she need a break after so many hours in one position?

"Celeste?" I pushed her hood back gently and peered at her face. There was no movement of her eyelids. Just the soft, slow breathing of someone deeply at rest. I tried reaching inside her cloak to find her fingers, squeezing them briefly to try to rouse her, but received no response. Even turning her body so that she rested on my other leg made no difference to her sleeping state.

She just rested her head against my other shoulder and drew up into my lap again. I tugged her hood back up over her hair and horns, tucked her head under my chin, and held her close as I set off again into the beginning of a new day. Mortals usually slept through the night, so perhaps this was normal?

Other than that once, I took no breaks, unwilling to sacrifice any time we could be moving. The shadow hounds bounding along beside me successfully cleared three more groups of ghouls, but as the sun rose higher, I released them back into the ether. I truly needed to reserve my energy now and not fight the tide of dwindling darkness. I still had hours to ride and was beginning to feel the drain. As the day wore on though, I became increasingly concerned when Celeste never awoke. Her slumber before the wedding had been magically induced as a kind of stasis to keep her illness from progressing, but they'd removed that from her for the ceremony. What if something was deeply wrong with her that my magic couldn't fix? I worried for the tenth time that maybe I had made the wrong choice in taking her away.

My grandmother's words were both a source of comfort and anxiety. *"She will not be immortal immediately, and though this disease will not continue for terribly much longer beyond the ritual itself, she will still be able to be killed for several years. Your only duty during that time is to protect her."* The disease couldn't last for too long now that my magic was inside her, but she could still perish. I looked down at Celeste and mentally willed my magic to spread farther, to work faster. I could do no such thing of course, but childishly, I tried anyway.

The sun had passed its zenith and I'd destroyed dozens more apparitions by the time the wall came into view over the horizon. I stopped at the tattered edge of a long-petrified forest and looked out over the badlands—a rocky, craggy landscape that was entirely devoid of vegetation as far as the eye could see. A hard packed road wound its way past low, strange rock formations toward an ancient fort known as the Fist of Heaven, which had housed a garrison of soldiers for millennia. It existed without a kingdom—a city-state all its own, supplied by tariffs from every nation within Faery. Its only purpose was to guard the Gate.

After the Great Migration, the old fae kings had encircled the Gate with a massive wall that stood imposing and stalwart on the horizon to this day—dwarfing even the nearby fortress. It rose several hundred spans into the sky and was dozens of spans thick, with only a single gap to allow people through. I could only imagine what they had intended to keep from coming through from the Boundlands, because the fae's written history was hard to come by from that time period and even my own people had little to say on the matter. Legends spoke of troops on dragon back, but that would have been long ago indeed.

I checked on Celeste one more time and considered my approach. I could show the guards my unconscious wife, hope they accepted our binding marks as proof that we were wed, and hope that they allowed me to take her through. That didn't seem likely. Not that they could physically stop me, but the amount of drama it would cause would be a nightmare. It was one thing to shirk my supposed duty to a social obligation people felt they were owed—such as attending my own wedding reception. It was quite another to be seen as kidnapping a woman from Faery against her will. Not to mention a member of a royal family.

I quickly settled on smuggling and removed the majority of my shadow cloak, stripping away enough that my mount and I could be seen, but that it still hung down my back to mark me as a reaper. I used a portion of it to cover Celeste so that she was hidden from view. It would already be seen as suspicious that a reaper would make use of the Gate, rather than our own portals, since I was "alone." Allowing them to see me coming from a distance would hopefully give them one less oddity to set them on edge since they would be able to hear the steps of my mount so near to them.

I kept a steady pace as I approached. The Fist was one of the few constructions I'd ever seen in Faery that favored function over form. It presided over its domain like an enormous gray toad, squat and wide, though it did have plenty of towers to be able to see both winged and mounted intruders from a distance. I noticed it didn't appear to have a single conventional window. Every opening within view was either an arrow slit or a murder hole.

Mortals had such a perplexing penchant for ending each other's lives early.

By the time I passed the fort, I could feel the eyes of the entire garrison upon me from all the watchers within. I trained my gaze straight ahead on the wall as I drew closer, its gap guarded by a dozen winged fae in full plate armor. These fae had no qualms with showing their true form to outsiders, being more inclined toward security than diplomacy, and wouldn't hesitate to make use of all their extremities if the need arose. Their helmets had been specially forged to fit around their antlers, with plates that dropped between them and interlocked with plates on the sides to cover their faces.

The leader raised a hand for me to halt, and I drew to a stop in front of him. His skin was a deep golden color that matched the tips of his feathers, and he was the only one of them that appeared to have much muscle on him. I waited for him to make his assessment.

"What is your name?" he asked.

"*Veardur,*" I responded. He didn't need to know my name. He already knew that it was sheer courtesy keeping me standing before him. That if I wanted to I could have walked right through him, his men, the wall itself, and then the Gate. And I might have, if not for the delicate mortal woman I held in my arms.

The fae commander's eyebrows drew together behind the eye holes in his helmet and his companions stood silently, taut and ready as he looked me over. Ready for what, I had no idea. Perhaps they had no experience with a reaper. It wasn't unheard of for entire groups of people to have never met one of us before, though any border guard should have been aware that border laws didn't apply to reapers. How could they?

His eyes scanned my body and my wraith one last time,

sliding right past the bundle that I held. "Go ahead," he told me, stepping back. The rest of his men followed his lead, clearing a path to the gap in the wall.

I spurred my wraith onward, wrapping myself in shadows and disappearing into the darkness between the walls the instant we stepped foot between them. Inside there was very little light from the sky above, the only real illumination coming from the Gate itself. I marveled at how fanciful it appeared with its archway of carved stone that was much larger than the utilitarian stacked-stone Gates within the Void or the quaint looking stone-arch Gates of the Boundlands. I took a deep breath to prepare myself, staring into the overcast skies of the town on the other side of the shimmering haze. I would be *incredibly* grumpy if my family were standing there waiting to erupt at me, knowing it would be a bottleneck in my travels. I was tired, and I wanted to give my new wife some peaceful rest, and I wasn't ready to deal with anyone else yet. I gritted my teeth and directed my mount forward.

The pins and needles feeling in my extremities as I passed through a fae-made Gate was something I would never grow accustomed to, but when I stepped through into the Boundlands there was nothing but relief as I found no one waiting for me but the dwarvish guards on the other side of the Gate.

I stripped away most of my cloak and addressed the nearest one. "What year is it?"

Chapter 8

Grim

"It's the 6258th Year o' the Axe, Master Reaper," the dwarvish guard responded in the thickest mountain accent I'd ever heard. He had long brown hair that he wore in a loose braid and deeply freckled, ruddy colored skin that matched his russet eyes. All six of his companions were similarly colored and matched his stout and sturdy build, nearly to the inch. All of them wore leather armor and held wicked looking halberds that seemed at odds with their placid expressions. "T'day is the 23rd o' Frostdays," he continued with his rolling lilt, graciously answering the next question he knew I would ask.

I did the mental math to translate their calendar into our own and was relieved to find that I'd only lost three weeks of Boundlands' time. Between that and the fact that my mother wasn't standing here waiting to tell me exactly what she thought of me leaving early, I could practically taste the triumph. There would be a reckoning, but not today.

"My thanks," I told the guard. "Is Master Blunthorn on duty today?" I asked him.

He perked up at the name. "Yasgrot Blunthorn?" he clarified. "I do believe he would be. Do you have need of him?" Mountain dwarves clipped their words in a way that occasionally took me a little more effort to decipher. *Do y'ave need o' 'im?*

"I do. If you could, please inform him that I'll be staying at Sorrow's Keep," I told him.

"I'll send a runner straight away," he said, motioning to another of the guardsmen who set off running for the messengers.

I nodded my thanks to him and the rest of the group and rode on through the tiny mining community called Granite Cross. It was nearly entirely populated by dwarves and gnomes and occasionally giants, nestled high in the jagged peaks of the Dragon's Teeth Mountains. The winds howled loudly and the overcast skies began to drizzle, but none of the townsfolk on the market boardwalks we passed seemed to care, having lived at this altitude for generations upon generations. I held Celeste closer and tugged her cloak and blanket tighter around her as I set off on the final leg of our trek toward my family's closest holding. My unease with her state of consciousness was like a slow burning coal buried in my chest, making it hard for me to breathe. Her pale face had taken on a bluish hue due to the cold and I turned her head toward my chest, hoping to lend her more warmth.

It took another hour of traveling through winding mountain pathways along the cliffs overlooking the Strait of Sorrows to reach the town of Bhalden's Post. The Dragon's Teeth didn't have much to physically sustain the populations that lived here, but the dwarves in this area and the giants that made a home in the enclave to the north made good business from the metals and stone they mined from deep in the mountains. Bhalden's Post was a relatively small outpost, but it did brisk business with traders who braved the dangerous passes year-round to bring in supplies for the miners. Even the eponymous Strait of Sorrows that sat below Sorrow's Keep provided little more than sea salt in the way of useful resources, with locals eschewing the cartilaginous, venomous fish that lived beneath the churning sea ice. Food from the lowlands was an easy trade for those seeking precious metals if you could haul it up.

The keep itself had been here before the outpost and was a product of the mountain it sat on. It was a collection of towers constructed of granite that had been carved straight from the peak, like most of my family's holdings. It had been managed by generations of Blunthorns—a local dwarvish family—whenever we stayed here, and their family was rewarded with a permanent spot on the Molchanov payrolls. The relief I felt as I rounded the final bend and saw the glow flickering in the great hall windows was a heady thing. Yasgrot, the current head of the Blunthorn family, had received the runner's message and sent servants ahead to open the keep and ready it for my stay. *Thank all that is holy for spectral messengers and for the Blunthorns too.*

I guided my mount along the narrow ridge that led to the stone bridge that spanned a deep ravine below and stopped in front of the iron castle gates. Carefully cradling Celeste's body in one arm, I reached behind me with the other to take hold of her belongings, then released my mount back into the shadows. I nearly staggered as we dropped into the snow, weary and aching from the long, cold ride. Several pairs of footprints had been left in tracks through the snowy courtyard and up the gray stone steps to the door of the main hall. I pushed the door open and was surprised to find Yasgrot himself adding wood to a roaring fire in the hearth. The smell of something warm and earthy hit me as I closed the door against the wind.

"Master Molchanov, welcome back, sir." He stood to greet me with a harried smile, revealing a clay pot hanging over the flames. He continued talking while he peeked under the lid and stirred the contents, his thick, green robes swirling around his feet from the movement. "I've brought along Brishta and Torindal to help open up the keep. It's sat vacant for several months this time so they're airing the linens and warming your bedchamber. Oh, and my wife insisted I bring you some of her root stew she was preparing for tonight. She always makes enough to feed an army, you know." *Sh' always makes enou' t' feed 'n army, y' know.*

I blinked at the barrage of words. Yasgrot's accent wasn't quite as heavy as the guardsman's was, and I'd known him for much longer as well, but even so, I had to focus on his speech more than my brain felt capable of at the moment. He shared the same brown, coarse hair and ruddy skin that the rest of the population here tended toward, though his beard was the longest of any other dwarves I'd seen—always worn in three thick braids.

While standing, he came to my mid-chest, a common height for his people, but he didn't have the heavy, brawny build of the miners and soldiers. He was efficient, and organized, and according to my grandmother, ran a very orderly household just like his father had before him. He liked to stop in and check on things himself, but as an older man, usually delegated the work to those in his employ. I was touched that he'd come himself and brought food from his own family's table as well.

"Brishta brewed some tea and left it over there for you." He gestured over his shoulder toward the heavy wooden table that was dark and glossy from age and wear. "There's some mulled wine, and some bread—it's not warm but I can warm it up if you'd like, and your stew is nearly finished heating through. Shall I send for a cook? I could—" His steady stream of words broke off as he glanced over his shoulder again to look at me. "Oh my! I wasn't aware you were bringing a companion." He replaced the lid on the pot and turned from the fire to get a better look at the woman bundled in my arms. I fought the bizarre urge I had to block his view of her or wrap her in my shadows again to protect her from his bewildered gaze.

"My wife," I explained to him. *My wife.* Her slight body was still lax against my chest, and I set down the sack of her belongings so that I could pull her hood back to get her some more air now that we were out of the frigid winds. I brushed my fingers across her cheek and my heart stuttered at how chilled she was. I cupped her cheek to try to warm her skin.

"Your wife?" he inquired, stepping closer, as if to verify my words. "Does she... need anything? Is she well? I can send for the healer in Bhalden's Po—" He froze for half a beat. "By *Balthor's beard*, she's a fae!" he nearly gasped, noticing her small antlers for the first time. "My goodness. Well, you would think I'd have seen one before with as close as we are to that Gate into Faery, but I never have. They just don't come through there anymore, and I'd always heard they stopped allowing their kind into our lands." He looked at me with wide eyes, as if I might have some kind of explanation. That wasn't exactly true, but it didn't matter. I just shrugged, not having any desire to discuss fae politics and societal norms with him.

"I stole her." That was simple enough.

Yasgrot made a peculiar choking sound that made me wonder if he might be unwell himself. "You *stole her*, sir?" His eyebrows shot up nearly into his hairline.

"She said she wanted to leave."

"I see." He seemed troubled as he looked at her, which added to my own concerns. Could he see something wrong with her that I couldn't? "And she lost consciousness when, sir? At the Gate?" His questions were timid, as if he were afraid of the answer.

"Shortly after our binding ritual." I shifted my left arm to show him the binding marks and the tenseness in his shoulders relaxed a little for some reason. "Nearly a full day ago," I explained further, and his shoulders tensed back up.

"Well, I do fear I know very little about high fae and binding rituals. I greatly doubt the healer will either, but I can fetch her for your... wife." He wrung his hands as he glanced around the room before calling for his two employees and rattling off a list of instructions for each of them. Torindal was sent for the town healer, and Brishta, a young dwarvish woman with a cheerful smile and a messy bun atop her head, ushered me into one of the bed chambers and turned down the bed sheets for Celeste. She added more wood to the fire in the hearth next to the bed and then dusted her hands off on her sturdy woolen dress while enthusing about how beautiful my new bride was before saying something about fetching the food.

I stood beside the bed feeling overwhelmed by the chatter and the activity and waited for her to leave before I laid Celeste on the bed. Brishta seemed like a nice enough girl, but all the staring made me uncomfortable. I wanted to protect Celeste from unwanted eyes. It occurred to me that I hadn't been subjected to this amount of physical contact with another person for this long probably since my infancy and was surprised at my reluctance to release her from my hold. Her soft, even breathing was something I could anchor myself in, but I felt at a loss to know what she needed.

I gently unwound her cocoon of blanket and cloak and lowered her to the bed as carefully as I could, consciously fighting the worm of panic in me that made me feel as though releasing her from my grip was some kind of abandonment. She just looked so small and frail lying there all alone in the giant bed, and I didn't know what to do. She'd been unconscious for a whole day, had nothing to eat or drink, hadn't even emptied her bladder, which seemed the most concerning. Wasn't that something mortals needed to do rather often? Didn't that mean she was severely dehydrated? Couldn't mortals *die* from dehydration? I'd never had to *keep something alive* before. This was entirely removed from my area of expertise.

I tried to remind myself that she did appear better than she had two days ago, even though it was obvious now that whatever healing potions they had given her before the ceremony were no longer working in her system. The skin under her eyes was no longer sunken, and now that she was next to the fire, her skin was returning to a more normal-looking hue. Her bones showed more than seemed healthy to me, but since the high fae often had a leaner build in general... maybe that wasn't too far outside the realm of her normal build. The feathers of her wings were badly rumpled from being wrapped in cloth for the ride, so I reached out to straighten them for her, marveling at the satin feel of her wings as I ran my fingers along them. She truly was beautiful to look at, I had to acknowledge, though I still resented that it seemed to be the thing everyone remarked on the most about her. And though she currently wore her beauty in that broken-flower way, she did seem to be healing, which helped to soothe my internal panic.

Her rest seemed at least to be a peaceful one, so I allowed myself to study her—this woman I was suddenly so bound up in. Her face was as "angelic" as her wings, with her small, sharp features, and large eyes with long lashes that currently rested on her cheeks. Her heart-shaped lips had a slight upturn that made me wonder if her dreams were pleasant, or if that was just her expression at rest. And there was a feminine gracefulness to her limbs that was evident even in sleep. But she was more than that. She had shown great strength of will and perseverance during our wedding ceremony, and I hoped, for her sake that who she was inside would come to be what she was known for rather than her physical appearance.

The desire to protect Celeste from prying eyes led me to draw the bed sheets over her when Brishta's footsteps sounded in the corridor. Her wings were a lovely part of her, but I suspected she wouldn't want them exposed like this to strangers, especially when she was so vulnerable.

"I brought you some stew, sir, and some of the broth for your love." I paused at her words, at the assumption that, because this woman was my wife, I loved her, and then blinked down at Celeste until Brishta pressed a steaming bowl of stewed root vegetables into my hands and set another on a side table. She came back with tea and some mulled wine and busied herself about the room while I stood staring in bewilderment until Yasgrot finally knocked at the bedroom door with the healer. The older woman couldn't find anything obviously wrong with Celeste, but she admitted that Yasgrot's assumptions were correct; she knew nothing of the high fae and equally little about reaper magic. She suggested that I support Celeste with fluids, keep her warm, and send for her again if her condition deteriorated.

I was unsure of what that meant.

Perhaps sensing my discomfort with the amount of people in the room, and seeing that they were unable to help anyway, the kind dwarves bid me farewell and left for the night with Yasgrot promising to send a maid and a cook the next day.

Once we were alone, I set down my bowl of stew and picked up Celeste's, dragged a padded chair around from beside the fire to the side of the bed, and settled in next to her. Taking the spoon, I gathered the smallest amount of the stew broth, tested it for temperature, and then tipped it ever so slowly into her mouth. Waiting until she swallowed each time, I spent the next hour sitting beside her and trying to make sure she got the fluids she needed.

I had no idea how to make this work. I was finally alone with this woman who was my wife, and yet, all I felt was incoherent panic at the fact that *I was alone with this woman who was my wife* and she was clearly still horribly sick and *I didn't know how to keep her alive.* I had never planned on having a wife in the first place. I raised another spoonful of broth to her lips and questioned yet again what I had been thinking to steal her away from people who knew her and knew about her medical issues. But I knew what I had been thinking—this precious soul was distraught and I wanted to please her.

But now what was I supposed to do?

Chapter 9

Celeste

I COULDN'T SEEM TO escape this dream of being swallowed up by shadows. It was a dream I was familiar with—something I'd dreamed again and again while being trapped in a sleep I couldn't pull myself out of. There was no up or down. I had no physical body to endlessly battle with. There was nothing but darkness pulling me down into its horrific, inky maw and swallowing me whole. That darkness had always frightened me, and it had consumed me over and over again no matter how many times I'd had this dream.

But this time something was different.

I was different.

The shadows that came for me this time were still powerful and ominous feeling. They were possessive and all encompassing. They still swallowed me down into the darkest chasm. But this time, instead of feeling powerless and afraid, I felt... comforted. Protected. Changed. The darkness was no longer a gaping maw of terror and despair. It was an obsidian fortress, it was strength, and it was part of me now. I floated in these shadows endlessly until a small, cool hand—much smaller than the one that usually cupped my cheek—pressed against the side of my face.

"Her temperature feels okay," I heard a soft voice say into the darkness. It was high and feminine with an accent I didn't recognize. "I know you're very anxious," she said gently, "but do you think you could pull your magic back a bit?" Her tone was so kind and encouraging that I couldn't help but want to do as she asked. I wasn't holding any magic, though. I hadn't been able to use my magic properly for years, not since my body had begun destroying itself. "A little more?" She raised her pitch at the end like it was a question. "It's so overpowering I can't feel much else in here."

"I'm holding no magic," his voice said quietly. *Him.* The one I was traded to in exchange for my life. The one who I'd been horrified to learn I was betrothed to from the moment my mother woke me and informed me I was to *marry* him, until I'd heard his first words to me, *"Is this what you want?"* His voice had been so distractingly decadent that I'd nearly forgotten to be afraid. When I'd finally understood him, I'd been terrified for another reason. Would he back out? Cancel the wedding? Would I finally die from my body's betrayal? But he hadn't backed out. He'd been infinitely kind to me, listened to my every word, and treated me with a tenderness that had shocked me. Vague memories of being held comfortably against his chest while riding fast, and the warm, clean scent of man with the barest hint of something sharp—like a cold fireplace—flitted unformed through my memory, but I couldn't hold on to them.

"Oh!" the woman said, sounding startled. "It's her! High fae have reaper magic?" The voice sounded a little more distant when she asked the question, as if the woman had turned away from me in the darkness.

"It was given to her during our binding," his voice said.

Our binding. My mind instantly shied away from the painful memory. Why hadn't Apollo been there to support me? His loss still felt like an open wound. And how long would my arm take to heal? The tightening of my betrothed's jaw as his veins had been opened had not prepared me for the stinging pain of the knife slicing through my flesh. I let my thoughts escape instead into the memory of how he had stood beside me at the altar and had borne me up with strong arms and his comforting presence, even as a complete stranger to me. I felt tears threaten in the darkness even though I had no eyes to cry with here.

"To... heal her?" the woman asked. There was no response that

I could hear and after a moment she continued. "Well, I can feel some other magic underneath yours, but I can't make sense of it. There's a *lot* going on here."

I listened, straining for his voice, but he didn't reply aloud before she continued, maybe in response to some unspoken question.

"Well, there are plenty of people that have more than one type of magic, obviously. Like myself, for instance. Or Jordan, with his vampirism that is layered over the fire elementalism he was born with... But this is *very* different to *anything* I've ever come across, Grim." *Grim?* Was that my new mate's name? I felt like it didn't match the name I'd been told, but my memories were like slippery eels in this dark place and I couldn't seem to catch them.

A brief pause left me alone in the darkness again before she continued in her thoughtful tone, as if she were analyzing something puzzling and speaking to herself as she did it. "There's some kind of shifter magic for sure, but I can't tell *what* kind. Normally I can get a sense of what animal a shifter becomes, you know? Like Sidney simply exudes magpie energy, and her friend Bane just *feels* like a panther to me. But this kind of shifter magic is much broader than that. There's also something I don't recognize that feels... defensive? Protective? It's hard to explain. And an elemental type of magic... maybe earth magic? And there's something that feels similar to animal communication. But I've never felt anything like this, so I could be wrong about all of it. It's all very scattered and chaotic compared to anyone I've ever felt before." I had a vague notion that she was talking about me, but I didn't understand the context or what she meant. My mind was having trouble making connections here.

"I don't believe that's out of the ordinary for her," he said, his voice curling through the darkness and sliding over me like a silk sheet. I'd never met anyone who possessed a voice like that. A deep, resonant baritone that made my breath catch and my brain stall out. I could have listened to him read the list that

77

Cook sent out to the shops. "The high fae are the oldest race of mortals from the Boundlands, and the elves, dryads, and all the other races are their descendants. Over time, as the genetic 'tree' diverged further from the source, your magic split off from theirs."

"Really?" the woman asked, sounding fascinated. "So, there was more magic in us the further back you go?"

"Yes, and no," he responded. "The high fae have more... generalist magic. As your races diverged your magic became more specialized. You are stronger in your specializations than they are, but they have a wider variety of magics at their disposal."

"That's so cool! I had no idea. I don't understand how that would work, though. So they can shift, but... ?" She left her question hanging.

A rustle of fabric and then he said, "Sidney could shift into a bird and live that way for the rest of her life should she desire to."

"I've never understood why she *wouldn't* desire to," the woman mumbled.

"High fae have a harder time maintaining one specific form other than their true forms, as Celeste is right now." I wondered how they could see my body when I couldn't even seem to find it.

"I see. Sorry, Grim. It's so exciting getting to see a new kind of magic I've never experienced before," she said with a sigh. "My brain hurts from trying to piece that genetic history together. It does seem promising to me, though, that your magic has taken hold of her so thoroughly, especially since it has healing properties, right?"

There was a long pause before I heard him audibly swallow and ask, "But why is she still asleep?"

Her tone was thoughtful and sympathetic when she said, "I can't be sure, obviously, but excessive magic use made me lose consciousness for a period of a few days like this once. My father swore it was my body healing from me being 'on the brink of death'—his dramatics obviously, not mine—but I wondered if it might have been some kind of protective mechanism from my body while my magic 'recharged.' You mentioned that she was extremely ill before, and noticeably so, but she doesn't look visibly ill to me now. So, I would say you had to have done *something* right. Maybe her body is protecting itself while she's healing, or she's trying to recharge her magic, or adapting to yours, or... any number of things. We can really only speculate since none of her healers, nor mine, had any idea what caused it."

He heaved a deep breath and then his voice was muffled, as if something were pressed over his face. "What if I procured another healing potion for her?"

"Oh, Grim. You poor, sweet man," she said with a good-natured chuckle. "It's like you've been given a potted plant with no tag." But then she composed herself and added more seriously, "I think I would be hesitant to add anything else to the equation right now, since you don't know what kind of healing potion they gave her back in Faery and you can't be sure of how one of ours will affect her."

"Why are mortals so complicated? How do any of you survive to adulthood?" he practically growled.

The woman's voice was full of patience and warmth. "You're doing a great job caring for her, Grim. She's going to be okay. And if she isn't, you send for me again and I'll do whatever it takes to bring you a healing potion for her."

"Thank you, Elara." His breathy whisper struck me deeply.

"Of course. Please bring her to meet us when she is well. Lysander has been asking for you *daily*," she said.

"Tell him I'll bring him a treat."

The woman's voice took on a teasing note. "No more treats. Between you and Sidney he's going to turn out to be the most spoiled child that ever lived." Her wry chuckle was an indulgent one.

His voice was softer, almost a whisper again when he said, "Thank you for coming. I know it wasn't easy."

Their voices were growing more distant as I heard her say, "It only took a few Gate hops to make it to Bhalden's Post, and your lovely Mr. Blunthorn was waiting for me... " And then, though I listened, they were gone and I was left drifting alone in the darkness again.

A BIRDSONG I'D NEVER heard before pricked me to consciousness, and I was alone when I opened my eyes. I lay in the bed for a long moment listening to the unfamiliar trill coming from outside the window and trying to make sense of my surroundings. The walls were made from a dark gray stone block, not the white stone of my bedroom walls, and yet the quilt that Nona—my paternal grandmother—and all her friends in her sewing circle had made for me as a baby gift lay stretched out across me on the bed that I was in. There was a muted blue velvet chair that sat empty near the bed, and a crackling fire filled the small fireplace to my right, with a stack of logs ready to go in beside it. A brown clay pitcher and washbasin sat on the bedside table. It was daytime, I had no idea where I was, and my bladder was overfull.

There was no bell to ring or rope to pull to summon the help, so I struggled to sit up in the bed thinking I could try to find the lavatory for myself, only to scream and recoil onto the bed again when a voice just to the left of me whispered, "You're awake."

Victor—seated in the chair next to me—flinched as if he'd been struck, his expression looking decidedly hunted.

"Where did you come from?" I squeaked, my adrenaline heightened in a way it hadn't been since I was a child. I lay panting from fear as I clutched at my chest, and his brows pulled down over his deep-set blue eyes as he frowned in confusion at my grasping hands.

"I've been here," he answered, clearly puzzled. A blush crept over his high cheekbones for some reason, the faint stain made all the more obvious against his paper-white skin. His hair was another stark contrast, dark as pitch and mussed, as if he'd spent a lot of time with his fingers in it recently, though he currently sat forward with his forearms braced on his knees and his fingers knit casually together between them. Even sitting, he was tall, easily taller than any fae I'd ever met. Everything about him was large—his jawbone, his bold nose, the cheekbones currently tinged pink. It was all in perfect, masculine proportion to the rest of him... but I couldn't help marveling over the substantial bone structure of his frame. His hands were long, his wrist bones thick, and he carried quite a bit of muscle in his arms and shoulders, yet he still was lean enough to be considered lanky. At least, I had thought so when I saw him from down the aisle.

The wedding came crashing back into memory in an instant. The towering soul-collector waiting for my pledge, who was *not* as lanky as he appeared from a distance once I was standing next to his imposing build. The darkened great hall, so different than every wedding that had ever been held in it before—normally full of bright sunshine. The bare-bones audience of family and what few dignitaries happened to be in the region already. The biting absence of the only person I'd hoped to be there for me. The dark magic that had torn through the room and my own veins before I had finally blacked out.

"What can I get for you?" Victor asked in a gentle whisper, his ice-blue eyes locked onto me with an intensity I was unused to. I could have sworn that chair was empty when I woke up.

I needed to slow my breathing and lower my heart rate. I took a deep breath and cleared my throat to tell him I was fine, because I didn't want to be a bother. But, realizing I was not, and with my own cheeks heating, I admitted, "I could use the lavatory if one is available." And I was starving, but that was a lesser priority.

His eyes widened in understanding before he started to stand and then froze. "I could take you to the restroom, or I could bring you a bedpan."

The sheer horror that rolled through me at the thought of using a *bedpan* in front of this shockingly handsome man—to whom I was not only a stranger but also *newly married*—was indescribable. "No, no," I practically wheezed out, trying to re-assure him without choking on my embarrassment. "The re-stroom is great." I was going to perish right here of mortifica-tion.

Victor stood from his chair, helping me to pull my blan-kets back. My injured arm was wrapped in white gauze, and I was wearing a simple, pale-colored nightgown I'd never seen before—it certainly wasn't something I'd brought with me. It wasn't even cut in a style I was familiar with.

"What is this?" I asked, feeling the loose weave of the soft fabric at my collarbone with my fingertips.

"The dwarves call it a shift," he explained. "It's worn for sleep-ing. I had to make some adjustments for your wings."

"You—" I started dumbly, unsure of how to finish my question without simply repeating him. I reached behind me to feel at the back of the garment.

"I cut some slits," he said, his cheeks flaming an even deeper shade of pink than before. "I don't know how to sew, but Brishta is working on some other shifts for you."

He had modified my nightgown himself? I couldn't tell if I was bemused or incredibly charmed. It occurred to me that he had probably been the one to dress me. I supposed he was—*techni-cally*—my husband, so my bashfulness was probably misplaced in that aspect and would need to be done away with entirely once we consummated our marriage. But... didn't he have any lady's maids to do such things for him?

But then I remembered that his lady's maids wouldn't be fae, and I cringed at the thought of having someone else handling my wings. If I could just put them away... I struggled to shift into my wingless form, but nothing happened. Changing forms required energy and that was something I was in short supply of, regardless of the fact that I had been sleeping for who knows how long.

Victor helped me to sit up and I noticed his own clothing appeared to be made from the same material as mine, just in a tighter, finer weave. His white shirt buttoned up the front but was cut in a casually loose style, and his dark trousers were similarly casual in appearance. He began to lift me from the bed, but I quickly assured him I was fine. Having him this close to me made my heart beat too fast and my head swim. I tried to tell him that, if he could just direct me to where I could refresh myself, I could walk there on my own. It only took me half a step to realize that the floor was coming at me entirely too fast and this was absolute folly on my part. I *could not* walk there on my own. Luckily for me, his reactions were much faster than mine, and he had me cradled in his arms before I became unceremoniously acquainted with the woolen rug. He didn't utter a word of chastisement.

The lavatory was simple but sufficient, and small enough that I could hold onto the wall for the time that I required some privacy, though it was far colder in here than it had been in his bedroom next to the fire. He was waiting for me when I opened the door again.

"I had some food brought up," he told me and then gently lifted me back into his arms, as carefully as if I were a porcelain doll. "Do you think you can eat?"

"I'm famished," I admitted as he tucked me back into the bed. Had he been sleeping here with me?

Victor nodded. "You haven't had anything but broth for the last several days, and not much of that." I marveled at the grace with which he moved when he paced to a tray that had been set up next to the door and began lifting lids from the dishes. "I wasn't sure what you would eat, so the cook sent up a variety of options."

"Anything is fine," I assured him.

He lifted an eyebrow as if to challenge me, but I'd been raised in the royal courts. We weren't allowed to have preferences, lest we risk offending a host on a diplomatic visit or while under public scrutiny at any of the numerous festivities. I'd been sent to bed without a meal many nights as a child until I learned to eat what was placed in front of me. It probably took me longer than it should have to learn my lesson, on account of Cook leaving out my favorite pastries for me to steal after everyone else had gone to bed. She could never abide a hungry belly. It was a good lesson, though, and had served me well at many public engagements. Food was fuel. Something to sustain us without being lingered over or quibbled about.

He peeked at a few more dishes and then lifted the entire tray, carrying it over to me and setting it on the other side of the bed. Sliding it closer to me, he climbed onto the bed next to me, sitting with one leg bent under him and began to explain the dishes. "This one is a morning pudding," he said, "and this is stewed cherries. There's toasted bread, curds, and I requested some meat too in case you eat that." He picked up the lid for the last one and replaced it much quicker than he had the other ones.

"You don't like it?" I guessed. He didn't answer except for a lightning-fast wrinkling of his nose, but then it was gone.

I promptly burst into laughter before I caught myself, utterly fascinated by his reaction.

His eyes flashed to mine, something sparkling in the depths, I thought, but I couldn't be sure before his gaze dropped back to the tray. He eventually lifted the bowl of pudding from the tray and handed it to me. "See if this agrees with you."

I accepted the dish and a spoon and ate a bite, feeling shy about eating in front of him while he watched me so intently. The pudding was hot, and rich, and I was so hungry that I nearly inhaled the next few bites. It got harder to support myself in a sitting position very abruptly, though, and my weakness became more evident when even holding the spoon up became too much for me.

"May I help you?" he asked, gently removing the dish from my hand and filling the spoon again for me.

"You don't have to do that. I just need to rest a bit, I think," I hedged, trying to ignore the hunger still gnawing at my insides.

"I've been doing it with broth since we got here. I don't see how pudding is all that different," he said lightly as he lifted the spoon to my mouth.

He had been... feeding me? While I slept? A strange affection flooded through me when I tried to picture this large and mysterious man attempting to coax broth into my mouth and cutting openings in my nightgown for my wings. I realized that he was waiting for me to open my mouth when he looked up from my lips and I quickly opened it to accept the food. Hot, sweet deliciousness flooded my mouth, and I couldn't help but give him a grateful smile while I swallowed, but all he did was continue to watch my face and retrieve another bite.

Chapter 10

Celeste

WHEN I NEXT WOKE, it was to darkened windows and a low-burning fire in the fireplace. The room was empty again, but I double-checked the chair beside me to verify that there was indeed no one in it this time. I nearly came out of my skin again when Victor rose from the window seat on the far side of the room. Was I simply not able to see him well when he was sitting still or something?

He froze when I screeched like a wild animal, his eyes wide. "Sorry."

I gasped for breath. "You just startled me," I said, panting.

"I'll try not to," he said, still stooped in his frozen posture. His shoulders were hunched, and a deep blush began to spread over his cheeks again. I hadn't been aware that it was possible for one of the powerful *Veardur* to appear bashful, but he truly did just now. He straightened very slowly, as if fast movements had been what set me off, and I tried to contain my smile. "Can I bring you some food?" he asked, turning to the tray on the stand by the door again when I agreed. He stared at the tray pensively when I told him I still had no preference, and then selected a porridge for me to try and climbed onto the mattress next to me again. I smiled at him gratefully, glad for the company.

After a few bites, he lifted the bowl from my hands without comment and replaced it with a dish of cheese curds, so I ate a few of those. But then he removed that one as well and placed the same pudding I'd eaten earlier into my hands.

"What are you doing?" I asked with a confused laugh.

"You like this one better," he said matter-of-factly. Both the porridge and the curds had been fine, hearty and savory. Filling. But the warmth and flavor of the pudding flooded my mouth at the first bite, and I couldn't help but sigh in pleasure. He rose from the bed to fetch me a steaming cup of some herbal brew. "The cook sent this up for you," he said hesitantly. "It doesn't taste good, but she says it's good for your health. You don't have to drink it."

I took the mug and sniffed at it, recognizing the familiar earthy, minty scent as healsall, a plant with medicinal properties that my own people used for helping with increasing our magical energy and as a general tonic. I'd been made to drink it often throughout my life, and he was right, it didn't taste good. But I drained the cup and handed it back to him, grateful for the sweetness of the pudding to cover the bitter aftertaste. I finished the pudding and ate a few more of the soft, pale-colored cheese curds before deciding I couldn't handle any more. "What about you?" I asked when I was full.

Victor lifted his gaze to mine with a puzzled expression. He didn't seem to talk much.

"Have you eaten?" None of the dishes had appeared to have been touched before I ate from them.

"Earlier," he said. "Do you need to use the restroom again?"

"No. I would love to get clean though, but I don't think I have the energy right now," I confessed. I'd managed to feed myself this time, which was an improvement, but my arms trembled rather pathetically when I lifted them now. My energy was spent. I was used to having to ration my energy even for daily tasks. It was something I'd learned to do early in my illness. And while I hated feeling unwashed and grubby in front of this handsome man who looked as though he'd been carved from white marble by the hand of God himself, I was already very familiar with the disappointment of having things my mind wanted to do but my body was not up to the task of doing. I wanted to ask if he had a lady's maid who could help wash me, as my parents did, but since I hadn't been introduced to one, I didn't want to risk embarrassing him if he didn't have one. And the thought of having a non-fae seeing me nude in my winged form felt deeply uncomfortable. Our wings were considered a sacred part of us, something no one but the high fae had.

Victor paused in thought for a moment, his mouth in a sulky, attractive line before walking to the mantle over the fire and retrieving a steaming pitcher. He settled it onto the small table next to me and stepped out of the room, returning quickly with an armful of bottles. "You'll have to tell me what to do," he informed me in a shy tone, settling them on the nightstand beside the pitcher. He picked up a toothbrush and used it to mix up a small amount of cleansing powder and water into a bit of paste while I stared at him and tried to muscle up the energy to work my arms again. "This part I can figure out on my own, I think," he said. He held the brush in front of my mouth with an expectant expression, and I reached to take it, but he tutted at me. "Open."

I opened my mouth, puzzling over the strangeness of having someone else brush my teeth. Even my maids didn't do that for me. He peered inside and gently cleansed my mouth with the minty tasting paste.

"Your mouth is very small," he commented with a frown, his eyebrows pinched together in concentration. After giving special attention to every surface, his brow smoothed out and he sat back as if satisfied with his efforts before handing me a cup of water.

I took a sip, and he handed me a bowl to spit in, staring at me with those piercing blue eyes. I couldn't bring myself to do it. I swallowed the foam instead, shuddering at the thought of spitting in front of someone else, let alone *him*.

He frowned at me but proceeded to take a cloth from a stack on the table, dipping it into the steaming pitcher before wringing it out. Starting with the corners of my mouth, he wiped my face, folding it over and moving to my cheeks and forehead, then wiping gently at my eyes with practiced motions. But then he faltered, as if unsure of what to do, a look of self-consciousness washing over his face. "I can... wash your hair," he offered.

It was such a sweet thing for him to suggest, and heavens knew I needed it, but I felt my own wave of self-consciousness when I thought of him touching my unkempt hair. It hadn't been washed since the morning of our wedding, however long ago that had been. Though, strangely there were a lot less tangles in it than I would have expected. "I can just wait until I feel better so it won't be so much trouble," I told him.

He frowned at me again, but I had no idea why. Maybe my hair was so unclean he found it distasteful to leave it unwashed for yet another day. I nearly drowned in shame before he said, "It isn't any trouble. I'm simply unsure of how to physically care for someone other than myself. This is the opposite of what I do," he said with a huff, sounding flustered.

I rolled my lips between my teeth, trying desperately not to laugh.

"What are you doing?" he asked, sounding mildly panicked. "Are you choking?"

"No, I'm fine," I told him truthfully. "What do you mean, 'the opposite of what you do'?" I asked, hoping to keep him going now that he was talking.

He waved his hand in the air. "I deal with *dead people.*" That sulky pout was back. "Caring for the living is a little beyond my purview. But I can learn," he quickly assured me. He must have seen the conflicting emotions on my face, because he reached out his long hand to trail his fingers down some strands of my hair in a familiar way I didn't expect. "May I?" he asked quietly.

How could I say no to that? I nodded timidly, having difficulty finding words with him touching me like this.

Victor narrowed his eyes at the bed for a moment, his own lips rolling between his teeth, before scooting me down and propping me higher on some pillows that he covered with a towel. A washbasin was placed behind my head. I tried to help him drape my hair backward over the towel he'd placed over my pillows, but he grasped my hands with a light touch and laid them across my stomach. "Rest," he instructed. Then, taking a clean cloth, he dipped it into the steaming water, wrung it out a little less than before, and then—starting at my scalp—began wiping it down the lengths of my hair. "See? I can figure this out," he muttered to himself. The hot water felt blissful, and my eyes started to drift shut immediately, but when he started to rub shampoo into my scalp they nearly rolled back in my head. It was all I could do not to groan in pleasure.

His fingers paused when I stiffened, trying to contain my rapidly accelerating heart rate at the feeling of his strong hands in my hair. "Am I hurting you?" he asked, alarmed.

"No," I wheezed. "It's nice," I babbled, trying not to gurgle. I was practically panting again, but not from fear this time.

"I feel like I'm making knots in your hair," he said absently. I didn't care. He could turn my head into one giant tangle as long as he kept up the rubbing.

"That's better," he said to himself, changing his technique so that his fingers reached farther along my scalp with each stroke.

I focused on my deep breathing, trying not to embarrass myself in front of him. This entire ordeal was mortifying but I never, ever wanted it to stop. What was wrong with me? I'd had my hair washed before! But eventually it did stop as he worked the lather down to the ends of my hair, then pulled the washbasin closer so that my hair could lay in it as he used the wet rag to rinse my scalp, dipping it into the warm water again and again. He could do this for the rest of my life, and I would never grow tired of it. Lifting my hair from the basin, he gently squeezed it to remove some of the water, then set the basin aside and pulled the towel up and around the wet strands, pressing as he went to soak up some of the wetness.

"Now what?" he murmured.

"Hm?" I wasn't capable of forming coherent sentences right now.

"I've... never done this before."

He could have fooled me. I opened one eye, and he was staring at my bundled hair with his eyebrows drawn together again.

"My sister talks about things like 'cream rinses' and 'conditioners' and 'hair masks,' but I admit I'm not very good at listening when she talks about it." His sulky frown shouldn't make me want to taste his lips. Had we kissed at the wedding? I couldn't remember, and that left an odd pang in my chest. I had to smile at his mildly grouchy tone. Siblings had a special way of getting under our skin, and my own brother would have been just as lost in a trial involving women's hair care products. "I usually put some kind of detangler in it," I explained, watching his eyes grow wide with horror at the additional mention of one more type of product, "but we can just let it dry, and I'll sort out the tangles later." My hair would probably be a mess, but the scalp massage had been so worth it. At least it was clean now.

Victor frowned at me again. Not as though he was angry, but maybe disapproving. "How do I figure out which one of these is a detangler?"

I rolled my lips between my teeth again. *Caring for the living indeed.* "Any kind of conditioner would be fine," I ceded, trying to make his task easier.

He was quiet for a bit as he stared at the cluster of bottles he'd brought in the same way my grandmother stared at her war maps. "I'm afraid I might have been overconfident in my assurance that I could 'figure this out.' What does conditioner *do?*" His tone was oddly distrusting, as if conditioner might be something scary. "And don't tell me it conditions, I don't even know what that means."

I lost the fight with my grin, enjoying his reactions and the fact that he was finally talking to me—something he didn't seem terribly comfortable with. I appreciated the effort. "It makes your hair slick and shiny."

The frown on his beautiful face deepened as he looked at my hair out of the side of his eye. "Wet hair is already slick and shiny."

"I know," I told him with a tired sigh, my mouth still pulled up into an involuntary curve. "It keeps it that way once it dries, too."

He began opening bottles from the nightstand and sniffing at each one, poking at the contents and eyeing them suspiciously. "I just don't know. What if we put something horrible in your hair? Wait—is this one it?" he asked finally, holding it out for me to see in the low firelight. When his shirt sleeve gaped open, I could see dark marks on his skin where he'd been cut during our ceremony. I touched the surface of the pale-colored cream and rubbed it between my fingers, noting the light floral scent.

"Seems like it," I told him with no small amusement. "You can water it down so that you don't have to rinse my hair afterward again." I watched him curiously as he placed some in a bowl and added water, stirring it in while maintaining a distrustful expression. "What do you wash with?" I asked him curiously a few minutes later as he was smoothing the watered-down mixture along my hair.

"Soap."

"I meant your hair," I explained with a chuckle. He had such glossy dark hair.

"Still soap." He stacked more pillows behind me and then lifted me into a sitting position while willfully ignoring my squawking.

"You use *soap* on your *hair*?" It was more of a protest than a question. Life was so unfair. My hair needed a minimum of four separate products a week or my wavy texture became completely unmanageable frizz.

He didn't answer me, focusing instead on combing through my hair in small sections, starting with the bottoms and working his way higher.

I watched him out of the side of my eye, not wanting to turn my head and disturb his efforts. It seemed I did anyway, as he paused when we made eye contact, lifting an eyebrow in question. "I thought you hadn't done this before." I supposed brushing hair out wasn't terribly complicated, but he was strangely skillful at avoiding creating new tangles with his comb in a way he hadn't been with his fingers earlier.

"I didn't think it would be good to leave your hair pinned

up as it was from the wedding while you slept," he responded, returning to his careful brushing.

I tried to picture him letting my hair down and combing it out as I slept, his eyebrows drawn together as they had been before. Clearly, he had no lady's maids. What a baffling situation. I found myself strangely grateful for this realization. True, it would mean that I would have more work to do for myself on a daily basis, but hopefully as I healed—if I healed—it wouldn't be too much of a burden to do so. The freedom of being able to do those things for myself was an odd thrill. Not having to wait on the maids' schedules to dress or bathe, or to worry about the listening ears and wagging tongues that eagerly carried all the latest gossip about the kingdom's notoriously infirm princess and her newest ailments beyond the palace walls by dinner time. No more "helpful comments" about how *this color* emphasized my sickly skin tone, or *that style* highlighted how underweight I'd become.

Of course, there would be some style or type of garment that was required of the spouse of a *Veardur*. They all wore simple, neutral colors, after all, so maybe I wouldn't have that much freedom in what I wore. I mourned a little for the loss of all the bright colors that I so adored, but duty and the importance of dressing for one's station was one thing I understood well. Hopefully he would help to guide me in that, since I wouldn't have someone to dress me any longer. But the thought of not having a bustle of women stripping me and dressing me and commenting on my body and fluffing my wings and pushing my hairpins in too tight... I let out a shaky breath.

Victor paused, his long fingers freezing exactly where they were in my hair. "Am I pulling too hard?" How was it possible this enormous, gravelly-voiced man, who felt so out of sorts at the thought of caring for the living, managed to handle me so much more delicately than my own caretakers?

My smile was tremulous but genuine. "No. You're being so gentle."

Chapter 11

Celeste

I'D LOST ANY SENSE of time. All I knew was that it was light outside when I finally woke up again. I darted my gaze around the room, expecting Victor to be there when I woke, just as he had the last two times, but even when I propped myself up in bed, he didn't appear. I felt a little silly, expecting him to still be there watching me sleep. And even more so at my disappointment that he wasn't. Would it be strange to have a crush on your own husband? I didn't think I was there yet, but...

Now that I knew where the restroom was, I thought I could get myself there on my own. *Maybe.* I climbed very carefully out of the bed, testing my ability to remain upright without the aid of a healing draught and half a dozen enchantments like I'd needed for our wedding ceremony. Even then it had been incredibly questionable to me whether I would succeed in making it down the aisle.

I gripped the edge of the mattress for a few steps, until I was confident I wasn't as dizzy as I had been the day before. The tray by the door was empty, save for a steaming pot of tea, and the room was silent other than the popping of low burning coals in the fireplace. The hallway outside was eerily quiet and devoid of people.

Once I found the lavatory, I did my best to avoid looking in the mirror, knowing nothing good would come from a close inspection of myself at the moment. My cheekbones would be too severe, my color too faded, and my wings were a horrible mess. I thought that I might actually have enough energy to shift to my wingless form today, but staying that way would be another story. I didn't want to push my luck when my energy was still so limited. After relieving myself, I took a blessed moment to really scrub at my body with the chilly water from the taps. We still hadn't made our wedding official with the necessary consummation, and I was sure my new husband would want to initiate that soon. The thought of him finding me unwashed for such a rite was mortifying. I paused at the bandages encasing my right arm. *Best to leave those alone for now*, I thought, afraid to see what was underneath. I did brave the mirror after replacing my clothing, just long enough to ensure my hair wasn't a disaster, but it only served to confirm that my feathers were as mangled as I knew they would be.

I padded quietly back down the hallway to the bedroom, noting the rough-hewn blocks that made up the walls and the high-arched ceiling. While I was truly grateful for the privacy, it felt rather strange to be so alone. The room was still empty, and I noticed that the side of the bed opposite mine was entirely undisturbed. Was he sleeping somewhere else? I didn't know why the thought of that made my stomach sink. Maybe he simply rose early and had straightened the sheets before he left.

As I poured myself a cup of tea to take back to the bed with me, a noise outside drew my attention to the window. When I crossed to the frost-coated glass and peered out, I found it looked down onto a snow-covered courtyard with stone walls surrounding it. Beyond those were rocky cliffs that dropped away into dark water filled with large chunks of ice. A tall man in a black cloak stood below the window, chopping wood. He looked about the right size to be Victor and he moved with the same kind of deadly grace that my new husband carried himself with, but he had his cowl pulled up for warmth and I couldn't see his face. I settled on the window seat to watch him work since I had nothing else to do, wrapping my hands around my cup of tea and pulling my wings around me for more warmth.

The axe he used for chopping was longer handled and much larger than what I'd seen used before, and the way he wielded it with such force and precision made my skin prickle. But then his tool changed! I leaned forward, trying to get a better look at it, but only managed to fog up the window so that I had to wipe it clean to be able to see again. His axe was smaller now, I was sure of it—still the night-dark color of the previous tool that he'd used, but the shape and size were completely different. I sipped my tea and watched, puzzled, while he tossed the smaller pieces of wood he had split aside, placed another large log on his stump, and then the axe in his hand *transformed again* into the larger weapon. After a few moments of chopping firewood, his hood dropped back, and I could see the man below was indeed my new husband. His magical tools were fascinating, but I was even more mesmerized by his movements. They were methodical, powerful, and practiced, but the force behind them was undoubtedly lethal. I pulled my wings a little tighter around me.

Back and forth he went, splitting a large log into smaller pieces, and then trimming the largest of those into even smaller pieces still, his tool changing size and shape as he went. The stack beside him had grown considerably when he flicked his hand and his cloak disappeared entirely, like mist on a hot day. There was nothing but trousers covering him as he stood in the snow, his breath fogging around him and the pale skin of his back glistening and damp as it dipped and curved over his muscles while he bent, stretched, swung, and stacked. He must have somehow heard my quiet gasp, because he turned and looked directly at me, finding me peering at him through the window, startling me just as much as he did when he materialized out of nothing—which is what I'd decided he must have done the previous times I'd woken to find no one. I knew the *Veardur* had magical powers involving the creation and disappearance of things, but I'd never understood it. A vague recollection of his mount—*a horse?*—suddenly appearing before us in the night as we left the palace tugged at my memory. There were a great many things about the *Veardur* that I'd never understood. It was said they could create their own Gates, and that they came for the dead. In very rare cases, they would occasionally guard people when requested—if they decided amongst themselves it was a worthwhile endeavor. They were feared, honored, and revered among the high fae. I'd only caught a glimpse of one a single time in the courts, long before I'd entered a room half-filled with them and then married one. His gentle treatment of me yesterday had lulled me into a false sense of normalcy, but seeing him like this today, completing such a mundane task in such an extraordinary way made me remember how little I truly knew about him.

His piercing blue eyes met mine for less than a second, lancing through me with a jolt of lightning, before he turned to answer the call of someone at the courtyard gates. I shrank back from the window, embarrassed to have been caught staring, but couldn't pry myself away completely.

The woman at the gate was far shorter than Victor, perhaps even shorter than me, but with a wider frame and stout build. She appeared stooped with age, and gray hair peeked out from under her cowl, but despite her evident seniority she still looked strong and hale. Behind her was a similarly sturdy-looking pack animal that might have been a donkey, held loosely by a rope attached to its halter. Victor's cloak reappeared upon his body the instant he turned to her, and he made his way to the gate to open it. He spoke to the woman, but I couldn't make out what was being said. I couldn't see her eyes from here either, but from the way her face was tilted as they talked, it didn't seem as though she was looking at him. Was she afraid? I didn't think she appeared to be, with a smile on her face as she lifted a cloth-wrapped bundle from her animal and held it out for Victor, just slightly off from where he stood. He spoke to her again and took the package from her, setting it down in the snow beside him and stepping after the woman with his hand held out to her as she turned away. She waved him off, causing his shoulders to hitch up, and when he said something else, she turned back to pat him on the arm, and then waved him off again. He stood and watched, visibly distressed, as she turned back the way she'd come, and he didn't budge until she'd led her plodding donkey all the way back across the narrow bridge that led from the gate. Even after he bent to pick up her package, he stayed and watched her closely until she was past the narrow ridge that wound around the face of the rocks and out of sight. Once she was gone his shoulders finally dropped and he pulled his hand down his face. His cloak billowed around him as he returned to the pile of wood he'd been creating, gathering an armful of split logs and carrying them, with his bundle, out of my line of sight. A few moments later, he entered our room. His expression as he greeted me showed a measured curiosity, a sparkle of something in his eye that he tried to keep subdued. His gaze flicked over me in the same clinical assessment I'd always received from my healers as he saw me sitting on the window seat, still clutching my tea.

"Are you cold?" he asked, setting his parcel on the tray with the tea as he eyed my tightly held wings. "I brought more wood for the fire."

"I'm fine," I answered automatically, working to loosen my muscles so that my posture was less stiff. It was a little chilly in the room, but I didn't want to admit that my bearing had more to do with nervousness than temperature. My elder sister had always been the brave one between us, the one who could launch herself into any situation with her head held high, not me. The two of us had always known that we would be arranged into political marriages. She'd looked forward to it; I'd simply accepted it. But this... wasn't what that was. My deteriorating health had caused my family to make a different choice—for which I was grateful—but I wasn't sure how to behave in this new situation. I'd expected to be betrothed to someone for a period of time and get to know them, be married to them over an elaborate ceremony during which we were able to become used to each other's presence at the very least. I would do my duty to my kingdom and represent my people's interests and bear an heir for my new husband but otherwise probably not feel much for him in any way that mattered.

It was all catching up to me now, as I sat here staring at a wide-eyed, pink-cheeked, bare-chested man who looked like the standard for masculine beauty wearing an oddly shifting cloak in a *strangely* quiet castle, that I was faced with a much different reality. Were there no staff at all? Why was he the one doing all the tending to me? Feeding me, cleansing my hair, bringing me wood—chopping it even. I was unused to this level of attention from any one person, and it made me feel... Well, I didn't know how it made me feel, but there was something fluttery in my chest and seeing the way the light from the windows played across his torso, casting shadows in the taut lines of his abdominal muscles, and the way his waist narrowed and dipped in just above his trousers... The room was suddenly much warmer than it had been the moment before, and he still hadn't built up the fire.

He set the logs in a neat stack on the hearth and added the last one to the coals before returning to his bundle and untying it. The cloth fell open to reveal smaller packages of food stuffs, all packed neatly in little clay pots wrapped in paper for protection. "Our cook had prior arrangements today, but she brought our food herself instead of sending it with a runner like I told her to," he explained in an indulgent grumble, but I didn't understand what he meant.

"Prior arrangements?" I asked dumbly. Even if she had been granted a day off work, wouldn't it have made more sense for her to cook his food here and then leave for the day instead of carting it by donkey from elsewhere? "Doesn't she live here?"

"No one lives here," he said absently as he opened a low cabinet in the back of the room and retrieved some porcelain dishes.

I blinked at that, feeling very slow. We had several palaces that we moved between throughout the seasons, but our staff always came with us. No one lived here, ever? I supposed that would explain why it was so quiet.

He must have seen my confusion, because an eyebrow lifted in what might have been amusement. "This isn't my home.

It's the closest holding my family owns to Faery. It's usually vacant unless we need to stay here for some reason, so I chose to stop here while you recover. We tend to prefer our privacy, and it's easier for us to employ a local family or two to come in temporarily when we're here. Helda cooks for us when we're here, but when we're not, she has other things to do." He filled two plates with food and carried them to me, handing me one and settling on the other side of the window seat with the other. "I am also capable of cooking for us, but not as well as Helda," he said wryly.

I quietly turned that information over while I studied the food, wondering where we would go from here and why he would know how to cook, but not wanting to pepper him with too many questions. He smelled faintly of salt air with a hint of sweat—reminding me that he also chopped his own wood—and I found myself glancing up at his bare chest through my eyelashes. He ate in silence, and I noticed his food did not match mine. I had an array of choices, but he had a pile of steamed greens with thick stalks covered in some kind of light brown sauce.

"You seemed concerned for her," I noted as I poked at my food, eating a bite of everything whether I knew what it was or not. I loved the deep timbre of his voice and wanted to hear more of it, to learn more about him and this place he'd chosen to bring me to.

"She is completely blind," he stated quietly as he pierced another stalk with his fork. "But she has been since birth, and she doesn't want assistance. I respect that, and the fact that she has lived in these mountains her entire life, but I would feel—" he paused for a moment and looked upset, searching for a word, *"unhappy* if she plummeted from one of these narrow ledges on an errand for me." The last bit was delivered in a decidedly grumpy tone, and I couldn't help but be struck by the strangeness of his surly elocution of such a morbid statement. He seemed as if his emotional reaction to such a tragic event were even more disturbing to him than the hypothetical event itself. "Maids and cooks will come in as we need them, but otherwise we will be left alone," he said with something like relief.

I frowned at him. "You have no guards?"

"I am the guard."

Chapter 12

Celeste

"I HAVE A REQUEST," I told Victor timidly over dinner.

"Anything." His quiet response was immediate and sincere as he looked up from his food. The feeling of butterflies in my stomach made it hard to continue.

"I would like to tidy my wings," I said when I found my voice, reaching up without thinking to run my fingers down one of the pinions on my left wing.

My husband's eyes snapped to my fingers and fixated on the motion with an intense concentration that made me shiver. But then he seemed to realize what he was doing and brought his eyes to meet mine with a little furrow on his brow that showed he didn't understand. Of course, he wouldn't.

"I can use hair combs for straightening them, but I don't have any wing powder," I explained, already anticipating how much this was going to baffle him after the conditioner confusion.

He must have seen the amusement in my eyes, because he narrowed his own eyes at me, weighing my words as if I might be making up such a product. I wondered who had been brave enough to tease this man with made up products and how often, that this was his first response.

I took pity on him and assured him, "I'm not making it up. I promise."

He turned his head just enough to look at me out of the corner of his eye, an expression I found oddly adorable. "And what does this 'wing powder' do?" he asked.

"It powders my wings," I told him while utterly failing to keep a straight face. His eyes squinted even harder at my admittedly suspicious behavior, so I relented. I didn't really know him well enough to tease him, husband or not. "It helps with water resistance and general maintenance. Any colorless mineral powder used for makeup would probably be fine." Wing powder as a specific product probably didn't even exist here.

He chewed on his own lip while lost in thought for a moment before answering with his own conundrum. "I could travel back to Faery alone to try to find you some, so that you wouldn't have to use the Gate again and travel so far to an outpost, but I don't want to leave you alone for that long." I didn't mention that he had left me alone for a long stretch today, but I supposed he had been nearby so perhaps that was different. But then I remembered that he'd told me time passed differently within the realms and we wouldn't have any way of predicting how much time had passed. No, I definitely didn't want him going back into Faery. He shook his head as if agreeing with my thoughts. "I will make sure you get some."

The next morning, he knocked on the frame of my open door while holding a small ceramic jar. I'd woken early to find the other side of the bed undisturbed again, had eaten some leftover pastry-things from the night before, and then set to work immediately on my wings. Better to do what I could while I had the energy, I figured. I'd needed to hold on to the table as I snapped my wings out several times, beating them as hard as I could to shake out any rumples and close up most of the openings in my feathers. And then I'd set to work on the most stubborn feathers with a stiff comb, smoothing out each one until it laid just right. I looked up to find him watching me work and gave him a self-conscious smile.

"You'll have to make sure this is the right kind of powder," he said. The familiar pink began to tinge his cheek bones.

"Oh, where did you manage to find some so quickly?" I asked in surprise.

He approached the small desk I was sitting at near the bedroom window. It had a matching wooden chair that didn't get in the way of my wings, and the old mercury glass mirror it held made me think it had seen more use as a vanity than a writing surface.

"I sent a spectral to Blunthorn last night and he had Helda bring some for me when she came to cook this morning."

I blinked at him in surprise. "Spectrals" were what we called the little spectral messengers that carried missives to another person for us in exchange for being allowed to absorb the magic that we placed inside of special stone chips for them. I was surprised to hear that they existed here, as I'd always thought they needed fae magic. I was also surprised that Victor was close enough to this Mister Blunthorn to send him a messenger. You needed a *literal piece* of that person for the spectrals to be able to find them, so if you don't know someone well enough to carry an old baby tooth or a lock of their hair, the spectral wouldn't be able to find them.

"Oh, please give them my thanks," I told him, taking the jar from him. I opened it to find what looked like a simple lady's setting powder inside, along with a powder puff, which would work perfectly for my needs. I told him that and thanked him, wondering what his Blunthorn man had thought of my *Veardur's* request for lady's setting powder and smiling at the mental image. "This was very sweet of you," I said, setting it down so I could finish with my combing.

"Always tell me what you need," he said quietly as he watched me preen with evident curiosity. "Is there something I can do to help? That seems like a lot of work." His voice was rumbly and deep, and his offer gave me a spark of pleasure.

I shrugged awkwardly and hid the embarrassment coloring my cheeks behind the wing I was tending to. "It isn't usually this much work," I explained, feeling bashful. "Day to day it only takes as much maintenance as someone's hair might. This has gotten particularly bad from me lying on them, so it's going to take a bit more work, like long hair would if it became badly tangled. But if you want to," I handed him another comb, "it would be helpful to do the back feathers where I can't reach."

"And what am I doing?" he asked, all business, as he took the comb and stepped behind me.

The prickling feeling at the back of my neck showed how aware I was of him being at my back, even though he hadn't touched me yet. I had to clear my throat before I could answer him. "Feathers have tiny hooks in the filaments called barbules, they help the feather to stay closed up and smooth. You can use the tines of the comb to rake them straight and close up the splits wherever you find them, like this," I explained, showing him a feather that had split and how to fix it.

He was so gentle I couldn't imagine how effective he was being, but I appreciated the effort. I smiled again at his tenderness, remembering all too well my whining protests at how rough my mother could be with my feathers when I was a little child. Or how we'd squawk at our friends when one tweaked a feather wrong.

"Does it tickle?" he asked when I chuckled at the memory, pulling his comb away.

"No," I told him, and he returned to combing. "Parents do this for little ones before they're able to, and then when we're children we tend to sit around and groom each other's feathers like this. It's a social activity, I guess. I don't know if girls here sit around and braid each other's hair." I glanced back at him, but he was too focused on combing to notice. "If they do, it's a similar thing. But little kids aren't the gentlest, and squabbles always started when someone wasn't careful enough with another person's wings. I was just remembering some of those childhood fights."

We never really stopped enjoying social grooming—we were a pretty touchy-feely people in general, I guess—but we became more selective about who we allowed to touch our wings as we grew up. It was a sort of bonding activity between close friends or with a lover, and though he couldn't have known it, Victor's offer to help me with mine was incredibly forward.

But it was a soothing ritual for most of us, and since the backs of our wings were difficult to reach and not particularly sensitive, friends would often sit for a chat and gossip while we helped each other with the harder to reach areas. We knew not to touch the underwings or specific places where they connected to our backs. But Victor didn't. When his fingers grazed the sensitive feathers closest to my spine, both of my wings twitched, and as my sharp intake of breath gave me away, I felt him freeze behind me.

He sounded startled when he asked, "Did I do something?"

YES.

"You're fine!" I reassured him with an awkward laugh, my voice pitched way too high to be believable. I took a shaky, deep breath, trying to ignore the way my body was reacting to his touch when he timidly resumed his feather stroking. But then he reached *under my wing* to steady it as he combed out a particularly stubborn feather and my whole body just lit up. I couldn't control the full body shiver at the feeling of his hands on me. I had to slap my hand over my mouth when my breath hitched. "Sorry!" I squeaked when he jerked his hand away. "We're just really sensitive there. It's not that you've done anything wrong." *It just feels way too good.* "I just wasn't expecting it, and—" I cut myself off, because I was babbling and he had stepped back with an alarmed expression.

"Forgive me," he said, schooling his face into a mask of calm nonchalance. "So sorry." He carefully placed the comb back in my hand without allowing his skin to touch mine at all. "I believe I have all the feathers smoothed out back here anyway, so I will leave you to finish without my interference. I will tell Blunthorn his delivery will suffice." He took another step backward before turning and walking from the room, his cheeks stained red and shadows pulling from every dark corner to wrap their inky tendrils around his legs as he left. The visual effect was startling, making his lower legs nearly disappear and then the illusion swirling up his body as he left the room.

I wilted in my chair when he was gone and rested my face in my hands, feeling the flames of embarrassment in my own cheeks at my clumsy reaction and scaring away my own husband with my nervousness babbling. After a few painful moments of wool gathering I finally straightened, glared at myself in the dimly reflective mirror, and set to work dusting the powder over my wings. By the time I reached the difficult places on my back I simply accepted defeat and did the best I could. That was all I'd been able to do for the longest time anyway.

I WAS MYSTIFIED BY how quickly I began to feel better. Obviously, I had been told that my husband's magic would heal me, but I hadn't truly understood it. Not after having been so unwell that I'd been practically bedridden for *years*. Most of my life had been spent battling with my own body. Victor's magic didn't necessarily make me any *stronger*, but it did seem to have healed the parts of my body that my immune system had so badly damaged, and that, in turn, allowed me to gain some of my own strength back. I watched every day as Victor changed the bandages on my arm, amazed at how the wound beneath was knitting itself back together so quickly. It was already nearly healed, though now there were "bond marks" as Victor called them, beginning to surface on the skin around it. I still needed naps throughout the day, and I had to be careful not to overexert myself, but compared to the state I'd been in for most of my adult life, it was a huge improvement. Massive.

Distrusting what I was experiencing was a regular struggle—like maybe it wasn't going to last and the bottom would drop out at any moment, and then I'd be back in that dark hole of magical stasis to keep me from dying. But when I was able to focus on the moment in front of me it was an amazing feeling, both being able to stay awake for longer periods and the pain I carried in my body slowly lessening until it was almost like it had never been there. I hadn't even realized how badly I'd felt until I began to feel better. I could even change forms for short periods now when I wanted to, which meant my magic was coming back.

Every morning I woke up to find a small flower on the night-stand beside my bed. I didn't know where he was finding blooms when there was still snow on the ground, but I enjoyed the little purple and pink blossoms immensely. The moment my eyes opened, I would look to the little cup of water on my bedside table to see what he'd brought me that day.

Still, the blankets beside me were never disturbed, and it left me feeling a little hurt and unwanted that he chose to sleep somewhere else at night. Even though we were married, I reminded myself often that we were still virtual strangers. Or maybe married *Veardur* didn't sleep together at night? I was too embarrassed and afraid of rejection to ask him outright. It soothed my heart some small amount to know that he was thinking of me and made the effort to bring me a little flower every morning before I was even awake.

I also started reading books that Victor began to leave in a stack beside my daily flower—works of fiction or histories that appeared on my nightstand like magic as well. My new morning ritual consisted of cleansing myself and then taking a book and a steaming cup of tea to the window seat to read. The birds flitting around in the courtyard quickly became a source of daily entertainment, even though watching them made me feel a little wistful. There were so many times when my brother and sister had talked me into flying off into the Black Woods with them to escape our tutor sessions as children. Since I was the youngest, of course I wanted to tag along with them, and then I'd continued to gallivant around in the treetops with Apollo, long after my siblings had outgrown such childishness. Our parents had truly had their hands full. Watching the little birds hopping around in the snow outside and squabbling over whatever they found made my heart a little sore at the memories, but I loved seeing their little daily dramas. In a matter of days, every time I cracked my window open, they came fluttering over to the ground below it for crumbs of bread that I tossed to them.

Each day I felt a little better, got a little stronger, and grew a little lonelier.

Perhaps because I didn't need as much of his help for getting around or caring for myself, Victor thought he didn't need to be around as often. Or maybe I'd embarrassed myself so badly in reaction to him that he didn't want to be around me. I saw less and less of him as the days passed and I hated it. Of course, he always made sure I had plenty of options for food, and somehow, he paid close enough attention to know which foods I preferred, even when I didn't pay enough attention to myself to realize it. The fire was always built up to the perfect level for warmth in the room, and he seemed to know when I'd finished a book or grown bored with it, because it would be replaced the next time I woke. He even realized I had been pressing his flowers in between the pages of the books to save them, because I would find them, perfectly pressed, beside the new ones. But any time I tried to engage him in conversation or ask him questions, he would look out the window and his eyes would turn white, and then he'd excuse himself and slink away like our grumpy palace cat when she'd been disturbed one too many times from her favorite pillow. *Although maybe "prowling lion" is a more fitting description for him,* I thought, when I considered the way his body moved and the air of authority he carried.

This morning he found me on the window seat, thumbing the brittle, yellowed pages of the book of poems I was reading as I watched the snow falling in wet clumps outside. The birds hadn't even come today. They were probably tucked away in the trees with their little feathers all fluffed out for warmth. It occurred to me that even though I was healing, not all that much had changed in my circumstances. I was still trapped in a bedroom all day. Sure, I was alive, but I was bored. And now that my oldest friend was gone and my new husband wasn't even interested in me, I was lonely. I'd been relieved at the thought of not having the maids around constantly, but at least they were *someone.* So when he knocked on the door frame, I didn't expect much. He slipped into the room when I looked up, looking uncomfortable as usual—his cheeks flushing pink at the apples and his gaze taking a meandering journey around the room before finally landing on me. I couldn't help letting my own eyes drink him in like he was water in a scorching desert. He might not have been much for company or conversation, but he sure was nice to look at. He swallowed three times before he spoke.

"It's snowing rather heavily."

I simply watched him, assuming that an unnecessary response might be seen as annoying chatter and he would disappear again. His gaze shifted to the window, and he stepped to the edge of the other end of the window seat, looking down into the courtyard.

"Your bird friends didn't come today."

I glanced at him in shock, surprised that he even knew how I felt about them since we'd never discussed it. "No," I finally responded. "I think they don't like the snowstorm."

He nodded, his eyes flickering between me and the ground outside. "Would you like one?"

I stared at him dumbly, not having any idea what he meant.

"A bird," he clarified. A quick flick of his fingers, and then darkness swirled above the other end of the window seat next to him, like a rolling plume of thick, black smoke, and then immediately settled into the shape of a large, black bird with a shaggy neck.

I flinched backward. One moment there was no bird, and the next there was, just like one of his ever-changing weapons. But the weapons hadn't been a real, living, blinking bird with shimmery black feathers who cocked his head to look at me. I vaguely remembered his mount, and how I had asked why it didn't move around. He had replied that it wasn't real, so this bird must not have been either. But it sure looked real.

Victor's face was as impassive as always, but his eyes showed a bit of a sparkle in the depths at my reaction. "Or do you prefer dogs?" He turned his other hand over and made a quick motion like he was scooping something from a bowl, and shadows around the edges of the room came together beside him and coalesced into the shape of a large, imposing dog. When its shape solidified, it sat placidly, ears pricked with interest while it looked at me. There wasn't a speck of color anywhere on its body, just short black fur covering its muscular, menacing build. It reminded me of the dogs that guarded the houses of very wealthy merchants in the cities.

I glanced between the dog and the bird. "Will they hurt me?" I asked.

"Never." He spoke with absolute certainty, and my anxiety about the animals began to ebb away.

"Does it have a name?" I asked timidly.

"Only if you give it one."

"Does it like to be petted?" My gaze flickered between Victor and the dog, though the dog simply sat with a loose, interested stance.

"If you would like to pet him," was Victor's vague reply. He raised his hand slightly and—like a puppet on a marionette—the dog stood and padded closer to me, with its tongue hanging out to show it was still relaxed. It stood next to me and watched me with soft eyes while I raised my hand and touched the side of its neck, marveling at the warmth and the texture of its fur.

"I don't understand how it's not real," I confessed.

He hesitated a moment before replying. "It is *real*," he said slowly, trying to find the words to explain. "But it's not a real *dog*. It's my magic, so it's an extension of me. It cannot do anything I don't want it to do. It doesn't need to eat, or drink. It has no will of its own."

I frowned down at the strange creature made of magic, who looked like a dog, and reached out to pet it a little more fully, watching as its tongue lolled further out of the side of its mouth.

"The rate of snowfall concerns me for Helda's safety," Victor said, interrupting my thoughts and drawing my attention back to him. "I would like to go to her and pick up our food for the day from her home instead of risking her traveling in this weather, but that would mean I will be away from the keep for a little while. Would you be okay with that if you have these to watch over you while I'm away?" He gestured to the creatures he'd created from the shadows.

"Of course," I told him. If he said they wouldn't hurt me, then I trusted him, and I thought it was endearing that he worried so much about the elderly cook.

"If you want them to leave, just tell them so and they will," he told me as he stepped away and left the room.

The dog turned its head to watch him go, but the bird hopped down the padded bench and settled in next to my thigh, pressing its little head under my hand for petting. As soon as Victor was out of the room, the dog stepped forward and plopped its heavy head in my lap, looking up at me with soulful eyes. I chuckled at the little magical beasties—whatever they were, they still solicited affection just like a real pet.

I wondered at his purpose in creating these for me. How long would they last? But at the moment, I found I simply enjoyed sitting with them and stroking them and enjoying their company.

Chapter 13

Celeste

ONE OF THE DOWNSIDES of feeling better and not needing to sleep as much, or as deeply, was that I started waking up in the middle of the night. Waking up alone in a pitch-black room felt too close to being trapped in my own mind with no one but myself to keep me company. Tonight, when it happened, I sat up in the bed gasping, thinking I was unconscious and needed to fight my way awake again. Not for the first time, I wished I'd been brave enough to ask Victor to make his dog again. Then even if he wouldn't stay with me, at least I'd have some of his magic.

Both the bird and the dog had vanished into thin air without warning shortly before he arrived back at Sorrow's Keep with a few days' worth of food for us. I'd been startled at the instantaneous departure of the creatures he'd created. I didn't know how they worked or how he controlled them or why they would have disappeared. It had felt good to keep a little piece of him with me while he was gone, but I had to wonder how much of them actually *were him*, as he had stated. The dog's goofy smile and wagging tail as I stroked its fur didn't seem particularly Victor-like to me.

I lay in bed, feeling the painful ache of loneliness settle deep in my bones. I did *not* want to go home to my family, not before giving this a real try with Victor, but I couldn't help feeling sad at the thought that maybe this was the extent of our "marriage." Maybe he felt like I was only my illness and he was merely my caretaker. He'd never known me as anything but a sick person. He hadn't known me before my health had inexplicably begun deteriorating and my magic had been lost to me because my immune system was destroying my organs. He didn't know how big of a deal it was that I could change my form again or get up and move around the room on my own. Even my own family, who had known me all my life, had begun to treat me as if this diseased version of me was all that existed. My brother, the first born, was the crown prince, the one all our hopes were pinned on. My older sister, beautiful and able-bodied, kind and brave, was the one who would secure the most promising marriage arrangement, whether for trading or an alliance or some other political gain. My younger sister hadn't survived, so my family was no stranger to grief. But me, I was the sick sibling. The one they were just grateful was still alive. The one they stressed over and worried about.

I wanted more than that for my marriage. I *needed* more than that moving forward. And Victor had told me to always ask for what I need. I didn't know what to ask for most of the time, but I decided right now I needed that big, warm, scary-looking dog who wanted my affection. Even if it wasn't real. After a few deep breaths to gather my courage, I slipped out from under the covers and lowered my feet to the thick woolen rug. The fire had burned almost completely out, which explained the darkness, but the room was still warm enough to be comfortable in my shift. I raised my hand, palm up, in front of me and focused my magic in it. Relief coursed through me when a small fae light fluoresced above my palm, just enough to illuminate the stone walls around me with a pale, soft glow. It had been so long.

Even with my little fae light pressing back against the darkness, the halls felt tomblike as I wandered down them all alone. Victor had told me this small castle had been cut into the side of the mountain and I could feel it in the cold stones and damp air. Even though I knew there were windows overlooking the ice-clogged strait, the rock walls were so thick it felt like we were below ground. Shadows above me clung to the vaulted ceilings of the hall in a way that didn't seem natural. I didn't know the layout yet or where he might be, so I tip-toed from room to room, peeking into the cavernous spaces and trying not to get lost. At one point, I found my way to the landing of a staircase, but I couldn't convince myself to descend into the inky blackness, though it most certainly led to the kitchens, or perhaps a root cellar, and not some dungeon as I imagined. I shivered uncomfortably at the thought and turned back to explore the other end of the keep.

None of the rooms had candles lit or a fire going, as I would expect to find in whatever bedroom he was sleeping in. Maybe he used fae lights as well? But I found none of those either. At the very end of the hall, I found a small library, and I eyed the towering shelves of books with a mixture of apprehension and awe. The shelves stood menacingly tall—heavy wooden pieces that looked as old as the keep itself. Here, too, the shadows clung to the shelves and ceiling, such that the tops of them couldn't be seen for the thick, viscous tendrils of gloom that hid the tops from my pitifully small fae light.

"Celeste?"

I shrieked like a hellcat, spinning toward the voice and trying with all my might to fling as much defensive energy as I could at whatever had spooked me—which was exactly none. No magic was flung. Several things happened at once. First, I realized I was a dummy and had been startled once again by my own husband. Then, in my futile effort to blast him with magical energy, I lost control of all my other magic, so my wings appeared and my fae light vanished, dousing me in complete darkness. And lastly, since I didn't have much practice staying upright lately—let alone whirling around like an overwrought top—I promptly fell on my backside, pinning one of my wings painfully between my body and the stone floor. It all happened so fast that even Victor couldn't catch me, though not for lack of trying. I suspect he could have made it in time if he hadn't been so surprised, but before I could even register the bolt of pain from my fall, he already had me back in the air with his arms around me. He clutched me tightly against his body, and I promptly burst into tears. Not dainty, quiet, demure tears. Big, gasping, sobbing tears.

"Celeste, what's *wrong?*" His own voice was a panicked gasp as he swiftly carried me a few steps and then lowered into a seated position with me perched on his lap. His hands smoothed over my body, feeling for injuries, and I flinched when he tweaked the wing I'd landed on. "Are you injured?"

I shook my head, knowing he couldn't see me in the darkness but unable to get any words out through my sobbing.

"Then why are you crying?" he responded quietly anyway, and I felt his hand gently clasp around my jaw and cheek, the way a healer might when inspecting an uncooperative child's eyes.

I cried even harder, unable to stem the flow of tears now that they had started. I was scared, unsure, lonely, lost, sad, embarrassed, intimidated, hopeful, and relieved, all mixed in together, and none of it made any logical sense. The words simply wouldn't form. "You just startled me," I finally managed to get out, unable to explain the other feelings properly to this handsome stranger from another world who had married me under bizarre circumstances.

He sighed, his warm breath fanning across my face, and released his hold on my face to pull me closer for a moment. "You have nothing to fear here. I will never let anything hurt you," he whispered. His chin rested on top of my head next to the curve of my antler and I curled my fingers into his shirt, momentarily mollified by his closeness and the sound of his beating heart.

"Why are we sitting in the dark?" I asked after sitting like this for a while, confused by the strangeness of the situation and my inability to see anything at all. It did make it easier to talk to him when I couldn't see his striking features watching me, though.

"Because you turned out your light," he answered matter-of-factly.

"But why are *you* in the dark?" I clarified. He had been in this dark library before I entered, and I must have passed him without seeing him somehow.

He was quiet for a moment before answering. "I find it comfortable, I suppose. But I don't think that's what you came to find me for."

Heat flooded into my cheeks. "I wanted to ask for the dog back," I made myself admit.

He didn't answer immediately, and his silence was unnerving. *Talk to me. Interact with me. Say something.* I was beginning to suspect that he didn't have a lot of experience with conversation, or maybe he simply spent a lot of time in his own head thinking things through before he spoke. "Because... you were afraid?" he finally asked, sounding puzzled. His fingers touched my chin again and lifted my face toward him. I couldn't see him, but I could almost *feel* his intimidating eyes tracking the tear marks down my cheeks.

"Can you see in the dark?" I asked, suddenly very sure that he could.

"Of course," he confirmed. "Answer my question, Celeste." The quiet command made my skin prickle with awareness. "Do you want the dog because you feel you need its protection?"

I tried to shake my head, but he had it caught in his hand. "No," I said, swallowing thickly and tugging my wings more tightly against my back for comfort. "I'm just lonely." My voice was so small I didn't think he would even hear me, but he did.

"Lonely," he repeated slowly, as if feeling the shape of the word in his mouth. "I shouldn't have taken you from your family," he said on a breath, his voice sounding shaken.

I blinked at his statement, confused by the conclusions he was drawing. I had specifically told him I wanted to leave the castle. I needed *out.* Now, granted, at the time I hadn't thought it was an actual possibility, but I didn't regret my request in the slightest. And I didn't fear for my safety or want a guard dog. Had he thought I needed one when he left? I simply *wanted* to be *wanted.* To have a friend or at least a companion. Tears began to leak from my eyes again, but at least this time they were silent.

"I'm so sorry," he told me, and I felt his forehead press against mine.

"No, that's not—" I didn't know how to explain without embarrassment, but I couldn't allow him to feel bad for doing exactly what I had asked. I squeezed my eyes shut, as if that would somehow allow me to hide from him. "You don't want me," I explained, hearing my voice crack and wondering if it were actually possible to die from embarrassment. The rejection and shame I felt in that moment surely could have put me out of my misery had it been possible.

"What?" That singular word sounded so baffled and out of place that if I had been capable of humor at the moment I might have laughed.

I was depleted though, in that moment. I'd burned myself through with the heat of my embarrassment and I didn't have it in me to repeat those words again. Completely drained and tired of being rejected, I gave myself permission to just let the tears flow.

The noise that he made was very nearly a growl, and I flinched and released my hold on his shirt as I was reminded precisely who I was sitting upon. He released my jaw, and I heard a low rattle and then a match was struck, held between his fingers before he reached to light a candle on the table beside him. I cringed at the light, but after a moment of adjustment I could now see the high-backed armchair that we were seated in, and the small stack of books on the side table in a language I couldn't read, and the walls and walls of books looming around us. But he took my face in his hand again and turned me to look at him, and his eyes were ice picks. "Celeste," he said, enunciating my name with excruciating precision. "What makes you think that?" That petulant frown was back, and his lips looked so soft. I'd never known anyone who could look so sinister and so tempting at the same time. This was the closest I'd ever seen to him looking upset, and a small spark of defensiveness flared to life in me.

"You aren't around very much," I finally answered, clutching my hands together tightly in my lap, and when he looked as though he might argue with me, I added, "and we're barely married."

His teeth audibly clicked when he snapped his mouth shut, and I could swear I felt his fingers tighten and release on my jaw. "What does this mean, 'barely married'?" His stare was always intense, but the way his narrowed eyes looked right now had me wishing the candle would blow out so they wouldn't drill into me quite so sharply. I tried to lower my gaze, but he lifted my chin to meet his eyes. There was something in them that I couldn't read, either a flicker of anger or pain.

I winced, hating the thought of either one of those reactions. "We haven't even consummated our marriage," I explained. Shouldn't that have been obvious? Did *Veardur* not... do that? That seemed unlikely. They had families and children, didn't they?

He stared at me with no reaction for so long that I wondered if he had even heard me and then blinked so rapidly I wondered if he was trying to reset his brain. "We—" he started, and then stopped with his mouth still hanging open, clearly aghast and at a loss for words. He struggled for several moments to sort his thoughts out before releasing my face to rest his elbow on the armrest, but dipping his head to make sure he had my eyes when he spoke. "You would want to do that with me?" he asked, seeming oddly skeptical about the notion.

I felt my brow wrinkle in confusion. Shouldn't we want to? He was my *husband*, but more than that, he was *hot*. Sure, he was a little frightening, but not because he was cruel or mean. It was just the nature of who he was. And he was actually rather lovely when he brought himself to interact. He certainly wasn't unattractive—he was built like a god and my stomach clenched just looking at his pretty, sulky face. I spent far too much time wondering what his lips felt like. Tasted like. Kissed like. Would he kiss with tongue? But I kept all those thoughts in my head and answered with a prim, "We're not married in my culture until we do." He frowned at me, scanning my face repeatedly for something, perhaps wondering if I were lying. "For all I know, my family might come and steal me back. They've already gotten what they wanted from our arrangement, after all," I warned him. I wouldn't put it past my mother to demand something dramatic like that, as upset as she had been about "losing me" to a non-fae.

He leaned closer, every muscle in his body tensing as his fingers gripped the armrest tightly, and a primal kind of possessiveness flared behind his eyes. "I'd like to see them try."

Chapter 14

Celeste

I WAS SUDDENLY A fledgling bird trapped in the gaze of a venomous snake as he watched me, and I had to remind myself to breathe. My entire body reacted to his arrogant, possessive tone—my cheeks heating and a strange swooping sensation building in my lower abdomen. I barely restrained myself from flaring my wings suggestively. He wouldn't even know what it meant, a fact which made my face heat even more. I was certain my flush had spread all the way down my neck, something he confirmed when his eyes dropped to my throat and lingered there.

"I think we should wait until you are well," he finally said when his gaze returned to mine. His pupils were so enlarged in the candlelight that they nearly swallowed his ice blue irises, and I watched as his eyes narrowed and his expression turned more thoughtful. The possessive gleam was still there, but there was something else in his gaze as he continued to consider me. I would have given anything to know his thoughts just then. "Let's get you back to bed, Doveling," he murmured. My shock at the endearment went entirely unnoticed as he licked the tip of his fingers and pinched out the wick of the candle, dousing us in darkness once again. He was careful of my wings as he cradled me in his arms, and his path to the bedroom was much shorter than mine had been to the library.

"Where do you sleep at night?" I asked him as he leaned across the unused side of the bed to lay me on "my side."

He folded my wings into a more comfortable resting position

before gently drawing the sheets up to my chin and carefully tucking them around my body, making sure that I was snug and warm. "I don't sleep," he responded absently, and then smoothed a wayward lock of my hair around my antler. He had already turned and was loading more wood into the fireplace by the time his words actually registered in my brain.

"You don't sleep at all?" I asked incredulously, propping myself up on my elbow and ruining all the careful fussing he'd done over the blankets. But how could someone survive like that?

"Not as mortals do," came his vague reply as he arranged the logs just so.

I stared unseeingly at his back as he rebuilt the fire, looking instead at the past few days—*or had it been two weeks?*—of our relationship through the lens of this new information. He hadn't been sleeping with me because he *doesn't sleep*. I didn't know how to reconcile that information with my hurt feelings. How does one come to terms with the fact that a wound they felt never actually occurred?

"Do you still want the dog?" he asked as he turned to me from the fireplace, unaware of the chaotic reshuffling of feelings currently taking place in my brain. The flames behind him grew and backlit the curve of his cheek so that I could see the frown he directed at my rumpled bed sheets.

I tried to smooth them back into place so that all his fussing hadn't been for nothing.

"Celeste?" he prompted when I didn't answer.

What had he asked?

Oh, the dog.

I dropped back onto the pillow rather forcefully. "I'd rather have you." The words were out before I could stop myself, a measure of my tiredness, perhaps. But they were true, and I couldn't take them back. The magical dog was a comfort, but it was second-best, and my attachment to it really came from the fact that it was a part of him.

His frown deepened further before he leaned down to brace his hands on the edge of the mattress and his expression was lost to shadow. "I would never desire to impede your personal autonomy, but other than by *your own choice*—no one will ever take you from me." This was delivered as a quiet statement of fact by a man entirely confident in his own abilities to defend what belonged to him. "Not my family and certainly not yours," he continued as he straightened and began unbuttoning his left sleeve. "You might not *feel yet* that you are mine, but that doesn't mean I don't. This mark," he stated, jerking up his sleeve to reveal the ink-black lines spreading out from the healed wound that lay beneath, "means that I have been bound to you for all eternity. Life and death will fade away and every version of this planet will crumble into dust, and I will *still* belong to you." He paused for a second to take a breath, and when he continued, his voice was softer. "I have been taught from childhood to respect the cultures of others, and because you are mine, yours is even more important to me. But you must understand that within my culture, and before the Creator who placed this magic within my people, there is no 'barely married.' I am yours. You have me," he finished gently, imploring me to believe him.

And I did, to a point. I knew it wasn't reasonable to expect this man I barely knew to feel close to me emotionally just because we'd gotten married. He still held himself away from me. So no, I didn't have all of him. Not yet. One thing I knew for certain was that if any consummation were going to occur, I was going to have to seduce him.

He seemed to see the doubt on my face, because he bent his leg and—with a sigh—seated himself on the bed beside me like he'd done when he brought me food to taste. "I'm yours, Celeste," he repeated, with slightly less confidence than he'd had seconds ago, and those strangely timid but earnest words were a balm to all my imagined hurts. I had to take a few deep breaths to keep myself from tearing up again. "What can I do to convince you?" he asked.

"Could you lie here with me for a little while?"

He looked at me as if I had two heads, so I tried to explain.

"I know you said you don't sleep," I said before pausing to

swallow, unsure of myself, "but do you think you could stay with me? Just until I fall asleep?"

"You want—" He raised his hands to gesture and then froze, his brain still working. Even in the dim lighting I could see his eyebrows pulled together in confusion. "I... uh... Sure. Yes." He looked so baffled as he glanced around the bed as if this were an entirely new concept for him. "Just a moment," he said as he stood to remove his outer shirt. Walking to the window, he peered outside, obviously searching for something while unbuttoning his top, and then, after he satisfied himself about whatever he was looking for, removed his shirt and draped it across the end of the window seat. He returned to the bedside and grasped the covers, holding them between his fingers for a beat, perhaps unsure if he wanted to be under them or on top of them. Eventually deciding on "under," he lifted the blankets and climbed onto the bed, settling himself rather stiffly beside me before laying the blankets back on top of himself. "Like this?" he asked.

I couldn't decide if I were more confused or amused, but confusion seemed to be winning out. "Have you truly never lain in a bed before?"

He was slow to respond. "I have. Just... never with someone else," he said, confirming my suspicions about needing to seduce him. I was still puzzling over how to go about that when he asked, "Why does this please you?" And I had to remember that he was asking about lying in bed together and not seducing him.

I thought for a bit about how to explain. "It's a comfort thing," I finally settled on. "People sleep together because we like being near the person we're sleeping with. When I was little, I would crawl into my big sister Kyra's bed nearly every night, because I hated being alone in the dark. And on the nights I managed to fall asleep by myself, I always woke up in the morning to find her in *my* bed."

"Oh." He was quiet for a moment longer before admitting, "I've seen lots of people sleep in a bed together, but I figured it was mostly for economical reasons."

SEDUCTION OF A PSYCHOPOMP

"For... what?" I asked when he didn't explain further.

"Beds are expensive," he said dryly. "I figured people shared so that they didn't have to buy so many beds."

I wondered if I would ever understand him well enough to be able to predict his train of thought.

We were quiet after that, with him gradually relaxing from his stiff posture beside me and me simply enjoying his presence and the sound of his slow breathing. Now that he was here with me, though, I couldn't focus on anything else. I was so aware of him that I felt almost jittery, so I closed my eyes and pretended to sleep, hoping to force myself to relax and not wanting him to feel like he had to stay with me all night. It didn't fool him, though.

"What is it like?" he asked in a whisper, a little while later. I opened my eyes, and he turned his face toward me, completely aware of my consciousness. "Sleeping," he clarified.

I thought about his question, wondering how to describe it to someone who had never experienced it before. "It depends on the type of sleeping, I guess. Regular sleeping feels like drifting. Sometimes you're not even aware you're doing it."

He was staring into the darkness, but his eyes narrowed slightly like he was trying to imagine it.

"And then, when we dream, it's like... watching pictures? In your mind? Sometimes about things that have happened to you, sometimes about silly things that could never happen. I've never understood how my own brain creates my dreams and yet I don't know what is going to happen next. How is it that I'm surprised by a dream that I'm creating?"

He obviously had no answer for me, and we lapsed into silence again, until eventually I began to feel self-conscious.

"I'm sorry. I talk too much," I said.

"I like to hear you speak," he told me quietly.

"Oh." My cheeks heated again, this time with pleasure. I tried to think of other things about sleep he might not know. "When I'm asleep because of the stasis, or when I can't wake up, it doesn't feel like normal sleep. Sometimes I know that I'm asleep, and it feels like I'm trapped. I'm all alone in the darkness, and I can't wake up no matter how hard I try."

"Is that bad?" he asked.

"I don't like it."

"You aren't alone anymore," he whispered after a moment of silence. He lifted his arm out from under the blankets and rested his hand on the pillow beside his face, palm up. An offering.

I reached over hesitantly and laid my fingers in his palm, and he gently closed his hand around them.

"Even when you sleep, I'm still here," he said, and my heart was so full it ached. "Goodnight, Angel."

I was almost asleep when I realized the silence didn't feel so uncomfortable between us anymore.

Chapter 15

Celeste

IT TOOK ME LONGER than I would like to admit to realize that Victor was still in the bed with me. Especially since he was sitting up and not exactly small or difficult to notice. But when I rolled over and nearly face-planted into his thigh, it made me jump, and I slapped my hand over my face to stop my scream. The sound of a page turning was loud in the silence.

"I worked *very hard* all night not to cloak myself, and I still managed to startle you," he said dryly.

"I'm sorry! I just wasn't expecting you to still be here," I said into my hands. I was surprised he could understand me from how muffled my words were.

"I can read here just as easily as I can in the library." He turned another page. "I simply didn't before because I thought you would prefer not to be disturbed while you slept. And that you might want some privacy."

Speaking of privacy... "I'll be right back," I informed him before standing up too quickly and needing to steady myself on the bed for a moment when my knees buckled. His head snapped up, and he was ready to snatch me up in an instant, every muscle taut until he saw that I had corrected my balance. I gave him a timid smile, and he relaxed by increments, watching me with a hawklike gaze while I carefully walked to the restroom to brush my teeth and cleanse myself.

I tried not to rush on my way back, delighted that he was spending time with me. "Where do you find flowers in the middle of winter?"

He cast a quick glance at the new little flower and raised an eyebrow at me but didn't answer.

"And what did you mean by trying not to cloak yourself?" I asked curiously as I climbed back into the bed. He couldn't avoid answering all my questions, could he? His gaze was fixed on my smile for a beat too long until he blinked a few times and cleared his throat. I think we both blushed, though I didn't understand why he did.

"I... it's an old habit of mine, to use the shadows even when I don't need them. I don't even notice when I do it half the time."

"You don't notice when you're making shadows?" My magic had been so difficult to use that I'd never really felt like I could use it without thinking. I hadn't even had enough magic to send a spectral messenger for years.

"Sometimes. Not *making* shadows, simply using them to bend the light around myself so that I'm not visible. I was a reserved child and didn't like attention, so I developed a habit of cloaking myself even when I didn't need to, just to direct people's attention away from me," he admitted ruefully. "But it startles you when I remove it, so I'm... trying to be better about it." The tips of his little rounded ears were bright pink, and he awkwardly rubbed his thumb along the edge of the dusty cover—another book written in a language I couldn't read. "But I startled you anyway just by sitting here in broad daylight, so I'm beginning to think maybe the problem isn't me."

I glanced at him in shock only to find him staring at me with the smallest hint of mischief in his eyes. He wasn't *smiling* per sé, but he could have been, if you squinted really, really hard. Was he... *teasing me?* Would wonders *never cease?* My smile spread across my face and happy butterflies swarmed my belly. "I've always startled easily," I admitted bashfully.

"We'll have to keep Levi away from you, then," he said, re-opening his book.

I turned to fluff my pillow and snuggled down into it, enjoying his company. "That sounds ominous," I replied.

"It's not," he said, watching me over the cover of his book

while pretending to read. "He finds amusement in a great many things, but one of his favorite pastimes is trying to spook a friend who also startles easily because she shifts forms when she does."

I groaned. My sister had also found amusement in jumping out at me to make me scream. I already felt bad for this poor friend of theirs, probably afraid of what was around every corner like I had been growing up.

He dropped his left hand onto the bed with his palm up again, and I'm sure I had hearts in my eyes when I took the offering and placed my hand in his with a grin. He didn't seem to emote much, but his eyes were sparkling, and even though his face was stoic he still seemed... happy. Which made me happy. His expressions were there, they were just incredibly subtle. A minute shift of an eyebrow, the slightest crinkling at the corner of his eyes, a so-faint-it-might-not-exist twitch of his lips. I drank up every understated expression like a parched woman. It was kind of pathetic really, but I couldn't bring myself to care.

He reminded me that there was food waiting on the tray by the door if I wanted breakfast, but I wasn't hungry yet, and didn't want to risk breaking the spell of this comfortable bubble. We weren't exactly cuddling, but holding hands in bed together and *talking* was a win in my book.

"Can you tell me about the mark?" I asked, scanning the lines of it with my eyes and wanting to hear more of his voice. I reached with my other hand to touch it, but he held his breath, so I took my hand back. I was curious about the image that had bloomed on his arm, but I didn't want to push him too much. When he'd bared it to me last night, it had reminded me how different it looked from mine. His skin had been perfect, smooth alabaster before the knife had marred it during our ritual, and now there were thin tendrils of black mist snaking their way into a shape like a half-dead tree. Mine didn't look anything like that. It was just a white scar where my cut had been and a few dark lines beginning to spread out from the newly healed wound.

"Mm." He looked down at his arm and twisted his wrist slightly, taking my hand with it as he watched the mark move along his skin. "It's the Tree of Life. It imprints in our skin during the binding ritual to show that our magic has left us and given immortal life to another."

"But why does it look half dead?" I asked. The trunk and the roots of the tree looked normal, but the canopy was split directly down the middle with leafy growth on one side and bare, skeletal limbs on the other. A large, thin, misty circle sat behind the trunk like a sun hanging low in the sky.

"Because I exist in both worlds."

I shivered at his words, unable to imagine that.

"Are you cold?" he asked.

I shook my head, amused at his protective concern. "No. Will mine look like yours?" I asked, pulling my own arm up to study the unformed image.

"I believe so," he murmured, staring at it with an odd mixture of curiosity and apprehension. "The pair that participate in the ritual always has matching marks as far as I know. It's always a Tree of Life inside a setting sun, but the mark is unique to the couple. Our trees won't perfectly match anyone else's but each other's."

"I think that's lovely," I said, looking at the forming mark with a new kind of appreciation. I couldn't feel it at all; it felt just like my normal skin. "How long will it take?" I glanced back up at him when he didn't answer right away.

"I don't know," he said with a small shrug. "Everyone I know was married long before I was born, and I never thought to ask."

I loved this. He was so fascinating to me, and though he was guarded, I didn't think he was being particularly cagey on purpose. He just seemed... quiet. Like he spent a lot of time in his own mind but didn't know how to articulate what he wanted to say. And perhaps, since we had forever, this was a gift. He was a puzzle I could tinker with for years and get to know a little at a time, treasuring each little kernel of himself that he shared with me instead of consuming him all at once.

"Do you have any other tattoos?" I asked, my eyes wandering over his soft-looking undershirt. I wondered if he would take it off to show them to me. Granted, I hadn't noticed any when he'd been chopping wood the other day, but a girl could hope, right? "Ah, no," he replied, hunching into himself shyly, as if trying to hide from my eyes. "My skin would never take a traditional ink tattoo. I heal too fast. The pigments would metabolize within days, maybe hours." He laid his book down beside me and practically oozed off the bed to get away from me while muttering something about getting breakfast. *Perhaps I flew a bit too close to the sun that time,* I thought as he piled tarts and fruit on a plate while looking hunted with his pink cheeks once again.

But Victor did make an effort to spend more time with me, even if he was a little skittish about being touched or having in depth conversations about himself. He showed me around the keep—there truly was only a hearth-kitchen at the bottom of the spooky stairwell and no dungeons to be found anywhere—and only disappeared once before taking me down to the library so I could pick out my own books.

Just a few moments after coming up from the kitchen, he'd stopped in his tracks, told me to stay where I was, created his shadow dog in the blink of an eye, and then pulled more shadows around himself and was gone. I was left staring at a black-furred hellhound made of nightmares and fangs, with a happily wagging tail and a dopey grin. I patted his head for less than a minute before he disappeared in a curl of smoke. A black line immediately split the air at the end of the hall. Purple light exploded out of the center in a circular ring, stopping just before it touched the ceiling or the walls, and Victor stood in the middle of it with an obsidian-colored staff in his hand even taller than he was. There was a lantern hanging from the top that emitted a soft blue light, and the black cloak he had begun to form around himself before flowed from his shoulders and flung shadowy tentacles out into the darkness behind him—some kind of rocky riverbank as far as I could tell. He stepped through the strange opening, and it collapsed into nothing behind him, disappearing as if it had never been there. I noted the snowflakes on the hood of his cloak and that his eyes had gone all white again. He approached until he was standing where he was before and stared down at me, blinking strangely with those solid white eyes. "Right," he said, shaking himself off and dropping his hand to his side as the staff disappeared and his eyes began to clear of their white haze. "The library." He nodded to himself and took a few steps before realizing I wasn't with him and turning to see if I was coming.

"Where did the dog go?" I asked, still rooted to my place on the stone floor and trying to make sense of what had just happened.

He stared at me as if not comprehending what I was asking.

"The dog. You made the dog again, just now, and then it disappeared when you came back." I pointed to the spot where the shadow dog had sat in front of me, probably looking entirely crazy, but I wasn't and I knew it. He didn't get to just do strange stuff and then pretend like it hadn't happened.

"Yes," he agreed. "I didn't want to leave you without protection, but it's faster to get back to you using a portal. When I step into the underworld to do that, my magic can't reach *this world* because I'm not in it."

I didn't understand any of that except that the hole he had made was a portal from the underworld. And that he wanted to get back to me the fastest way. Why was that so cute? I flicked my wings before I caught myself and barely stopped from grinning.

His cloak of shadows was slowly disappearing from around him, ebbing away from the ground up so that it looked like thick black cloth draped over his shoulders that faded into murky looking shadows before vanishing altogether before it touched the ground. "Did you want me to make it again?" he asked, clearly puzzled. At least we were together in that.

"No, that's okay." But it was nice to know he could make it for me whenever I wanted. "Where do you go when you have to leave so suddenly?" I asked as I stepped up beside him and we started back toward the library. I trailed along beside him, taking two steps for his every one, and noticed the hitch in his step when his gaze swung to peer at me out of the corner of his eye. He did that a lot.

"Outside." We stopped at the library door, and he gestured me inside like a gentleman. Now that it was daylight and there was sunshine filtering in through the high, arched windows, the room didn't feel so eerie.

"And what were you doing outside?" I asked as he led the way to a back corner of the room, praying that he wouldn't shut down and return to his silence. *Talk to me.*

"Removing vermin," was all he said before bending down to the bottom of a row of shelves. "These are all of the books in *Sanrin*," he explained, referring to my native tongue as he gestured to the few lower shelves. He retrieved a large book—an encyclopedia of plant species in the dwarvish realms that had been translated into *Sanrin* for some reason—and handed it to me. It looked ancient. "Most of the rest here are Common Tongue," he said, "which you speak very well. Do you also read it?"

I assured him I did, though admittedly my Common tutor was the one I ditched out on the most growing up. If I'd known I was going to be living in the Boundlands as an adult, I might have tried harder to pay attention. Common was still spoken in my kingdom, but not as much as *Sanrin*. And definitely not written as much.

"How many languages do you speak?" I asked as I scanned the rows and rows of shelves that created little corridors throughout the room. While I did see a lot of spines with Common Tongue titles, there were quite a few languages I didn't know, too.

"Most of them. I never counted the exact number. I suppose it depends on how different a dialect needs to be before you consider it a new language."

I turned back to stare at him, blinking repeatedly. *Most of them.*

"And... there are dead languages I don't speak at all but can read quite a bit of, and I don't speak all of the human languages in the Void," he amended.

The encyclopedia was heavy, so I wrapped both arms around

it and carried it to a table near a hearth at the front of the room, settling in with it while Victor drifted among the bookshelves looking for something in particular. I stared at the empty hearth for a bit, imagining how lovely it would be to sit with Victor and read by the warm glow of the flames. I didn't know how to start a fire—our servants had special tools to light fires, and I wouldn't know how to use one even if I had it—but at least I could load some wood into the hearth. Victor was always the one doing everything for me here, so I rose, deciding to make myself useful.

I only managed to get two small logs into the firebox before I felt his hands smoothing down my wings as he gently tugged me away. My eyes widened at the sensation of him touching me in such a familiar way, and I turned to find him trying to guide me back to the table. "Rest, Doveling. This is my job."

I let him guide me but frowned at him as I sat. "I wanted to help."

"And I'm still concerned about your ability to stay upright. I want to take care of you. Rest, please."

It was hard to say no to that, but as I watched him arrange wood in the fireplace and start it by using little sticks that smelled of sulfur, I felt rather useless. "Can I at least retrieve the tea from our rooms for us?"

He raised an eyebrow at me while he waited for the flames to take hold, and then, rising, said, "When you have more balance and strength."

I nearly argued, but as soon as I opened my mouth, he tutted at me and gave me a playful scowl that made me clack my teeth shut. Did I think the man didn't emote? That haughty look made me bite my lip and clench my thighs. I locked my muscles to keep from flaring my wings as he left the room and just about held my breath until he returned with the tray of tea and cups. He even had my quilt neatly folded and draped over his arm.

He unfolded the quilt and tucked it around my shoulders before pouring me a cup of tea and placing it in my hands. Then, after pouring himself one, he took a seat in front of me, dragged the stack of three books that he had selected across the table, and began to read. I watched him drinking from the dainty cup out of the corner of my eye and smiled to myself.

The fire crackled beside us as we sipped our tea in the old library, and I managed to find all the flowers that Victor had been bringing me—little cliff-side plants that bloomed in the snow, somehow defying the poor soil, salt spray, and bitter cold to produce sweet little blossoms in the dead of winter. But I couldn't pay attention to the text because somehow his hand had brushed against mine, or mine against his, and then his fingers had closed around mine and we were holding hands. And that was how we spent the next couple of days. Whenever I wasn't sleeping, we were huddled together in the library reading books, him reading whatever it was he read in various languages I didn't understand, and me reading specific texts that he selected to help me learn more about the cultures here or—at my request—to broaden my understanding of Common Tongue. But always holding hands.

His hands were surprisingly demonstrative. He would appear to be thoroughly engrossed in his texts, his brow wrinkled in concentration and chewing on his lip—but his fingers would trail along the inside of my wrist or brush tenderly against my sensitive palm. And his fingers were so long. Silken skin with slightly firm pads from the weapons he wielded, strong and delicate at the same time. I shivered when his fingertips feathered along the bones of the back of my hand, drawing patterns around my knuckles or stroking gently along the thin skin between my fingers.

I would be reading a passage about grammar variations among modern elvish communities and his hand would sneak across the table to tangle with mine. Every time we laced fingers, I would feel a secret thrill, reveling in the way my body warmed and tingled just from the feel of his skin against mine. It was truly bizarre. I had held hands before. I'd even kissed several boys growing up. Nothing had ever felt as erotic as this. It got to the point where just seeing his fingers twitch made me short of breath.

I noticed that, if I spoke, I had his full attention. He would listen to me talk about anything, but when I asked him about himself, he had a hard time answering with more than a few words and seemed almost bashful. It was very strange to me that someone so powerful and fearsome could be shy, but I couldn't deny what I was seeing with my own eyes. But what I'd taken for aloofness and possibly even disinterest at first truly appeared to be an acute case of introversion. He didn't ask me questions often, but when I did speak, he listened with complete focus, able to recall exactly what I'd said later with perfect accuracy. It was the strangest thing. If he was so interested in me, why didn't he *ask* me anything? But he rarely did, simply taking what was offered and cataloging it away instead. It was flattering and baffling all at once.

Then I discovered another way to get his attention. We were sitting in the library nibbling on tiny cakes and sipping tea by the fire and I—having crept my way around the table to be closer to him over the past few days—was slowly working on getting him used to my touch in places other than his hands. He was focused on another book from the stack he'd built beside him. This one had illustrations of people contorted into strange postures scattered throughout the pages. I was pretending to be engrossed in some political drivel about goblin territories he'd seemed surprised to see me pick up. I probably should have been a little more careful when choosing my prop. I'd started with "absentmindedly" caressing his fingers while I "read" before trailing the tips of my fingers across his palm to his wrist, drawing non-existent shapes along his skin as I went. I was curious to see if I could give him a dose of his own medicine, honestly. He'd had me squirming in my seat for days with flushed cheeks and hard nipples while he'd sat here stoic and impassive. I might have thought it didn't have the same effect on him as it did on me, but his fingers twitched in the tiniest of spasms, and as I trailed my hand higher up his arm his skin tightened into prickled gooseflesh. I reached his binding mark, the image that represented our marriage to one another, and began to lightly trace the contours of the image. The tip of the roots and up the trunk of the tree. The bare branches on one side and the lush foliage on the other. His breath hitched, and when I raised my gaze to meet his, I found he was staring me dead in the eye, his pupils completely dilated and his expression as hungry as a wolf.

Chapter 16

Celeste

I DREW MY HAND back slowly, skimming my fingers down to his wrist as I wondered if, perhaps, I'd bitten off more than I could chew. His fingers caught mine when I reached his hand, and he held me trapped in his gaze like that for several more moments before heaving a rasping breath, a reminder that I'd forgotten to breathe as well. When he finally turned his head back to his book his eyes followed last. He returned to reading with an audible swallow, and I lowered my gaze to stare at his hand still laced in mine. I sat still as a statue beside him since I didn't entirely understand his reaction, but I was incredibly intrigued and filed it away for future inspection.

By the time dinner came, I'd managed to shake off the tense feeling between us. Perhaps it was just me feeling that way, I didn't know, but I began to wonder if I had made a mistake in pushing him as far as I had. I knew it was greedy, but I wanted his body *and* his heart. I wanted to be a proper husband and wife. I didn't like the thought that my family wouldn't see us as truly married in the state of limbo we were in. I'd thought before we married that the most I could really hope for in an arranged marriage was a companionable relationship and wanting more wasn't in the cards, but I wondered what it would take for me to win the rest of him in addition to his hand. Maybe a spirit guardian's heart couldn't be won. Hearts were something I didn't have a lot of experience with. I fell asleep pondering this dilemma, which probably wasn't the wisest thing because it affected my dreams.

"Celeste." Something brushed my cheek. "Celeste, wake up. You're crying."

I sucked in a gasping breath, grateful beyond measure that he'd pulled me from that nightmare. I'd been right back in that agonizing moment where I realized that my mother hadn't been mistaken when she relayed to me, as I was being dressed in my wedding gown, that my closest friend had left the city and wouldn't be attending my ceremony. I'd been absolutely convinced that she was wrong. *Apollo is my oldest friend,* I'd thought. *Of course he would want to see me off when I left, even if he didn't care about weddings.* We'd played together and gotten into mischief since we were little children. He'd been the golden child, the court's favorite little ringlet-haired pretty boy who'd snuck me silly books and hung all my terrible paintings on his walls. We'd talked about *everything.* He knew it was a scary moment for me. He knew why I had to do it. *Of course he'll be here,* I'd thought. We'd *always* been there for each other. I'd entertained him with puppet shows when he'd flown too close to the cliffs and gotten caught in an updraft as a child, requiring that he convalesce for weeks while his leg and wing healed. When I'd become ill, he had visited and filled me in on all the latest drama between our peers.

When the doors to the great hall had finally opened to reveal my new husband, I had been wracked with anxiety, even in my determination, and Apollo had been nowhere to be found.

The sharp sting of betrayal slowly settled into a melancholy ache, but I couldn't stop my tears from flowing, much to my *Veardur's* distress. Victor wiped at my tears with his thumb, desperately trying to smooth them away as fast as they came. "You dreamed?" he inquired anxiously as his large form leaned over me, blocking out the flickering firelight.

I reached up and wrapped my hand around his, stilling his frantic movements and holding it to my face as I nodded. His closeness was a balm. I felt cocooned by his presence, and it made me feel safe. I'd been so hurt by my own best friend. My only friend, really. But I'd thought I was doing a good job of moving past it. Or at least starting to.

Victor's voice was quiet as a breath and almost timid when he asked me, "What can I do?"

It was so desperately sweet that I started crying even harder. How was it that this man who probably hadn't even known I existed several weeks ago cared more about my feelings than the person who knew me as well as my own siblings? I just needed to be held and I should have asked, but I felt too shy. I reached for him and wrapped my arm across his lap since he was hunched over me from where he sat beside me. He answered my silent request by lowering himself until he lay next to me in the bed and wrapping his arm over me and my wing to pull me against his chest. I pressed my face to his throat and tried to stem my tears.

"You... want a hug?" he asked, sounding apprehensive.

I nodded against his neck, not trusting my voice yet. Most people would call this a cuddle, but "hug" was close enough.

His entire body was stiff, but after a few seconds he gathered me closer and settled his chin on the top of my head. I smiled against his throat. He wasn't so bad at this after all.

"What happened?" he whispered into the darkness.

I gave myself time to settle before answering, noticing the way his fingertips began to trace the shafts of feathers along the back of my wing and his steady breathing calmed my own. There was a painful lump in my throat when I swallowed, but I tried to explain anyway. "My friend hurt my feelings," I summarized.

His fingers stilled against my back. "In your dream?"

"No. I was just remembering it in my dream," I mumbled.

His hand tightened against my feathers so slightly that I might not have noticed it if my wings hadn't been so sensitive. "Tell me, Doveling," he whispered, and I shivered at the promise of vengeance I imagined in his voice.

I pondered the best way to explain what had happened without boring him with what probably sounded like a childish emotional dispute between friends. But then, he rarely requested that I tell him about myself or my past, though he seemed to pay strict attention to what he could glean from my behavior. "I have—" I stopped and had to restart. "I *had* a friend. My best friend. His name is Apollo." I waited a beat to see if he would have any reaction to me having had male friends, but when he didn't, I continued. "We've known each other since we were toddlers. Babies, really." Apollo was the only son of a nobleman my father was close to, and his whole family had been friends with ours for generations. "We spent our childhoods playing together, and when I began to show signs of illness, he was the only friend that went out of his way to spend time with me. For years he was my *only* friend, because I couldn't get around much anymore and he was the only one who visited me regularly."

Victor tucked me more firmly against his chest, and then turned his head so that his cheek was pressed atop my head, antlers and all. His hold was tight enough that I had to struggle to breathe, and it was exactly what I needed.

"The day of our wedding, I was woken up and told that he'd left the city and refused to attend the ceremony."

"I don't understand," he said after letting my words sink in for a while.

"I don't either," I admitted. That was part of why it had hurt so badly. Other than my family, I had no one who had supported me the way he had. "He didn't even say goodbye. My mom just said he couldn't watch me marry somebody else." And my mother had been *irate* on my behalf. She told me she had explained to him personally why I was being arranged to marry Victor specifically, and that she was as upset as he was that I was leaving Faery, but it was necessary to *save my life*. Privately she had ranted that he was selfish, or he would have cared more about my life than what he wanted, and cowardly for leaving without even telling me himself. But I couldn't even bring myself to be angry with him. I was just hurt.

My parents had never considered him for my hand back when it was assumed I would marry into an alliance. The queen had no need for an alliance with his house as we already had one, and my mother grumbled that it was clear to anyone who watched us that we weren't a love match anyway. And she was right, at least I had thought. I loved Apollo deeply, but not in a romantic way. He had attempted to kiss me once in our teens, in that horribly awkward way that young teens do, but I'd found it like kissing a brother, and told him so immediately. I'd always felt a little guilty for not returning his feelings, and wondered if maybe I could have grown to have romantic feelings for him eventually, but it just never felt right. Not only that, but as my only close friend at the time, I couldn't risk losing my friendship with him. He had told me that he understood and that our friendship was more important to him, too. My siblings had both grown up too much for our games and childish things; they had duties to the crown that I was beginning to realize I wouldn't be able to shoulder with them. Apollo was all I had.

"Is that why you were crying at our ceremony?" Victor asked, and my heart sank like a stone.

"It was," I said, cringing in his arms. "I was also nervous," I hedged, not wanting to admit that I had been *terrified* of him. The doors had opened, and my eyes had skittered away, searching for my friend for support, for his nod of encouragement that meant everything was going to be okay. "But I'd only just been told shortly before, and I couldn't accept it until I saw for myself that he truly hadn't attended. I'm *so sorry*, Victor. I can't imagine what you must have thought of me, weeping uncontrollably like a child at our wedding." My cheeks were burning hot with shame. I was an emotional person in general—I'd always been teased by my brother for crying so much. It was my body's reaction to any emotion that felt too big for me, regardless of if it were sadness or anger or happiness.

"I thought... you were lovely," Victor whispered into the darkness, startling me. "Your skin was almost glowing. Your dress was the most beautiful garment I'd ever seen. I was completely taken with your eyes. I thought you looked like a queen."

I have no words for the warmth that suffused every molecule of my being. How was it that this man saw me so differently than I'd seen myself? The generosity and kindness of his soul humbled me. I didn't deserve this person.

"And if I ever meet your Apollo, it will take enormous restraint not to open a portal to the underworld beneath his feet," he murmured, returning to his lazy exploration of my feathers.

"What?" I asked, unsure if I had heard him correctly and not knowing him well enough to know if he was joking. Surely he was joking.

"Don't worry, Doveling. I do have enormous restraint," he said, and I could hear the wryness in his voice even without trying.

I pulled back and propped myself up on my elbow so I could see his face, though truthfully, I couldn't see much in the fire-light. Wiping my own eyes, I studied his, but he didn't give anything away. "Please, don't hurt my friend. Former friend. Whatever you want to call him," I told him, just to be sure. I had no doubts that this man could end Apollo's life in an instant.

He took a breath and released it in a sigh that sounded clearly put-upon. "If you insist," he muttered.

"I do." I wished I hadn't been blindsided by Apollo's absence right before my wedding, though I couldn't blame my mom for telling me the way she did. I'd been asleep for so many months that I didn't even know I was getting married until she'd woken me up that morning. When else could she have told me? And it wasn't like she could have just not said anything. I definitely would have noticed he wasn't there. But my biggest regret was my reaction. "I'm truly sorry for allowing my sadness to mar our ceremony," I told him sincerely.

He reached down and took my left hand, toying with my fingers as he answered me. "It wasn't exactly the ceremony you were expecting anyway," he said, and his eyes looked strangely soft in the shadows. "You had your arm sliced open midway through. Most little girls probably don't grow up dreaming about that."

I smiled at him as I thought back to my childhood fantasies. "Probably not, no," I said with a self-deprecating chuckle. "My fantasies were always about dressing up in a flowing gown and kissing my tall, handsome husband." Granted, my fantasy-husband was never anywhere near *this* tall, and he had usually been some shade of glittering pink or golden brown with enormous gossamer wings. *You know, like most little fae girls,* I thought with an inward smirk.

Victor's eyes were practically sparkling. If I squinted really hard, I could almost see the wrinkles in the corners. He *wanted* to smile. Was this his version of laughing at me? I was delighted.

"Well, at least you got the flowing dress and the tall husband part," he said thoughtfully.

I laughed in disbelief. "And you're handsome!" He was so handsome. He had to know he was handsome. He was *gorgeous.* "Wait a minute!" I gasped. "Did we not kiss at our wedding?" I could feel that my mouth was hanging open, but I couldn't manage to clamp it shut.

His gaze dropped, and he glanced off to the side in a shifty expression.

"Victor. Tell me we kissed at the wedding." My family was going to be so horrified.

His eyes went wide, but he only made eye contact with me for a fraction of a second. He probably wasn't used to being chastised, but this was grievous. "We did," he said, but he didn't sound at all convincing.

"Why do I feel like you're lying?" He was totally lying.

"No, we did!" he insisted. "I touched my lips to yours."

The noise that came out of my throat was closer to a squawk than any kind of speech. "That's not a kiss!" I finally responded.

He huffed, and I could have sworn he rolled his eyes at me. "That was the point. I'm not going to kiss someone who isn't conscious enough to consent."

My eyebrows pinched together in my confusion. "I—You—It was our *wedding,*" I stuttered. "It's part of the marriage ceremony!"

Victor scowled at me from where he lay on the pillow. "The fact that you don't remember if I kissed you or not tells me I made the correct choice."

This was outrageous. "We're not married," I told him as a taunt and then flopped back onto my pillow.

It was his turn to prop himself up. "We are married!" he insisted indignantly.

"We're not. My family is probably going to pop up any moment and drag me back to Faery." I wasn't entirely teasing. Hadn't he ever been warned about making bargains with the fae? My family was no exception. They very well could do something like that just for the slight. But I knew I'd hit my mark when he leaned over me with that scowl still on his face and said, "I'll kiss you now, then."

I raised my eyebrows and waited, which probably wasn't the most welcoming expression, especially since I was still blotchy-faced with red-rimmed eyes from crying. But Victor didn't seem to notice any of that. He was staring at my mouth as if trying to solve a mental equation. I couldn't help but huff a small laugh. "Have you ever kissed anyone before?" I asked, the sudden realization dawning.

He met my gaze with that shifty-eyed squint again. "Obviously."

"*Other* than when you 'kissed' me at our wedding," I clarified.

He didn't answer for a long moment. "Does the top of a small child's head count?" he asked slowly.

I melted into a pile of goo. *He'd truly never been kissed?* The odd mixture of hesitancy and petulance on his face suddenly made more sense. "You're thinking about it too hard. Come here." I reached up and took him by the chin, tugging him down until his lips brushed mine.

He lingered there for half a second before pulling back to look at my eyes.

I burst out laughing. "I'm not going to bite you. Kiss me," I coaxed him, tugging him down again and raising my chin to meet him partway. His lips grazed mine, and I nibbled on them with my own. They were as soft as they looked. I kept it gentle, light, allowing him to get used to the feeling of my mouth on his. I explored him carefully, enjoying the slip slide of our lips and matching my breathing to his. The scent of him in my nose and the heat of his body over mine was a delight. His breaths started to become shaky, and I didn't know if it was desire or nervousness. I decided to end it with a hint of what was to come and darted my tongue out just enough to taste his bottom lip before releasing him.

His head jerked back a few inches, as he narrowed his eyes at me in the dark, and I laughed delightedly. "That's how it's done at a wedding," I told him. "You don't kiss me like you kiss your sister."

"I don't kiss my sister," he said petulantly, dropping to the pillow beside me again.

"I think we need more practice," I said, trying desperately to say it with a straight face.

"I think you need more rest."

I failed at keeping my composure and grinned until I fell asleep.

Chapter 17

Celeste

"I DIDN'T THINK ABOUT how long my family might take to bring your trunks when we left," Victor murmured the next morning as he finished securing the buttons on the back of my dress for me.

"What do you mean?" I asked, raising my gaze to meet his in the dingy old glass of the mirror.

His eye contact was a flicker, there and gone as he focused on his task. "If I'd known they were going to take this long to rejoin us I would have brought more than three changes of clothing for you." He frowned at the final button in thought. "Would you be comfortable with me asking Yasgrot to send a tailor? They could come and measure you for some new outfits," he offered. "They won't be like the style you're used to from home," he cautioned, "but maybe they can make something you will like."

I quirked an eyebrow at him. "As long as they fit, I'm fine with whatever you would like for me to wear," I told him with some amusement. True, I would miss the cheerful colors I often wore back home, but my clothing choices had never really been my own. Clothing was to keep the body warm or cool, sometimes to preserve one's modesty, and to declare your status and role within the courts. Although I was no longer within the courts, I still had a role as this man's wife, even if it wasn't as an ambassador for my kingdom.

He still hadn't released my button even though he was finished, and his expression grew concerned for some reason I couldn't understand. "I would like for you to wear whatever pleases you." His gaze flickered to mine again before skittering away, a blush touching his cheeks. He seemed even more shy than usual this morning.

I didn't know what to say to that. Was this some kind of test? My pleasure had nothing to do with my duties.

He saw the conflict on my face and released my button to place his fingers on my elbow and turn me toward him, gazing down at me in the morning light. "Your preferences have value," he told me. "The things we love make us who we are. You are allowed to want things. Ask for whatever you want, and I will do my best to provide it for you."

I heard the words he said. They made sense as verbal sentences. I still didn't understand. "But why? Preferences just make us picky," I said with a frown, repeating the words that my father had recited to me every time I complained about anything throughout my childhood. He had no time or patience for whining from multiple children and no desire to be embarrassed in front of courtiers by childish complaints. Unless you wanted to be the subject of gossip for every noblewoman with nothing better to do, you ate what Cook gave you with a smile on your face and wore what your maids dressed you in with confidence and grace.

"And you're allowed to be picky," he said, as if it were completely obvious and of no consequence. He lifted his hand to press his fingertip to the crease between my eyebrows, smoothing it out with a gentle motion, and more than my forehead relaxed at his touch. "You have been taken from your culture, your language, your land, and your people. Everything here is new and different. If you were to separate from your body, the things here from this land are not what your soul would show me in the memories that made you happy or brought you joy." His eyes were piercing, and he spoke with emphasis that showed the importance he placed on his words. "Our preferences are things that make us happy, and your happiness matters to me."

I stared at him in silence as there was no chance of me finding proper words to speak in that moment, so I simply nodded and then wrapped my arms around his waist, pressing my face against his chest. His body stiffened but eventually he brought his arms around my back as he had last night.

"Does the tailor have a shop?" I asked into his shirt when he finally relaxed.

"I would assume so," he answered hesitantly.

"Could we go there instead?"

He didn't answer, but when I tried to pull back to look at his face, his muscles tightened again, and he slid his hands down my shoulders to hold me closer instead.

"Is that not allowed?" I asked with a sinking stomach. He'd just told me to ask for whatever I wanted, but maybe this wasn't what he'd meant. Maybe there were rules about what that could include.

I felt his neck recoil as if he'd been struck and he released me enough to pull back and look down at me. "Of course it's *allowed*," he said, sounding slightly offended.

"Then why didn't you answer me?" I asked, not liking the uncertainty I felt when he didn't respond. I pulled my wings tight against my back and stepped back to cross my arms.

He released me with reluctance. "I was thinking."

The pink that bloomed on his cheekbones was the only thing that kept me from feeling as perturbed as I might have been normally. That and the fact that the shocking blue of his eyes made it hard to think straight. And the fact that he had seemed to enjoy hugging me. He was hard to be frustrated with.

He took a deep breath and released it slowly. "But *yes*, if that's what you want, of course we can visit the outpost."

My mouth pulled down to match the concerned frown he wore. "What's wrong with the outpost?" I asked, wondering what he knew that I didn't.

He studied my face, a look of apprehension creeping across his features before he closed his eyes for a beat and opened them, his expression once again impassive and calm. "You won't be truly immortal for several more years," he explained gently. "It makes me... *nervous*"—he said the word hesitantly, as if trying it on for size—"to have you outside the safety of the keep. However, I have no desire to own a caged bird, so we will visit the outpost."

"Is it so dangerous here?" It was difficult to judge for myself what kind of risk we would be taking, as I had never visited the Boundlands before and knew little of the people. The *Veardur* were the fiercest warriors in Faery, so much so that we counted ourselves lucky that they found mortal politics beneath them and refused to fight in our wars, so his concern made me nervous.

Victor's eyebrow quirked in what I was beginning to recognize as a tell for his amusement. "As a collector of the dead, I'll admit my perception of mortal risk is probably skewed. I'll keep you safe."

I searched his face for any sign he was displeased with my request, and eventually nodded when I found none.

Just a short time later we were together on the back of a horse made of shadows, riding through the snow outside the keep. The horse—or wraith, as I reminded myself, no matter how real it felt to the touch—was vaguely familiar to me as the mount we'd ridden out of the Dawn Palace. My memories of that night were fuzzy at best. Victor had offered to create my own mount for me, but I didn't trust my control of a creature made of magic, so he had me seated between his thighs with his chest pressed to my back. I was grateful I had regained enough magic to put my wings away and maintain my fae form, because I could feel his warmth even through my cloak like this, and I smiled, remembering his timid kiss last night. His fists rested on his thighs while loosely gripping the reins, but every time the horse shifted, he raised his arms enough to ensure I wasn't jostled. This horse was huge, much larger than the irin we rode back in Faery, and its long strides carried us quickly along the winding path into Bhalden's Post. Victor explained as we rode that, while it was a relatively small outpost, it contained plenty of traders due to its location near the mountain pass. His deep voice just behind my ear as he stooped close enough to be heard made my heart race even more than the knowledge that I was riding a wraith.

The chilled air bit at my cheeks, but he'd bundled me so thoroughly that I was otherwise comfortable nestled in front of him, and the views of the surrounding mountains—Dragon's Teeth, he'd called them—were as breathtaking as they were foreboding. The mountains I'd known from home were merely rolling hills compared to these stark peaks and rocky drop-offs. There was something beautiful in the icy, jagged rock here, but maybe that was just my excitement about being able to get out of the keep and explore somewhere new.

The outpost wasn't terribly far. It was a little village made up of small stone or wood buildings that was sheltered by its location between the sheer rock faces of the surrounding ridge. There were multiple blacksmiths with three-sided buildings open to the elements, fitting shoes to stout-looking donkeys with loud clanging strikes or hammering away at their metal tools. Boot repair shops and leather smiths dotted the line of buildings as well, and there was a butcher who had frozen cuts of meat hanging from the front of his store. Other than the blacksmiths we didn't see many merchants, making it the quietest merchant row I'd ever seen. Not a single person called out to the few people passing by us in the road. Most of the stores didn't even have signs. You were just expected to know where to go, I supposed.

Our black horse approached a wooden building with a small square sign painted only with the image of a needle and thread, coming to a stop in front of the wide wooden porch. "Are you ready?" Victor asked. He wrapped his arms around me protectively and then my legs were suddenly dangling in midair as the horse disappeared and he stepped to the ground in a single fluid movement. He climbed the step to the porch before setting me on my feet, then tapped the snow off of his boots. As he pushed open the front door, he asked someone inside if this was the tailor's shop Master Blunthorn had recommended. He drew me under his arm as he engaged in a rapid-fire conversation with a man whose voice sounded like tectonic plates moving, but I only caught Victor's words. I had no chance of understanding the man's responses with as deep as his voice was and the way he ran his words together so that there weren't any breaks in between them. He must have given the answer Victor was looking for, because he led me inside and then stood over me while conversing with the dwarvish man for several more moments.

I had no experience with dwarves other than the few glimpses I'd caught of the ones who ran the keep. This man was only as tall as me but four times as thick, and he looked like he'd been built of pure muscle. He wore fine, heavy robes that looked well-made, and his coarse, dark hair was pulled back into a single braid that was thicker than my upper arm. His dense beard covered skin that was a deep bronze color with a distinct reddish cast. Behind him were bolts of fabric crammed into every possible inch of shelving that covered the entire wall, floor to ceiling. Most of the options were muted colors, and there were lots of grays and browns, but I did see a light yellow and a pretty bird's egg blue peeking out of the stacks.

Victor stayed close, standing directly behind me to the point that one might have said he was hovering. I tried to pay attention, because he was asking questions about production times and fabric types, but it was all very overwhelming. Besides, I wasn't used to having any input on my outfits, anyway. The man held up several garments for me and tried to talk to me about cuts and colors, but even though I was nearly positive he was speaking Common Tongue, I couldn't understand a word of it. I looked up at Victor with wide eyes and wanted to melt into the floor in embarrassment.

His hand squeezed my shoulder in a reassuring way, and he tilted his head toward the tailor as he spoke to me. "He wants to know if you have a specific style you want or a cut you prefer. Do you have specific clothes that you find the most comfortable?"

I started to shake my head but then stopped myself. "Tight sleeves. Fitted top. Something I can move in on the bottom?"

The dwarvish man rattled off a few sentences, and Victor

agreed to whatever he said. "Do you have any brighter colors?" Victor asked him, making me glance up at him in surprise.

The man disappeared into a room at the back of the shop and came out followed by a woman smaller than him, both carrying bolts of cloth in a rainbow of hues. He waved me forward as they laid them out across his wide countertop and Victor told me, "He's saying you should touch them."

I stepped forward cautiously to feel the ones he gestured to and marveled at how soft some of the fabrics were. The girl who had joined him passed me another sample, and she had the most cheerful smile I think I'd ever seen as she handed it to me. She was much younger than the man, and her hair was frizzy instead of coarse, but she kept it plaited in a braid as well and shared the same reddish undertones in her skin. She tried to show me her own dress, but I couldn't understand what she was saying other than her gestures at seams or the neckline, and Victor was busy talking to the tailor. *Maybe coming here wasn't the best idea*, I thought, crestfallen. But the girl was undeterred and started speaking more slowly and trying to enunciate using single words which I could finally understand with her accent. She pulled out bolt after bolt of fabric for my inspection, always with a pleasant expression and an encouraging nod when I touched them. Her friendly disposition made me feel like she wasn't judging me, and that she was having fun with the challenge of figuring out what I liked.

"Measure you?" she asked, picking up a measuring tape and gesturing at my torso.

"Sure," I agreed, happy to finally be able to contribute in a way that didn't involve talking, and stepped away from the counter so she would have room to move around me. Victor let his conversation with the tailor lapse, watching every move the girl made as she wrapped the tape around my body and noted down each measurement. "Surely you've been measured before," I told him with a tiny, teasing grin. His hovering was strangely reassuring, but did he really expect this sweet woman to harm me with a measuring tape?

He eyed me with a raised eyebrow before apparently deciding that the tailor's assistant was safe enough, then went back to his conversation with the tailor. "Anything she wants, simply let Master Blunthorn know to settle it with the Molchanov accounts," he told the man quietly.

"Your husband?" the assistant whispered with slow, careful enunciation while tipping her head at Victor. She had an amused smile for some reason.

I nodded in response, feeling an odd sense of pride fill me at being able to claim such a striking man as "mine."

An impish grin spread across her face. "New marriage?" she asked, squeezing her fingertips to the pads of her thumbs before tapping the gathered fingertips together.

I frowned at her in confusion until she made a kissy motion with her lips while glancing to make sure Victor wasn't paying attention. I tried not to laugh and nodded. "Yes, a new marriage," I confirmed before rolling my lips between my teeth to contain my grin. *With our first real kiss only last night.*

"I make you extra," I thought she said with a wink and a mischievous light in her eyes. She chattered something about "him liking it," but she spoke too quietly and too fast for me to catch it with her accent, so I simply nodded. "Colors?" She held up various bolts with some of the bright colors she'd brought out at Victor's request, and they were beautiful, but I was so overwhelmed with all the choices that I had no idea what to pick.

"She likes this one," Victor said, pointing to a sea foam green that I'd been eyeing—how did he know?—"and this one," he added, selecting a soft, sunshine yellow that my hand had kept drifting back to.

"You like this, too?" she said slowly, holding up a lovely pale purple color that reminded me of thistle flowers, and I agreed. "Matches your eyes," she told me with a sweet smile, and I was so grateful for her kindness.

We left after arranging to have the finished pieces delivered, and as we rode back, I had to lean against Victor. I was thoroughly exhausted and mentally drained, but I was proud of myself for venturing out and exploring something new. As we balanced together on the back of this horse made of shadows and gazed out across the mountain spires in the distance, I found myself looking forward to more days like this with Victor.

We were almost back to the keep when an unexpected wave of fear washed over me, my heart breaking into a sprint and my skin prickling in alarm. Victor's left arm came around my waist to hold me steady as his mount came to a stop without needing to be told. A low oath behind my ear was all the warning I got before the air around me seemed to darken and a flock of crows burst out of the shadows pooling across the ground beneath us. They dashed into the sky and swooped back down into the rocky cliffs above us, screaming and cawing in a riot of feathers as they attacked something hiding between the rocks.

"What—"

"Ghouls," Victor interrupted as a tall, black scythe formed in his right hand.

I turned to glance at him over my shoulder, but he was staring up into the cliffs where the birds slowly took to the sky again before winking out of existence one by one. "You have ghouls here?" I asked. That explained the fear that I'd felt—they couldn't be seen, but we could feel them.

"Banshees," he confirmed. "Among others. Every realm has them, but they aren't as much of a danger to the other races as they are to you." His eyes were paler but not pure white yet, and darkness flowed in billowing swaths from his shoulders.

I pondered that as the wraith began to pick its way down the path again, and I made sure I paid better attention to my physical and emotional responses now. "Why are they more of a danger to me?" I asked. I tried to access my defensive magic, reaching and flexing, hoping to help protect us if needed, just in case. But there wasn't anything for me to use. I was completely dependent on my husband, something that made me both humbled, grateful, and upset all at once. "A *healthy* high fae can blast a banshee out of existence," I groused, acknowledging that

I wasn't there yet.

"Correct," he agreed. "But all fae are *also* more vulnerable to their predation, not just you. The other races have sturdier connections between their bodies and their souls. The high fae live a little closer to the spiritual veil, physically speaking."

"What does that even mean?" I asked, my confusion eclipsing even my effort at vigilance. I pictured my soul becoming untethered and drifting away from my body. The thought was horrifying.

"In a practical sense, it means the humans have no magic at all, but as long as they're alive they generally have very little to fear from the spirit world because their bodies protect their souls." He leaned against my back as he searched the path in front of us, and his voice dropped into a low grumble. "Which is convenient for them because the Void has some of the most disgusting spirit predators in existence." He dropped back into the saddle and loosened his grip on my waist, nudging his mount to a faster pace. "Your people are on the other end of the spectrum," he continued somewhat absently, "with the least protection physically, but the most access to the old magic. The other races all fall somewhere in between. This type of banshee seems to be attracted to high fae in particular, I think. They were all but extinct when your people lived here—or so I've been told—but I've killed more of them since we've been at the keep than I've ever seen."

A chill flooded me as something clicked in my brain, my mind flashing back to all the times he'd suddenly excused himself mid-conversation and disappeared. *"What were you doing outside?" ... "Removing vermin."*

Another familiar wave of adrenaline hit me just before Victor's arm tightened around me again and he swung his scythe in a blur of shadows in front of us. The feeling faded before he had even settled himself back in his seat again. A gesture of his wrist preceded an entire pack of black dogs taking shape from the shadows along the path and joining us at a swift trot all the way back to the keep.

Victor kept me close to him for the rest of the evening.

Chapter 18

Celeste

"HAVE THERE BEEN ANY more banshees?" I asked, wrapping my arms around myself as I approached Victor in the library the next afternoon. I couldn't suppress the shiver that shuddered through me at the memory of the fear and adrenaline that had warned me of the ghouls' presence yesterday, or Victor's explanation that *my soul wasn't as sturdily attached to my body* as the other races' were. What did that even *mean?* The very thought had all kinds of horrifying implications. I might have been mentally flailing about it since waking this afternoon.

"None today," he said, raising his eyes to meet mine over the top of his book and lifting his hand to gesture with long fingers at the overly large armchair across from him. His eyebrows drew together as he studied me. "Are you cold?" He closed his book such that his finger held his place and started to reach for another log to add to the fire, but I shook my head.

"Can I sit with you?" My voice sounded pitifully small in my own ears.

"Of course—" he started to say, his hand extending once again toward the high-backed chair across from him, but that wasn't what I meant.

I gently moved his arm aside and climbed into his lap.

"Oh," was all he got out as he raised both arms and inched toward the backrest to give me more room. I didn't want more room. His arms stayed up as if he were unsure where to place them while I struggled to get comfortable. "What—I—okay." He was clearly at a loss as to what I was doing clambering into his chair with him.

I shifted around in his lap until I was pressed against him and finally able to lay my head on his chest. Once I was there, I melted into him, feeling safe and relaxed for the first time since we'd come home. I'd been so exhausted yesterday after we arrived that I'd fallen into a fitful sleep and remained that way until late this afternoon. The errand had taken a lot out of me. It had been good to get out and push myself, but my body was still weakened. Between the exertion, the social interactions, and the adrenaline from encountering the banshees on the way home, I'd been completely depleted of energy. Replaying the feelings of fear the banshees had caused was a normal side effect their power had on people, but it had ruined my sleep, which I'd been in desperate need of.

"Where are your wings, Doveling?" he finally asked, his voice solicitous as he settled his free hand on my shoulder and began smoothing it down my back.

I simply shrugged and cuddled closer. How could I explain that shifting forms and conjuring feeble little fae lights was the only magic I could wield right now, so I wanted to practice what I could in hopes of building my strength? It sounded pathetic. "Will the ghouls still try to eat me once I'm immortal?" I asked instead. Ghouls were horrible creatures—invisible parasites that ate a person's magic, and when that was gone, sometimes ate their *souls*. "Why do they even want me if I don't have very much magic right now?"

Victor's hand paused on my back as he answered in his deep, soothing voice. "I think it's more about the type of magic than the quantity," he murmured. His hand squeezed my shoulder in a reassuring way. "I don't know the answer to your question about immortality, but I suspect they won't be as dangerous to you then. We can see what my grandmother knows when she comes back." I involuntarily shrank into a smaller ball as I remembered the woman who had cut into my arm at the ceremony. And whom he'd purposefully defied, at my request, by taking me from the castle. He misunderstood my anxious response and tutted at me, smoothing his hand down my spine again. "I will keep you safe, Angel. I promise."

And I believed him. This man was a gift. He had become my safe place and my favorite source of comfort. Even though I didn't like the thought of being so utterly dependent on anyone—especially the way I was on him—I couldn't think of a better person to have to depend on.

As the fire crackled beside us, casting its warm glow across his alabaster skin, the panes of glass rattled behind us in the ancient windows. "It's just the wind," he reassured me quietly when I flinched. "You're safe here."

I nodded against his chest, and my mind began to drift to the way it always felt as though he was *so aware* of everything around him at every moment. And the way he wielded such immense and dangerous power with what seemed like so little effort. He shielded me as a matter of course, it was ingrained to protect me not only from harm but from even the smallest discomfort. I pondered the way he spoke to everyone we encountered with thoughtful manners and gentle deference, regardless of their station—or the fact that he could end their life in the blink of an eye.

And I remembered the way his muscles had felt pressed against my back and his lips had felt so silken touching my own. I think, somehow, I had already become addicted to him—or at least was well on my way—to his quiet strength and his considerate nature, and like an addict I needed just a little more. My fingers curled into his shirt like they had a mind of their own and I found myself turning my head to his chest and pressing my lips to the muscle there beneath the smooth cloth of his shirt. I was so focused on his slow, rhythmic breathing that I couldn't have missed the way he held his breath each time I pressed my mouth to his body.

I inhaled deeply as I drew my nose across his collarbone to his neck, savoring the now-familiar scent of him that mixed with wood smoke and the ever-present salt air from the strait below. The skin of his neck was soft and warm, and I could feel his blood racing in his veins as my lips brushed over the artery there.

The tiniest intake of breath—a gasp?—proceeded his full body shiver as I gave in to my craving and pressed my mouth more firmly to his throat. His fingers spasmed reflexively, causing him to drop the book that he'd been resting on the arm of the chair. It landed with a thud on the thick rug as I kissed my way up to his jawline. I wanted to test the firmness of the muscles here with my teeth, but I settled for a gentle nibble with my lips that left him breathless anyway.

I pulled back to study his face—his striking, deep-set blue eyes under sharp black brows, his beautiful, sulky lips, the pink stain of heat beginning to mar the unnaturally pale hue of his skin. I knew my own pupils were so blown out that I probably looked like I'd been rolling in pixie dust or some other illicit pain killer. I certainly *felt* like I had been. "May I kiss you?" I asked him, staring at his lips with something akin to desperation.

"Is that not what you've been doing?" he asked, lifting his hand to trail his fingers along my jaw, and I couldn't help but lean into his touch. I raised my eyebrows at him as he guided my mouth to his own with the tips of his fingers under my chin. If he thought *that* was kissing...

I was going to consume him.

His lips were as plush and silken as I remembered them, but even better than that was his finger still lingering under my chin and the shaky breath he exhaled as I tasted him with the gentlest of kisses. I wouldn't be able to restrain myself with him forever, but for now I met his hesitancy and softness with feathered kisses like the caress of a butterfly's wings. I waited, testing and tasting and learning him as slowly as I could bear, meeting his energy with like energy so I didn't scare this shy man away with my eagerness. I pressed my palm to his chest and felt his heart thundering beneath his heavy rib cage, traced his sternum up to his throat and felt the way his Adam's apple bobbed against my thumb, slid both hands over the caps of muscles on his shoulders, squeezing gently and appreciating the strength beneath my fingers.

His own hands slid up my back to my shoulder blades, trembling so slightly that I might not have noticed except that I was so focused on his every movement. Every sigh, every shift, every beat of his heart. So, the little involuntary moan that slipped out of his throat when I licked his bottom lip? It hit me like a lightning bolt.

My heart burst into a sprint of its own as his fingers trailed up the side of my neck and slid into my hairline. Where his kisses were tender and sweet, mine grew hungry and seductive. I turned, clinging to his shoulders, so that I was no longer seated across his lap but straddling it, endeavoring to get even closer and feeling my skin heat everywhere we touched. One hand cupped the side of my face, the other pressed gentle fingers into my back, anchoring me to him as his breath fanned across my face. I was losing my hold on my restraint; licking and tasting until he opened his mouth to let me in. The sensuous slide of his tongue against my own was everything I needed and not nearly enough.

He groaned as I sucked the tip of his tongue into my mouth, sending a frisson of need straight to my core. His hands tightened on me, and I slid my greedy hands up into his hair, carding the silky, raven-dark strands through my fingers before gripping them to pull him closer. We were both panting, his chest pressing into me as he heaved for air and his lips seeking mine as earnestly as I sought his. He was a quick learner, all of his hesitancy replaced by arousal—as demonstrated by the thick, hard evidence of his wanting that pressed up between my thighs. Had I ever wanted to combust from a simple kiss? His eyelashes dipped even lower, fanning across his cheekbones as he broke our kiss in a low gasp when I rocked my core against the delicious hardness in his lap.

And then a prim cough behind me made me yelp like a whipped pup and sent me scrambling out of his chair in horror. Of course, I was tangled up in him and would have sprawled across the floor if he hadn't caught me and set me to rights. He held me steady in front of him as he bent himself double on the chair, refusing to let go and allow me to give in to my urge to flee in embarrassment. We were both breathless, but at length, he cleared his throat and sat up. Keeping one hand locked around my wrist like a steel shackle, he tugged me gently to the side so he could see Madam Helda, our elderly cook, where she stood in the entrance to the room.

I couldn't understand much of what she said, but Victor nodded as she spoke to him, even though he had half his face covered with his other hand and his cheeks and the tips of his ears were the reddest I'd ever seen them.

"Of course," he told her. "I would be happy to help."

I couldn't follow the conversation, something about needing more wood in the kitchen and some whisky for a recipe. My own face felt like it had been coated with whisky—the stinging heat was suffocating. My whole body was hot as I studied my shoes and the pattern of the rug around my feet and sought to get my breathing under control.

After her conversation with Victor, she turned to leave, and he gave my wrist a reassuring squeeze. "She needs me to carry in some wood and make a request for some things from Yasgrot. I'll be back in a moment," he said, standing and straightening his clothing before drawing a hand through his hair to fix the mussed strands.

I bit my lip as I watched him go, noting that not *all* the evidence of our dalliance was so easily erased. A whimper escaped my lips as I collapsed into the high-backed chair with my hands over my face. I sat like that for several moments, vacillating wildly between unhinged hilarity and utter mortification, until finally dropping my hands to gaze into the flames with a thousand-yard stare. My rumination was short-lived, however, because the book that Victor had dropped caught my eye at the edge of the hearthstone. I reached for it, fearing an errant ember might singe it, and noticed that it was one I'd seen him reading before. The writing was a strange script, nothing I was capable of reading anyway, but the illustrations were... *interesting*. Various images of inked figures contorted into increasingly confusing sexual positions graced each of the pages, and I found myself tilting my head this way and that, trying to understand what I was looking at. This was clearly an educational book about intimacy, and though I'd had the same classical education as anyone else my age, I didn't recall anything like *this* ever being included. Was he... uneducated about sex and trying to learn? This seemed like an odd way to go about it. I looked around and spotted a small stack of books near the chair, and they all appeared to be full of diagrams and explanations about different ways of achieving intimacy, though none so explicit as the one I held. I replaced his stack and carefully laid his current read on top, feeling like I was snooping but also immensely fascinated. Maybe his skittishness was just nerves and lack of knowledge. Maybe I should just take the reins and—

Footsteps in the hall alerted me to his return. He carried two trays of food into the library and set them on the table near the door with a clunk.

I waited for some kind of greeting, or acknowledgement of how awkward that was, but he seemed to be mentally stuck somewhere in the space between hilarity and mortification just as I had been, staring into the middle distance in the exact same way. It probably didn't help that he still appeared to have a partial erection. I rolled my lips between my teeth to try to control the giggles that wanted to slip out. "I'm sorry!" I said, my voice pitching high as a laugh slipped out, and I slapped my hand over my mouth to stifle it.

His eyes snapped to mine but that was the only movement he made. His facial expression might have been interpreted as a scowl, but I was beginning to think that was just his face. My husband had resting scowl-face. The blush in his cheeks had begun to fade but now it returned with a vengeance, making me laugh even harder.

"I got a little, um—" *Unhinged.* "—overzealous," I settled on, aiming for prim and falling far short. The movement of me lowering my hand to clasp my fingers together caused him to drop his gaze long enough to break the feeling of being pinned. He raised a hand to drag his palm down his face, and then uncovered the trays without comment on my earlier antics. *Like climbing up on him and thoroughly mauling him in front of the help.* "Helda had our food prepared already, so I brought it up." If he was aiming for prim, he'd nailed it.

I could think of something else I'd rather do instead of having dinner, but he seemed like he was intent on collecting himself, so I moved to join him at the table. *Patience. I am trying for patience. Very poorly.*

I took the seat that he pulled out for me and watched him through my eyelashes as he took a bracing breath and then sat himself as well. My plate was a collection of foods he'd noted I showed enjoyment of, except for one small portion of a meat I didn't recognize. His plate appeared to be full of steamed roots and cubed winter squashes. "What is this?" I asked, gesturing to the mystery meat with a fork from the tray.

"Deer," he answered. "Helda brought some up from her butcher to see if you might like to try it."

"Oh!" Not mystery meat at all then. We ate deer all the time in Faery. "That was kind of her."

Victor nodded and began eating his vegetables. He handled his silverware with the utmost grace, and it occurred to me that he would have fit right in at a palace dinner. Just watching his hands made my neck hot again. I struggled to control my ardor and redirected my attention to our meal.

"Do *Veardur* not eat meat?" I asked, eyeing his plate. He'd wrinkled his nose at the meat he'd brought me one time, but I figured maybe he just didn't like that dish. Come to think of it, I'd never seen him eat meat of any kind.

"This one doesn't."

"Not at all? You don't like the taste?" I knew a few fae that didn't eat meat, but it was usually because they had trouble digesting it. I couldn't imagine that would be a problem for an immortal, but there was much I still didn't know about his people.

He gave the food on my plate a small frown and appeared to

suppress a shudder. "I don't like the concept."

"Of... killing animals?" I guessed. That seemed odd for someone who saw so much death, but perhaps he didn't want to add to the tally? The queen employed multiple hunters to supply us with fresh venison, and it was a highly revered position within the courts. I tasted a bite of the deer meat, and it tasted fine to me. The sauce was a little strange, containing spices I was unused to, but certainly edible. I took a sip of tea to wash it down.

"Of eating someone's decomposing flesh carcass," he said crisply.

I choked on my drink, causing him to look at me in alarm. I waved him off while I coughed up my lungs into my napkin and then wheezed out, "Well, when you put it like that!" I grimaced. "It's not *decomposing*," I disagreed in horror.

He made a sound that might have been a scoff, but I saw a spark of mischief in his eye as he raised an eyebrow. "Any flesh that's not alive is already beginning to decompose," he said matter-of-factly.

"Stop calling it that! It's *meat*." He was teasing me! I was disgusted but trying not to laugh again. I raised my nose in the air in an imitation of haughtiness. "And you make it sound like we eat *people*. We only eat animals."

He poked another of his vegetables onto his fork and answered blithely, as if it were of no consequence. "And you may continue to do so."

"But you won't?" I asked, my own eyebrow lifting. I poked a bit of the venison and lifted it toward him in offering.

This time he did shudder, his shoulders lifting in revulsion. "Not if I can help it."

"Does it bother you if I eat it?" I asked, lowering my fork. I didn't want to distress him. Why had he even served it to me if it bothered him?

His gaze shot back to mine in confusion, and his eyes softened as he looked at me. "Of course not. Many populations eat meat. I just don't want it myself." The twinkle returned to his eye. "I will provide you with all the decomposing flesh carcasses you want."

I gasped and hit him with my napkin, and I swear I saw the corner of his lip twitch up right before his hand snaked over the corner of the table to hold mine.

Chapter 19

Celeste

THE GARMENT MADE FROM tiny scraps of pastel purple and white lace wasn't what I was expecting when the tailors delivered a package late the next day.

I'd gone to bed early the night before, not able to make it long past dinner when exhaustion took hold of me again, but I'd woken to birdsong this morning, feeling pretty good.

Then I'd endured another torturous day of nothing but erotic hand holding that made me want to scream. Every touch, every lazy movement of his thumb skimming the sensitive skin between my thumb and forefinger, made my heart beat faster. I didn't understand how he could get me so worked up with nothing but his fingers brushing along mine, but I'd never felt so repressed in all my life.

After dinner, I'd been brushing out my wings in the bedroom mirror to ready for sleep when Victor returned from taking down our dinnerware with a small package. "The tailor shop sent this for you," he said, setting it on the desk in front of me. "Your order shouldn't be ready yet, but maybe they had something already made. I'm going to help Helda load up her donkey for her commute home, then I'll be back," he explained with a pause at the door as he left again.

I smiled at the way he doted on the older woman—who had made no mention of interrupting our make out session—and returned my attention to the package. The thick brown paper tied with string was easily opened, but once I had the parchment spread out on the desk, I wasn't sure what I was looking at.

Straps of lavender-colored ribbon and purple and white lace didn't look like any of the garments we had discussed at the shop. Strands of pearls connected in multiple places and fabric flowers decorated the lace here and there. Some kind of high fashion? Or... lingerie? I found a card tucked into the garment and opened it to reveal tiny script written in Common Tongue.

A gift. Congratulations on your new marriage! Your order will be finished shortly.

Sincerely,

Inga – Perfect Fit Tailor Services, Bhalden's Post

My eyebrows raised as I held up the straps of ribbons and lace. I'd never owned any lingerie, but that was what this appeared to be: very, very skimpy lingerie. Inspection of the inner seams showed that it did appear to have been pre-constructed, and then specific seams were altered to adjust the size. I stripped out of my sleepwear and after a few tries figured out that several of the ribbons wrapped around my upper thighs and rump, and a second piece had ribbons that wrapped around my back and chest to hold up my breasts, along with a gauzy mesh lace that backed the fabric flowers to "cover" my nipples. Several strands of pearls draped from both the top and bottom, but the two pieces were unconnected. It was, indeed, a perfect fit. And absolutely scandalous.

Inga was the name of the woman who had taken my measure-ments. *"New marriage? I'll make you extra. He'll like it,"* I recalled her saying with a happy wink and a mischievous grin. Had she sent this? Or had Victor requested it? Was this his sign that he finally wanted to join with me and become a *proper* husband and wife?

Footsteps sounded in the hallway before I had time to react, and Victor froze two steps into the bedroom, his eyes widening the tiniest amount as he stared at me.

"This is what was in the package," I told him, confusion clear in my voice as I turned toward him and fingered the silk strap that came over my shoulder. "Did you order it?"

Victor didn't respond except to slide his gaze up to meet mine from where it had lingered on my torso, his eyes widening even farther, but I was getting better at reading him. As far as responses went, that was the equivalent of a stuttered, "Wha—what?" *Not him, then,* I decided. *A wedding gift from the girl in the shop who had giggled about us being newly married.* I decided to tease him a little anyway, and I could feel the mischief on my face as I fluttered my wings in a flirty little flickering motion.

That got more of a reaction out of him. "What is it?" His voice was hoarse.

"Lingerie," I stated, but my voice pitched up like it was a question.

"Lingerie?" he repeated, his focus drifting downward to take in my garment again.

I felt a little silly standing here, dressed like this in front of him, with him being fully clothed. But he *did* seem to like it. "So that's a no, then? You didn't buy it?" I took a step toward him, and his eyebrows came together like he was doing intense mathematical equations in his head.

He started to shake his head in denial, but only got as far as turning it to one side before he seemed to get stuck, still looking terribly confused as he stared at me out of the corner of his eye.

My smile was probably blinding. This was *fun.* I'd never seen him so flummoxed. Perhaps if I had looked for *his* reaction on our wedding day, rather than being afraid and searching for support from Apollo, this was what he might have looked like when I'd entered the great hall for our ceremony. It made my heart ache to have missed it. The thought occurred to me that I had been afraid of death for so long, and I hadn't even really been living.

Now here I was *flirting* with him.

What is it about proximity to death that makes someone feel more alive? In this moment I felt *so* alive. "Are you sure?" I asked as innocently as I could, knowing I was doing a terrible job keeping a straight face. "Men purchase lingerie for their lovers, right?" I teased, knowing we couldn't really claim to be lovers yet, but enjoying the process of getting there. "For their *wives?*"

I settled on, probably laying it on a little too thick, but he didn't seem to notice.

He was too busy having an aneurism or solving the mysteries of the universe or whatever it was he was doing while staring at my tits. It's not like he'd never seen them before. He'd cared for me while I was sick, bathing and dressing me. But I had been unconscious then, and he had probably seen himself as my caretaker more than my husband. Even after I'd woken, he'd been gentlemanly to a fault, turning his gaze away even as he helped me dress. Now I was practically offering myself up on a platter for his viewing.

His eyes snapped to mine, flaring in the same way they had when I'd traced his tattoo a few days before. It made me pause to consider that maybe his reaction was less about the tattoo itself and more about what it stood for. He may not have known what to do with me or what it meant to be a husband yet, but he *liked* that I was his wife.

I decided to test my theory, stepping close enough to touch him again, and trying not to let my nerves get the best of me when he didn't step away. "I believe it was actually a wedding gift from the tailor girl. She said my *husband* would like it," I said, stressing the word. I laid the nail of my first finger near the top of his binding mark and dragged it lightly down the tree from the top of the leaves to the tip of the longest root. I looked up at him through my eyelashes to find him looking dazed.

"Does he?" I prompted, and he responded with a silent nod. "I think I'm going to need your help to take it off," I whispered.

He gave a rough exhale, and when his eyes focused, they were decidedly hungry. I wondered what kind of beast I had unleashed. How does one seduce a reaper? At least for this one, I decided to appeal to his desire to provide for his wife. His need to protect me and give me space to heal had been warring with both his own personal desires and his desire to give me what I want. And so I voiced very clearly what I wanted. "I want you to make me your wife. *Properly.*"

His pupils bloomed so large the pretty blue ring around them was scarcely visible. Still, he spoke through a mouth that barely moved, as if he thought moving any part of his body might make him lose control. "You are my wife." I suspected if he had a tail, it would have been swishing.

"In my culture."

He was silent as he considered this, his gaze making a circuitous route over my form. Not in a lustful way, as one might assume, although that part of his brain was definitely engaged. His expression was suddenly detached in a way that made me think he was judging my fitness for such activities. Was I well enough? That had been his stipulation before, after all.

"Okay." The word was the quiet click of a lock turning over after weeks of trying to open it.

I blinked at him, unsure if I'd actually heard him agree. "Really?" I asked, studying his face to see if he'd truly meant it.

He nodded slowly, a single movement. His posture was stiff, and he stood preternaturally still. "Yes," he said. "I'm at your service." His eyes were maelstroms of desire, locked onto mine and pulling me into their depths. Nevertheless, he made no move to touch me.

I narrowed my eyes at him, wondering what his game was, and considered the books he'd been studying in the library. If he was unsure of how to go about doing this, then perhaps he was simply waiting for me to take the lead. He certainly didn't seem... reluctant. I suspected my husband was somehow even more nervous than I was, which, strangely, made me feel even less nervous about it. I decided to start with something we had already found some measure of success with and work from there.

"I think we should practice kissing again," I told him, infusing my words with bossy confidence.

His eyes narrowed slightly. "Do I get to choose where I practice my kissing?"

I blinked at him, not expecting that. "You have somewhere you'd like to kiss me?"

"Yes," he answered simply. I waited until he dropped his gaze from mine to the side of my neck and raised a finger to brush the skin there. "Just here."

Sparks of delight shot through me, and I shivered at his touch. He'd been thinking about kissing me? "Then do," I told him breathlessly.

He bent slowly, tilting his head until he could graze the delicate skin at the base of my neck with his lips. My heart was already racing as he raised his hands to touch my face and arm, only making contact with the lightest pressure from the tips of his fingers. It was the softest, most feather-light kiss I'd ever experienced, as if I were the most fragile flower bloom in existence. Heat coated my neck as he released a small sigh, and the next press of his lips was firmer, and then firmer again as he began to make his way up to my jaw. I felt his tongue dart out to taste the skin just below my ear, and I sighed his name as I arched to give him more access. At least... I thought I'd sighed his name. What I'd actually said was "*Husband*," and I didn't realize it until he'd groaned in response. He practically melted into a puddle, moaning into my neck with a husky, humorless chuckle. Stepping around me while continuing to work his way over my jaw to kiss my mouth, he backed toward the bed while gently drawing me along with him. We broke our kiss for him to seat himself on the mattress, and he quickly removed his jacket while toeing off his shoes.

I decided to help with his shirt, tackling the tiny buttons under his chin and working my way down them with lightning speed, only pausing once they were finished to run my gaze across his chest and abs. "How are you real?" I asked, feeling dazed myself. Every muscle was taut and defined. He looked powerfully strong and trim, the firelight casting each curve and dip in sharp relief.

His expression was almost bashful. He wanted to cover himself back up. My mind flashed back to how he had immediately donned his shadow cloak the day Helda had arrived at the gate while he was chopping wood. I wondered briefly how hard he was fighting against his instinct to cloak himself now in front of me and smiled. "Victor, this is... How are you so muscular?" I knew he was a guardian of some kind before I met him, but in the weeks I'd known him he hadn't seemed inclined to exercise for the sake of it.

"Physical combat training is as important as magical," he murmured and raised a single shoulder in a self-conscious shrug before scooting back toward the headboard, then gesturing with a finger for me to join him.

Hell yes it is, I thought to myself, climbing onto the bed after him and trying hard not to drool on his abs. He guided me onto his lap after propping the pillows against the headboard and leaning back on them, and I lifted my wings to give him room to draw his knees up behind me to support my back. He watched me with bedroom eyes as I hooked the pads of my fingers into his collarbone and then dragged them softly down his torso, feeling the muscles under his satin skin and the faint smattering of hair that dappled the middle of his chest and stomach.

I didn't ask, I just took. My eager little fingers savored every inch I could touch. I watched his stomach flex and his shoulders bunch. His pectorals couldn't be real. They had to have been sculpted by God himself. I'd never seen anyone so well built, so starkly handsome, so beautifully masculine. So *mine.*

He must have seen the possessive gleam in my eye, because he released a shaky breath and raised a hand to touch my face, gently tugging me toward him. His mouth met mine in a tender kiss, his lips parting the smallest amount, and when the tip of his tongue grazed mine, it was so hesitant I had to fight back happy tears. He was such a conundrum. Deadly, powerful, gentle, shy.

I kissed my way down his jaw and nipped at the side of his neck, finally giving in to my desire to test the firmness of the muscles here with my teeth. Suckling and kissing my way down his throat, I enjoyed seeing the way his delicate, pale skin marked up with every bite. How long would the marks last? I felt like I was claiming him for anyone else to see. We already had our binding marks, but some long-buried instinct made me want to do this thoroughly. How many places on his body could I mark as mine with tongue and teeth and lips? I locked my mouth onto the muscle at the base of his neck and lingered there, sucking lightly, and the groan he released was *electric*. His hips tilted in search of mine, and my nipples tightened as I arched to press them into his chest.

"Come here, Angel," he breathed, touching my elbows with the tips of his fingers and directing me upward with the lightest pressure. I pulled back to look at him and his gaze was feverish as he looked at my body. "Take this off." His voice was rough as he stared at the straps of lace that arched over and around my breasts.

I reached up to the tiny hook on my right side and unlatched it with one hand, letting the lace and flowers fall away.

His exhale came out in a gust. After a moment of silence where he didn't appear to breathe at all, he said, "That too." He indicated the bottom portion with his chin as he gazed at the straps around my thighs and ass. The embroidered purple petals afforded me virtually no modesty anyway.

I unhooked that too, and the pearls and petals slid to the bed.

"Thank you," he whispered, ever polite, and the gentle pressure from his fingertips on the backs of my arms directed my chest up to his face. He didn't ask, but he also didn't *take*. Not like I had. His hands were feather-light on my skin, completely opposite of my greedy little paws that claimed and cupped.

His lips, too, became the faintest pressure on the inside of my breast. His hot breath was a stronger sensation than his touches on my skin. "I love the noises you make," he told my breast as I arched against his mouth seeking more contact. I realized I was panting just as heavily as he was. The more I pressed, the more he took, and when I shifted so that my nipple was in front of his lips, he fell on it like a man starved, licking and suckling until I was writhing against him with my grasping fingers in his hair. His own fingers never increased their pressure, simply guiding, directing, keeping me where he wanted me, but always as light as a breath. His mouth and my body writhing against his was all the sensation I was able to focus on. The slightest pressure directed me upward again, and I pushed up to only my knees until I was kneeling over him as he kissed his way down my ribs, down my belly, until he reached the juncture between my legs. "May I kiss you here?" he asked, his eyes flicking up to meet mine.

Chapter 20

Celeste

MY MOUTH DROPPED OPEN. Was this something he'd read about in one of his books? This seemed like advanced—

He inhaled deeply, his nose barely bumping the mound of my sex, and lust lit his eyes. There was a curiosity and a confidence in them when he looked at me next that helped to soothe my nerves.

"Okay," I choked out. "If you want—"

But he was already nuzzling at my inner thighs, and I had to brace my hand on the headboard above his head at the sensation. His nose tickled my mound as he inhaled again and pressed gentle kisses there before trailing his fingers around the tops of my thighs to my opening. "Can I touch you here with my fingers?" he asked, raising his gaze again to meet mine through his inky eyelashes.

"Yes," I breathed.

Still, his touch was gentle. He directed my thigh over his shoulder and then parted my opening with his thumbs, holding it open as he kissed me *there*. His hot tongue darted out before I was ready—far less tentatively than it had inside my mouth—and slipped right through the seam of my folds. I squealed and nearly jumped out of my skin, and felt his mouth curve in amusement against my opening as his tongue flicked out again and again, laving my clit and slipping past it to dip into my opening. A hot swirling sensation like he was licking a lollipop was quickly followed by him pressing his lips around my flesh and suckling. It was the filthiest kiss I'd ever had in my life and all I could do was hold on to the headboard with both hands and whimper as he alternated between swirling and sucking.

He increased the pressure of his tongue until I was seeing stars, one hand bracing my weight on the headboard, and I realized I'd moved the other—it was gripping his hair with my nails in his scalp. I was desperately grateful that there was no one else in the keep to hear the high-pitched noises falling out of my open mouth. The leg I was kneeling on began to shake as I gave into the lustful urge to rub myself against the increasing suction and pressure of his mouth, until he finally gave in and caught my thigh in a tight enough grip to keep me up, holding it against his chest to keep me upright. If he was concerned that I might not want this, the vice-like hold I had on his hair was surely enough to mollify him. He was meeting every rock of my hips with a hot thrust of his wet tongue, and I suddenly came so hard I think my heart stopped. I know my brain did. My neck and chest flushed hot as I began to convulse inside. Every muscle in my body locked up as I orgasmed, arching over his head and desperately trying to be gentle with his face. Fierce aftershocks hit me multiple times as he continued to lick and kiss me, until finally I had to pull away and beg for a reprieve. He seemed reluctant to let me go.

"Hm. Does that count toward kissing practice?" he asked crisply after I collapsed back against his thighs, my knee slipping off his shoulder, my head propped against his bent knees.

"Yes." I was still shivering with aftershocks. I would agree to anything he wanted right now. I couldn't even chastise him for the mildly smug look on his face. He wasn't quite smirking, but you could tell he *wanted* to.

He surveyed his handiwork as I lay cradled against his thighs, my wings spread haphazardly on the bed, his eyes practically smoldering as they roamed over my body. "I think I like you like this."

"I think I like me like this, too," I said, my words slurring as if I were drunk.

"Shall I 'service you' again?" he asked, with humor in his eyes and a hint of laughter in his voice, then leaned down to press another kiss to the top of my breast.

"Yes, but not like that," I told him, getting my knees back under myself and pushing up to a sitting position so I could lift up enough to open his trousers. His abs tightened as I worked open the button below his navel, but he kept his gaze on my face. "Is this okay?" I asked him when he lifted his arms away to give me room to work.

"It is," he confirmed quietly, his eyes still hooded and his breathing picking up again as he lowered his arms to the bed. He gripped the blankets on either side of his hips as I tugged his pants down.

Here is the pink skin I'd been looking for, I thought with a smile, remembering my childhood daydreams about a pink-skinned fae prince. My daydreams had nothing on this, though, and my grin faded before I quickly forced it back. At a glance, his cock looked too large to close my hand around it—which was intimidating to say the least—and much longer than I had been expecting. I'm not even sure what I'd been expecting, but I tried not to let my surprise show, lest he change his mind and decide I wasn't well enough for this after all.

"Can I touch?" I asked, and my heart sped up when he nodded.

"I'm yours, Angel," he said simply.

Before I could question myself, I reached out to feel it and ran my fingers down its length, marveling at the smoothness of the skin and how hard it was to the touch. Surely it had to be painful with his flesh being this hard. A glance at his face told me he very well might be in pain, his expression one of deep concentration. His breathing became more broken as I touched and fondled, exploring the slight curve of it and the thick veins that wrapped around its length. The sack underneath was soft but firm, drawn up tightly against his body. The glans at the top was particularly sensitive, causing him to clench his jaw and breathe through his teeth when I rubbed the pads of my fingers over it. Even the veins in his arms stood out as he gripped the sheets beneath him. Poor man was definitely in pain. I tutted at him and hoped what we were about to do would help him to feel better.

I watched his face as I raised up and centered his length at my opening, dragging the tip through my wetness multiple times to ensure it was well coated. I'd heard enough stories to know that would help with his size. His breaths were harsh, and his jaw clenched harder as he gripped the bedding even tighter with desperate fingers, trying to restrain the little movements his hips were beginning to make. But I found I liked the movements and got distracted as I began to roll my hips. A little more exploration had me chasing the feeling of his fat glans circling my opening and pressing through the folds around my clit.

"Ah, Doveling," he choked out, hissing through his teeth. He flexed and released his muscles, fighting himself as he panted for air. "Can I—may I touch you?"

I broke into a fit of giggles. "I'm currently sitting on your penis," I said with a laugh, rolling my hips again as if perhaps he needed a reminder. *Such a sweet man.*

He released the blankets and slid his hands up my legs, finally beginning to cup my thighs, caress my hips, cradle my breasts. Even the slight roundness of my belly received attention as he coddled every curve he could reach.

I took his hardness in my fingers again, lining him up with my opening and testing how it felt as I pushed him inside of me. I gasped as the thick, firm head of his cock entered me, stretching me immediately as I lowered myself onto it as gently as I could. Victor's head tipped back, eyes shut and mouth dropping open as his fingers tightened on my thighs. I rose up again, then lowered myself a little farther this time, allowing him to fill me a little more with each successive motion. I looked up to see him watching me through his eyelashes, the tendons in his neck standing out from the tilt of his head. A mild flare of pain made me wince and I hesitated to wait it out, but his hands quickly pulled me up enough to remove the pain.

"Are you okay?" he asked hoarsely and waited until I nodded. "Go slow," he instructed. His entire body tensed as I lowered myself onto him again, his eyes hazed over in concentration as I waited for the pain to fade, and after a few deep breaths it started turning to pressure and fullness instead.

As I began to relax, I realized he was practically trembling with his efforts to keep still and not cause me more pain.

"I'm okay," I assured him, but he lifted a hand to pinch his temples as if he too were in pain.

"I can't unknow this feeling, Celeste," he groaned, dropping his hand back to my hip as he arched against the pillows. "This is—" He couldn't finish his sentence. His eyelids fluttered as his breath caught in his lungs. He made a choking sound and his hips spasmed as he fought to control himself.

I set my hands against his chest to help me balance and kept most of my weight on my knees, testing the feeling of him inside me again. A little sore, but not necessarily painful. "You can move," I told him, and his response was instantaneous. Still gentle, but he *moved*, his hips driving up into me reflexively.

He wheezed out a sharp breath as he thrust into me. "Is that okay? Are you hurting?" His eyes were feverish, and his cheeks flamed.

"I'm good. This is good," I assured him.

Little by little, his hard cock burrowed deeper into me with each thrust, until finally, he was hilted entirely within me and I was able to seat myself firmly on his hips. I took a moment to explore the strange sensation of being filled so completely, something I'd never experienced before. I felt like I could feel him in my lungs. "I'm okay," I assured him again before he could ask, concern written all over his face.

And I was okay, but I would never be the same again. It wasn't even about the *act* itself. His tenderness and vulnerability, being this close to him and seeing him entirely unbound, taking him *into my body* had changed me somehow. Again, something I hadn't expected but wholly welcome. I knew exactly what he meant when he said he couldn't unknow it. *This* was why my people believed that a couple weren't married until they had come together like this. Well, now we had, and he was truly *mine*, in the culture of both our peoples.

I found that, if I rolled my hips in the same way I had when he had been pressed outside of me, I could get the same stimulation as before, but now it was even better because he was filling me, rubbing places I hadn't known existed until just now. His pubic bone gave the perfect amount of pressure when I shifted my hips *just so*.

"God, I could listen to you make those sounds every day of my life," he breathed, driving up into me with little movements even as I rocked my hips against him, increasing the pressure on my clit and directly causing the staccato cadence my keening was beginning to take on.

I wanted to do this for hours. His hands caressing my breasts, fondling my hips, plucking at my nipples. He'd apparently remembered my reaction to his touch on the underside of my wings, now reaching with purposeful fingers to trail his fingers up my back and through my feathers. It was his face, though, the pleasure and pain and vulnerability there, that pushed me over the edge. The rolling pressure of his hips driving into me one more time caused a tensing inside of me that triggered a wave of pleasurable contractions as I came again, this time on his cock. My muscles clenching around his swollen girth seemed to completely overwhelm him, and he gasped like he'd been shocked, his thrusts becoming hungry and wild. His ragged breaths culminated in a broken gasp as his torso curled up against mine and his cock swelled impossibly further and spasmed inside of me. It was heaven. Bliss.

He came back to himself slowly—his hot breath on my neck, his cheeks stained pink, and looking at me like I held all the secrets of the universe. "Are you okay, Angel?" he whispered, bringing his knuckle up to brush it down my cheek. All I could do was smile with my heart in my throat as it threatened to escape my mouth and tell this man everything it felt about him.

And I may not have won the war for *his* heart yet, but I knew in my bones that I'd won a battle.

I HAD SOMEHOW CREATED a monster.

It was a thrilling monster as far as I was concerned, but Victor seemed distressed by the change in his body and how his physical need for me had flared to life seemingly overnight.

"This can't be normal," he practically growled to himself, vexed with the constant erection he seemed to be sporting beneath his trousers. He was agitated and concerned by the fact that his body seemed to have awakened to a new base need that left him throbbing and uncomfortable multiple times throughout the day.

I could only try to smother my giggles in response. As far as I knew, that was indeed the normal reality of many men, but he seemed so anxious about it that I couldn't help but want to help. I'd started it, after all. And in fact, I found that milking his cock to provide him relief had become one of my favorite activities. And he enjoyed "servicing" me too, but I think I found a special pleasure in assisting him with his... *troubles*. As such, over the following week, he had taken me while I sat on the library table, bent over the library table, him sitting in the high-backed chair, me folded in half on the library rug, with his hand over my mouth in the shadowy alcoves that lined the hall, against the closed door of our bedroom, and several creative positions on the bed. If Helda or Yasgrot weren't around, he had my legs in the air and I was crying out for him. If they were, I was furtively draining his balls in a dark corner somewhere while he panted and groaned over me. It was the best week of my life—even if he seemed positively dismayed at his sudden need for me.

"Doveling, this can't be healthy," he hissed at me in a whisper-shout as I tried to see how much of his erection I could fit inside my mouth. He'd gotten that annoyed look on his face just moments prior that said his cock had grown stiff again and he couldn't concentrate on his language studies, so I'd lured him to the stacks in the back of the library and found his cock to be rock hard and hot to the touch. His cheeks were perpetually stained pink these days, the blood rushing to them a telltale sign he was struggling with the tightness in his groin again that he needed my help relieving. And I was delighted to do it. Watching the helpless pleasure take over his hard expressions of vexed frustration was an aphrodisiac all its own. The way all his indignant aggravation would melt off of his face as I took him in hand or into my body only made me want him more.

"Angel, please," he said in half-hearted protest as I tried out a bit of suction around his cock, and his hips bucked ever so slightly. His gasping breaths and quiet moans of pleasure made heat pool in my belly and between my thighs. The light begging just made me even more enthusiastic. "You could choke," he said, but it came out breathless.

I tried relaxing my throat but didn't find much success there, so I settled for light suction and just taking him to the back of my mouth instead. I wrapped my hands around the base of his cock to make up for the rest of it.

His jaw dropped open slightly, and his mouth moved as if he were trying to speak but couldn't quite find the words. "Oh, god, why is this so hot," he finally choked out from above me as he gripped the shelving for support.

I was just starting to find my groove when he decided he couldn't take any more and pulled out from between my lips, picked me up to standing, turned me around, and flipped my skirt over my back—one that had been delivered in a lovely bundle a few days ago by Inga the seamstress. He pushed down on my back to guide it into an arch so he could enter me more easily, and as I braced against the shelves myself, my head lolled to the side as he pushed into my heat and began to thrust. This was my happy place; tucked away in a secret spot with Victor, making love and listening to his soft, broken breaths. We'd learned pretty quickly that when he entered me from behind, he needed to manually stimulate my clit to make me come, and it didn't take long before his warm fingers were digging through the folds of my skirt to find my clit, rubbing the sides of it in a rough rhythm that matched his thrusts. My cheeks immediately heated, and I felt my nipples tighten. I wouldn't last long like this, and he could tell by my breathing that I was close.

"That's right, Angel," he purred against my back as he rubbed at my clit and buried himself inside of me again and again in long, luxurious strokes. "My personal angel. That's my good girl."

I came so hard he had to cover my mouth again.

Chapter 21

Celeste

"THEY'RE HERE," HE WARNED me in a low voice the next evening as he leaned against the ledge of our bedroom window box, silently watching his family arrive in the courtyard below.

I had been curled up in our bed early, drawing in a sketch book he'd requested Yasgrot procure for me after I mentioned I used to paint, but my anxiety spiked at his words. "We should be down there to greet them!" I said, dropping my haphazard sketches of little flowers and starting to climb out of the bed.

He lifted a lackadaisical hand to stay me. "There's no need. They will come to us," he replied, mild annoyance threading through his voice.

His assertion only amplified my horror—these people were his *family* and we needed to make a good impression. They'd only known me as a weeping ball of nerves, and then I'd asked their son to directly disobey what he'd been asked to do. *And he had.* "Victor, what if they hate me?" I whisper-shouted at him, whirling in mental circles, unsure how to prepare to greet them. We should have food. I wasn't even dressed properly! "I'm the one who asked you to leave!" I'd already made a terrible impression. We'd snuck out of our own very public wedding, and it was *my fault.* I was terrified to have to face my own family eventually, but at least I knew what to expect from them—Mom would be irate but would forgive me because she loved me, and Dad would refuse to talk to me for a period of time but then go back to everything being fine, no discussion necessary. The queen, well—I would get an earful from my grandmother for sure. But I had no idea what to expect from his family.

And for us it had been *weeks* since we left, but it would only have been days—possibly only hours—for them in Faery since time didn't pass the same there.

My husband turned to look at me like I had two heads. "Why would they—"

The heavy wooden door to our bedroom swung open with a *bang* as it forcefully slammed into the stone wall. "Knock, knock, motherfucker!" A young man about our age stood at the entrance to our room, a black cloak of shadows swirling about his feet. He looked remarkably similar to Victor, same lean build and scowling expression, only a hand or so shorter and with a slight wave to his chin-length dark hair and more roundness to his face. "Do you have *any idea* how much *ranting* we had to listen to after you kidnapped your wife?" he said as he glared at my husband from the doorway while gesturing wildly at me. "Hello, *said wife*," he said to me as an aside before returning his glower to Victor.

A smaller—though still taller than me—woman pushed him into the room from behind. "Move, dipshit. Her name is Celeste," she said tartly as she stepped around him and then held her hands up in the air theatrically, cackling at the top of her lungs. I recognized her as his sister, who had stood as witness at our wedding. "It was *amazing*. I can't wait to tell you about all the drama. Great work. I'm so proud. Hi, Celeste," she added, but before I could respond, another man—thicker across the chest than the first one, and with shorter hair—pushed in behind her to all but shout at my husband over the top of their heads.

"That was *not* great work! What the hell, Vitya? You can't just steal people and ditch out on your own wedding. It's just not done! What is wrong with you? Mom is *furious.*"

I recoiled against the headboard, unsure whether I should hide or stand up for my husband as the other man started ranting in a language I couldn't understand. I cringed away from the shouting, but no one seemed to be paying me any mind. A glance at Victor showed he was entirely unconcerned. In fact, his expression looked *bored*. He picked at a fingernail with his thumb, something he did occasionally when he was thinking. I'd learned to read him well enough that I think I would have been able to tell by now if he was upset, and I could only find annoyance reflected in his face.

"Victor Molchanov, you are in So. Much. Trouble!" The three at the door stepped aside—veritably skittered out of the way—for a woman with a slight build who shared their same black hair. Her eyes were lit with fire, and she had her hands curled into angry claws like she wanted to strangle my husband. My heart rate skyrocketed until I caught a glimpse of his expression again. He'd worn his signature bored scowl as the others had entered the room, but for this woman, presumably his mother, though I'd not been introduced to her, his expression softened slightly. Everyone looked so young it was hard to tell at a glance how they were related and what generation they belonged to.

"Everyone out," came a familiar voice from behind the small crowd of people, and his sister was the first to slip away, with shouted instructions for Victor to come find her later as she left. The two men also stepped back, making room for the last woman in a deferential way, but not actually leaving the doorway. The bigger man glanced at me and gave a little nod of greeting, even though his face was clearly unhappy. The woman who had performed our wedding ceremony stepped into the room to stand between Victor and the rest of them, her sharp eyes taking us in quickly before turning to the three others.

She pointed at the two men—*brothers? cousins?*—and said "Go home, or go find your own room if you wish to stay here in the keep. Find Yasgrot and give him a tally of whomever is staying, and request that he have the princess's trunks brought up from the courtyard." She had a stronger accent that didn't quite match the rest of them, his mother's speech only bearing a mild form of it. After watching everyone else leave, she turned to his mother and patted her shoulder tiredly. They looked like they could have been sisters. "Milata, darling, I know you're exhausted. Go home. I will deal with it." She started to wave a hand dismissively until she noticed the bigger man still lingering in the hallway. "Out!" she repeated to him, pointing an accusatory finger. Then, firmly ushering out his mother—who also gave me a nod of greeting as she went before returning her glare to her youngest son, which made me feel even guiltier—she peeked into the hall and then shut the door with a decisive click.

She heaved a sigh before turning and greeting me absently, and then headed to the chair in the corner of the room. Her hair was bound in a practical twist at the back of her neck, and she wore a real cloak made of cloth instead of a conjured one of shadows. She shared Victor's dark hair and fair skin like the rest of them, but her build was slight like his mother's. Her features were sharp like his, but though he had a very slight hump at the top of his nose, hers was more hooked in shape, giving her a slightly hawkish appearance.

My arm burned at the memory of her cutting into my flesh, and I had to fight to keep from shying away from her as she took her seat in the armchair next to the bed. It was his grandmother, if I recalled correctly from what my mother had told me while I was being prepared for the ceremony. But I couldn't see how this woman could possibly be his grandmother. Our people aged slowly, but just like his mother, she looked like she could have been our age.

Victor watched her in silence from his spot at the window until she was seated. "Tea?" It was the first thing he'd said since they'd arrived inside the keep.

She settled into the chair, groaning as if she was far older than she looked.

"Yes, dear, that would be lovely. Three cubes today if you have them." She watched as he poured her a cup of tea and began to stir in some sugar. "Vitya, that was *wrong*."

His hands froze over the cup. "I put three cubes, just like you—"

"Not the *tea*, Victor. Leaving!" She huffed an exasperated breath and then glowered at him from across the room. "I would have *never* suspected you to be capable of such deceit." I flinched at her words, wondering if I should come out and confess my part in it, but fearful of interrupting them. I wished I'd had the forethought to discuss what to say and do before they'd arrived. Strangely, he relaxed from his tense state and returned to stirring her tea, before carrying it over to her while she continued.

"Your mother is incensed. Celeste's mother is outraged," she said, gesturing blithely toward me.

"Careful, it's hot," he said, handing it to her slowly.

"Thank you, dearest," she said softly, cradling the cup in her hands and taking a moment to enjoy the warmth. "I don't abide such disobedience, you know."

"Of course not," he agreed amiably, stooping to kiss the smaller woman on her temple.

She blew on her tea as he returned to his place at the window. "You have tarnished our people's reputation as unbiased, dutiful servants among the fae."

That got my hackles up. Victor had done *nothing* but what I'd asked him to do, and he'd been entirely virtuous and dutiful since the moment I'd met him. Well, until I'd seduced him, at least, but that took *weeks*. I curled my fingers into my blanket, not knowing if I should speak in his defense or hold my tongue. He wasn't upset or angry. He didn't even look particularly chastised.

"How dreadful," he murmured.

"You caused much doubt among the Morningstar family as to your ability to care for their daughter," she continued, making my anxiety spike again. They wouldn't... They couldn't make me leave him now, could they?

"And I, well—*I'm* going to be laughing about it for at least the next few hundred years," she continued before taking a careful sip of her tea. I wasn't sure I'd heard her correctly until I saw Victor's reaction.

Victor raised his eyes to meet hers and flashed her a smile. The man *smiled*. I'd never seen such a beautiful thing in my entire life. It was the brief, self-satisfied, affectionate grin of a little boy who'd gotten caught with his hand in the cookie jar and knew without a doubt that he'd be eating that cookie. It was the brightly glowing morning sunrise after a particularly long night. It lit up his entire face for a brief, glorious second of incandescence. My lungs ceased to function. You could have knocked me over with a feather.

His grandmother returned his little grin with a mischievous-looking one of her own and chuckled to herself. "It was quite the coup," she said, sounding thoroughly impressed. "But we have to pretend that you've been reprimanded within an inch of your life, for your mother's sake, or the jig is up." She sighed, turning to me. "And how are you holding up, darling Celeste? You look *much* better than the last time I saw you. How long were we gone for?" she asked, directing that last bit to Victor.

"I was gone three weeks. I'm not sure how much longer your stay was. We arrived here maybe five weeks ago," he suggested, folding his hands in front of the long line of his body as he leaned against the wall.

I was having a hard time following the conversation, having been dazzled so thoroughly by Victor's unexpected smile moments earlier. I hadn't yet been able to shake it off when she turned her attention to me again, expecting a reply.

"Oh, I—um, I'm fine. Thank you for asking," I stuttered out pitifully, having a hard time tearing my gaze away from her grandson.

"I'm so glad to hear it," she told me kindly anyway. "After living with our magic day in and day out for a thousand years, it becomes rather commonplace. Mundane, even. But seeing its effect on you is remarkable," she said, studying me. She turned to Victor briefly and said, "You did very well caring for her, Vitya. Not that I doubted," before turning back to me.

"Vitya?" I asked, glancing at him. His family kept calling him that.

"A diminutive," she explained. "May I see your binding mark?"

I realized I was clutching my arm against my chest and forced myself to let her have it, leaning forward to show it to her.

"One of many this dear boy is subjected to," she muttered as she leaned over my arm to look closer, and I realized she was still talking about his nickname. "When he was a baby we would call him Vitüshka."

I broke into a wide grin, looking past her to my husband as I imagined a soft, tender, baby version of him being doted on by this woman as she called him "Vitüshka."

She made a comment about how the mark was filling in nicely before looking up and following my expression to her grandson, who was watching the two of us with rapt attention. "I can see this was a match well made," she said with smug affection, before patting me on the arm and releasing it. She turned to Victor. "I trust the hormone surge hasn't been too unbearable?"

Victor's eyes snapped to hers, and there was no mistaking the dawning horror within them. "The *what?*" he asked, his words like the snap of a whip.

She hesitated in confusion before responding. "The surge of hormones after the binding is finalized."

"Is *that* what this is?" he asked, all of his distress from the past week bleeding into his words, his face a mask of irritation.

"Oh, dear. Please tell me you received some education about 'the birds and the bees,' dearest. I'm afraid this conversation is quite outside of my wheelhouse. I always left these kinds of talks to your grandfather."

Victor practically sputtered with indignation, the most flustered I'd ever seen him. "Of course I know what... *that* is. But no one mentioned anything about a surge of hormones. I've felt like I've been going through a second puberty." His voice was still low, but his tone was acerbic, and I worried how his grandmother would respond, but again she surprised me.

"Well, now you have some ammunition to volley back at your mother when she comes for your hide," she suggested lightly. "The hormones will settle down... eventually. It's been too long ago now for me to remember specifics. Perhaps ask your brother." She drained the last of her tea and handed him the cup when he stepped forward to take it, putting it away and returning to lend her a hand as she stood. I climbed off the bed to stand beside her as she rose and helped her straighten her woolen cloak. "I think I will take a day or two here to rest and catch up with Yasgrot on the local happenings," she told him before turning to me and placing her hand lightly on my healed binding mark again. "Welcome to our family, Celeste. We will not try to replace the one you already have, but now you are included in ours as well. It appears Vitya's magic has already begun to correct your malfunctioning organs, yes? It will take you a while yet to be back to your full strength I think, and several years for your cells to fully turn over for you to reach full immortality, so please be careful with yourself in the meantime." She lowered her voice to a murmur and met my eye. "I know the handfasting was an awful thing, but you were strong, and so brave. You did so well. And you've weathered the worst of your healing already, I can tell. I'm very proud of you."

I nearly melted into a puddle on the floor as she leaned in to press her cheek to mine and kiss the air. All I could do was look at her grandson with watery eyes and my heart in my throat. He didn't seem ready to let go of the revelation about his body's response to our "finalizing" the binding, by which I assumed she meant consummation.

"Do watch out for Nikolai," she told him as she passed him. "He blames you for having to listen to two days of Milata's haranguing."

Victor didn't seem concerned about her warning, but I couldn't help but feel concerned. I didn't know which one was Nikolai, but would he hurt us? I felt extremely on edge, and Victor seemed to notice, as he reached out to take my hand and draw me against his chest. "Please remind them that Celeste isn't used to people stepping through walls," he said dryly as his grandmother reached the door. "And that she sleeps at night," he added as an afterthought.

"I'll do my best," she responded, though she didn't sound

entirely hopeful.

I relaxed my posture against him as we watched her go, comforted by his warmth and his arm around me. "Well. That explains that, I suppose," he grumbled when the door clicked shut.

I glanced up to find him glowering at the floor before he raised his gaze to mine, looking rather put out about the fact that no one had warned him about his reaction to our first joining. I bit my lip and tried not to laugh, failing entirely and hiding my face against his side instead. He huffed at me, clearly vexed with all of this, but that just made my grin wider. I turned my arm so I could peek at my binding mark, wondering what the effect of his family being here would be on our relationship dynamic.

Victor took my arm in his hand and smoothed his thumb down my binding mark in a way that felt both comforting and protective. I marveled at the way the mark itself had changed over the last week, the vague shape of a young tree sending out roots farther down my arm. It was growing, just as we were. My stomach churned with a mixture of happiness and nerves.

Chapter 22

Grim

CELESTE HAD A HARD time falling asleep once we went to bed together—a ritual I'd finally become accustomed to and begun to find strangely enjoyable in the last few weeks. Her nerves and concerns made her twitchy and kept her mind from settling fully for long into the night. I briefly considered trying to help her settle through physical means, as I'd found that she relaxed substantially after being stimulated to culmination. It would be difficult to keep her from being heard by my family members now that they were here, and I knew from her reaction to Helda's interruption while we kissed that others being aware of our coupling would be an entirely unwelcome circumstance for her. I felt the same. No matter how quiet I kept her, though, they would be aware, simply due to the nature of our senses. Even now, I could hear them moving about their rooms—my grand-mother's quiet murmurs in the kitchen, my sister splashing water on her face in a bathroom. Celeste's stiff posture as she lay with me made me even more hesitant to attempt such a union, though I had found her eagerly receptive to my urges surprisingly often over the last week. Tonight, though, I merely gathered her into my arms and held her close until she finally relaxed into sleep and my mind drifted to other things.

On the one hand, my family's return meant that I no longer had to maintain my constant vigilance. The spirits in the region seemed to be coming out of the woodwork in search of her magic. There had been a disturbing number of the cadaver-ous-looking ghouls around since we'd arrived. I'd had to step away and quietly dispatch dozens of them, striking them down before they could come anywhere near the walls of the small castle or its inhabitants. It was a relief to know that we were now surrounded by people who were similarly equipped with the senses and abilities that I have. That I was no longer the only thing standing between my wife's delicate soul and the parasitic creatures that seemed so intent on *hunting* her.

Even so, I felt unfairly resentful of my family's return and their intrusion on the personal peacefulness Celeste had found, as well as the tentative relationship that we'd begun building with one another. Yes, I loved my family and was grateful for their safe return, and yes, I had departed our wedding against their wishes and left them to deal with the fallout. But... *they* had decided that I would marry this woman and handed her into my personal care. I didn't regret my actions.

That said, I spent the entire night trying to ignore the uncomfortable sensation of heat and tightness demanding attention in my groin, unwilling to wake her up for relief even though I knew she would receive me if I asked. I could have gone outside to blow off steam by sparring with Nikolai—and to make him pay for the unnecessary flamboyance with which he entered our quarters *uninvited* upon their arrival. Loudly slamming doors when you are perfectly capable of walking through them was nothing short of drama for drama's sake, and Celeste had jumped nearly a foot in the air at the offensive sound.

Not that he'd noticed.

But I didn't want to leave her. She liked it when I stayed close while she slept, and I'd grown rather fond of this quiet time spent watching her dream and listening to the soft lull of her breathing. It was a special kind of torture having her warm, soft body pressed against me all night, calling to mine for hours on end. I'd never understood this intense craving people seemed to have for the affections of their partner, but the slow journey to understanding I'd been on with Celeste had taken a forceful leap forward the first time we joined physically. Then I hadn't just understood—*I'd known.* The unexpected rush of bonding chemicals that poured into my brain in the moments following our first act of making love—a euphemism I hadn't realized was literal until that moment—had caused a distressing shift in my emotional state. *And physical state,* I thought with a grimace as I shifted to try to find some relief from the frustrating erection that seemed to plague me constantly now.

My mood plummeted every time Celeste flinched in her sleep, her facial expression contorting into that tiny frown that told me her dreams were not pleasant ones. I watched her, presiding over her sleeping form throughout the night like a dragon jealously guarding its precious treasure. The idea of living beings as a dragon's hoard was no longer as silly an imagining as it might have been to me once. I'd never personally felt any desire to sleep, but when the frown melted away and her peaceful expression returned, I wished for the first time that I could join her in her slumber and see her dreams with my own mind. But since I couldn't, I was happy to be here with her, guarding her from both the outside world and her inner dreams. She tossed and turned but I held her close and murmured quiet nothings into her hair until she calmed.

By the time morning came I'd already made up my mind to take Celeste and leave again as soon as she was well enough. I didn't know when that would be, but the infusion of my family members clearly had her on edge. In the meantime, though, since I wouldn't be able to pacify my baser urges within the tight hold of her intoxicating body, I would happily work off some of my frustration by beating my cousin into the ground with whatever means of combat he found most desirable.

I rose with an irritated growl when I finally heard Brishta, the servant girl, deposit a tray of food outside the door, adjusting my maddening erection through my pants before I retrieved the tray to plate a meal for Celeste. Leaving the prepared meal on the desk near the bed, I slipped from the room while she was still asleep and headed for the kitchen, knowing my family would be lurking about, waiting for me. It would be better to get these conversations out of the way before she was awake to witness them. My mother was the first to find me, silently taking a place at the table across from me as I sipped my morning tea. I loved my mother, and it pained me to have angered her.

"I'm sorry I disappointed you," I told her honestly when she didn't speak but, instead, simply stared at me with the same unspoken wrath I'd received the few times I'd gotten into a fight at school as a child. I *was* sorry that my departure with the princess had inevitably caused trouble for both of our families, even though I didn't regret doing it. Because if no one else was going to put her well-being first, then I felt justified in removing her from the situation. But that didn't mean I didn't care about its effect on my mom. My father hadn't arrived with her, which meant he wasn't angry with me and had decided to skip out on the rebuke and return directly to their estate. Though we didn't really age, he liked to pretend he was too old to be "gallivanting around" all the time or burden himself with unnecessary familial disagreements.

My mother's face softened a little, but only a *very* little, as she regarded me from across the table. I poured her a cup of tea and handed it to her. She accepted it with grace.

"What were you thinking, Vitya?" Her words held censure, but she also truly wanted to know.

I flicked my gaze to her as I refilled my own cup of tea and then replaced the kettle on its tray. "I did what was best for the wife you entrusted me with," I told her mildly, before blowing on my tea. "And I would do it again."

She slapped her open palm onto the table in frustration but never got to voice her opinion on the matter because my cousin came barreling down the stairs into the kitchen at that moment.

"I thought I heard you!" Nikolai said, pointing at me. "Courtyard. Now. You and me. Let's go."

My mother nearly snarled at him for interrupting her, and I rolled my eyes at him trying to act like he was being a tough guy due to some imagined slight over me leaving. His expression was stern, but anyone who knew him could see that his eyes were sparkling with excitement at the prospect of sparring.

He was practically bouncing on his toes. But I would join him today. I did feel like I owed him for being subjected to all the angry quarreling after I left. *Even though the man lives for drama.* And it would be nice to have some kind of physical outlet for the frustration building within me, even if it wasn't the one I wanted.

I drained the last of my tea and set my cup on the table as I stood to follow him outside, nodding at my mother to acknowledge her grumbles of irritation and gesturing to Nikolai to lead the way. "Why does this please you so?" I asked him with a sigh as we traipsed down the short staircase to the courtyard.

"Because you never have time to spar with me and now you have nothing but time, so you can't make excuses not to," he told me as the door banged shut behind us and we stepped out into the crisp, cold air. Our boots sank into the soft earth beneath the thin layer of melting snow. "No portals. No ranged weapons," he declared.

"You have a lot of rules."

"No blades, no weapons changing, and no magic blasts," he added.

I slid my gaze to him as he dropped into step beside me when we reached the center of the courtyard. "What *am* I allowed to use?" I asked, half expecting him to declare a fisticuffs match like some old-timey boxer.

"Staffs," he announced, stepping in front of me with a mischievous glint in his eye. Quarterstaffs and baton fighting had always been his strongest fighting styles. Shadows were already beginning to swirl around us as we amassed our magic, and I had my staff conjured before he'd settled into his stance. The staff I formed was nearly a foot taller than me and a full two inches thick—larger than Nikolai's, which only reached the height of his eyes. He always complained that larger weapons were unwieldy, but I preferred the longer reach. "Compensating for something?" he quipped.

I raised an eyebrow and waited for him to get on with it.

My cousin opened the match by swanning about as usual with

a showy little flourish, spinning his staff high over his head as if it were a war scythe. I went straight for his vitals, aiming for a hard, direct hit, mid-torso, forcing him to bring his staff down to guard himself. If he wanted to fight, we were going to fight. The clack of our weapons impacting echoed dully off the ragged stone walls surrounding the yard as we began our dance. He grunted with the effort of repelling my attack, and I slid my hands down the haft and pivoted, bringing it around behind me as fast as I could to aim another blow at his head. A hard hit would hurt, possibly even break bones, but we healed fast enough that I had no real fear of *truly* harming him. I didn't hold back at all, and I knew he wouldn't either. If he could bash my head in, he was going to try.

He knocked my staff away and brought the back of his own at me, finally beginning to take it seriously. His movements were flowing and practiced, reminding me that he had one hundred years more experience with this form of combat than I did. But having been stationed in the Void, I used it more purposefully than he did. And I used a brute-force fighting style that he *hated*.

"Gah," he growled as he contorted his body to dodge the end of my weapon when he failed to deflect it in time. "You always do this. When did you get so bloody *big*, Vitya?" he groused.

"Twenty years ago."

"Blink of an eye, really," he bit out before I knocked his staff away from me and managed to land a hit on his thigh. He pivoted from stance to stance with steady, measured steps while I buffeted him with a burst of quick, powerful, rapid hits that left him unable to do anything but defend. The end of my staff connected again, this time with his right hand, and he responded by flinging himself to the side and bringing his own staff around in time to clip my shoulder. My entire focus narrowed down to the pinpoint goal of driving him backward so I could take advantage of my extended reach and push his strike zone away from me. The cold, the wind, the distant waves, the churned-up mud and snow all faded away as I spun and struck and dodged and fought. I briefly wondered what he would do if I summoned shadow hounds—he hadn't forbidden those—before I finally got him back into a defensive position, fending off my strikes with every ounce of his concentration.

On my next swing, a concussive burst of magic hit him from my left side, and I stumbled as the arc of my staff met nothing but air as he was thrown, bodily, across the courtyard. He impacted the far wall behind us, hitting the stones with a low thud and dropping into the muddy, churned snow at the base of the wall in a boneless heap. "Ow," he said, sitting up to rub his head.

Shocked, I turned to find Celeste standing barefoot in the doorway to the keep, still in her sleeping shift with her hair in wild disarray from her slumber. Her wings were out—spread wide in an obvious threat display. She was an avenging angel, her chest heaving for air and fire in her eyes, her cheeks stained pink from the cold and her teeth bared in fury at my cousin. She looked *magnificent*.

"Do. Not. Touch. Him." The words she growled at my cousin carried clearly across the courtyard and my eyebrows nearly rose into my hairline.

"She broke the rules," he complained before plopping himself back into the snow to catch his breath.

I was pretty sure this meant she was well enough to leave now.

Chapter 23

Grim

"Where will you go?" my grandmother asked from where she sat behind a heavy, ornate desk located in one of the keep's lower-level drawing rooms. There were half a dozen ledgers spread out in front of her and a forgotten plate of partially eaten breakfast that had been delivered to her just after my mother left to return home. Nikolai was pretending to convalesce in one of the armchairs near the drawing room's large fireplace while Brishta wrapped his head in a swath of clean, white gauze. Yelena sat in another armchair openly judging him, her elbows propped on the armrests and her fingers laced in front of her chest, her mouth turned down in a disgusted grimace.

I tore my gaze away from the bizarre spectacle of Brishta fussing over my immortal, nigh-impervious cousin while he sprawled in his armchair, happily soaking up all the attention, and blinked down at my wife, trying to order my thoughts so I could answer my grandmother. Celeste was tucked under my arm on the couch opposite the armchairs, absolutely mortified—with her face hidden in her hands, wings gone, and wearing a dress from the trunk my family had delivered from her home. "We could... return to my apartment in the Void," I suggested, looking up at my grandmother. I knew as soon as the words were out that it wouldn't work. If ghouls were a problem here, they would only be worse in the Void. And even though Celeste would no longer *die* in a land without environmental magic, that didn't mean she would be comfortable there.

Grandmother Zdenka's face paled, and she looked at me like

she questioned my intelligence.

"Or... we could go to Dry Gulch?" I tried.

Yelena interjected, "Why Dry—Oh, right. That's where your mortal friend is." She waved a hand dismissively, suddenly distracted again when Brishta tutted at Niko as she finished with his bandages and bustled out of the room with a peppy goodbye. "How long are you going to let this farce continue, Niko?" she asked after the door clicked shut. "You're not injured."

"I was!" he objected, opening his eyes briefly to glower at my sister before closing them again to bask in the warmth of the fireplace.

"I'm sorry!" Celeste muttered for the eightieth time from behind her hands. She'd spent the entire morning apologizing, and my cousin was loving every second of it, hamming it up in the worst way. I gently squeezed her to let her know all was well. No amount of telling her he was fine had made any difference.

"But you're not injured anymore," Yelena scoffed. "Blood or no blood, the wound is gone already, so why are you being such a twit? Victor's given you worse knocks on the head in every match you didn't think to hobble him so thoroughly."

Niko only bothered to open one eyelid as he lounged indolently in his chair. "Not every match," he retorted haughtily. "She wanted to bandage my head." He gestured toward the door where Brishta had left and shifted to cross his legs at the ankles. "Was I supposed to tell her no when her bosoms were two inches from my face? The woman can bundle me up like a mummy for all I care."

My grandmother raised her hand to forestall my sister's reply, closing her eyes while taking a bracing breath. "How would you get her to Dry Gulch?" she asked me, clearly done listening to the bickering. "Will you go the long way?" She was referring to travel within the Boundlands, which *would* theoretically be the safest choice for Celeste.

"She's not well enough," I said with a slight shake of my head. Extended travel would be too hard on her while she was still recovering—several grueling days of riding down out of the mountains and then over a week by train to the other side of the continent. Our best option was to use the Void Gates. I'd never had to travel extensively this way myself, but I would have to learn. Celeste would never be able to use the underworld portals as reapers do—that was a one-way trip even for other immortals not born to our people.

My grandmother sighed, understanding immediately. "I'm not sure how I feel about her being in the Void, even for a short time, but that's my nerves speaking and not my trust in your abilities, Vitya." She pressed her lips together and studied my new wife in silence for a time before addressing her. "I'm incredibly pleased that your magical abilities have returned, Princess."

Celeste lowered her hands and balled them in her lap, still clearly embarrassed but straightening her shoulders and engaging my grandmother as she continued.

Grandmother Zdenka's voice was gentle. "I want you to be able to use your magic at that level to help defend yourself in the coming years if something were to happen and you needed to do so. I am distressed, however, that you felt frightened enough to use your magic like that even with our family surrounding you as we are. What can we do to help you feel safe?"

"I wasn't worried about myself," Celeste responded. "I thought they were trying to kill each other!"

"That's... not entirely inaccurate," Nikolai grumbled to himself.

"I had no idea they were merely sparring. They were moving so fast that everything was a blur. I heard you warn Victor about watching out for his cousin—"

"Rude." He shot an irritated look at our grandmother, who ignored him entirely.

"—and that's all I could think about last night. I woke up to find them fighting and suddenly my magic was just *there* and I used it." She turned to Nikolai with a plaintive look painted across her face. "I'm so sorry. I really am."

I narrowed my eyes at him in warning and Yelena slowly

moved to grip her armrests with tense fingers, clearly ready to leap from her chair and strangle our cousin with her bare hands. "I'm fine! I'm fine. All's forgiven, darling. It hurt for mere seconds, no more," he assured Celeste with a rueful smile as he adjusted the silly bandage on his head. "I would never try to kill our Vitya. His siblings are old and boring."

Grandmother Zdenka sighed and pinched the bridge of her nose. "I understand your need to get away from... all of *this*," she told me, waving her hand vaguely to encompass the whole room, "but please keep her safe."

I SAT ON THE window seat studying the route that Elara had sent me for our Gate travel based on the Gates she used to reach Bhalden's Post after I first arrived with Celeste. Gate hopping as a means of long-distance travel between the human world and the magical realm was not a straightforward endeavor like the portals through the underworld were. Gateways were permanent and had been created over time without any real order to their placement. This meant we would need to travel via multiple Gates scattered throughout both realms to end up where we wanted—to get from Bhalden's Post to Dry Gulch would involve stops in Amsterdam, São Paulo, and Seattle within the Void, as well as Snowgard and Oar's Rest here in the Boundlands.

I reached out absently to run the backs of my fingers down Celeste's wing feathers when she stepped closer to pick up her box of trinkets, noting the way she shivered and her eyes filled with hunger as I drew my hand back.

"You're doing that on purpose," she pouted before shaking her wings out. She paused, lingering by my side while holding her little box, and glanced at the closed door. "They're truly not mad at me?" she whispered. It wouldn't help, the whispering, but there wasn't anything we would say that I wouldn't have said in front of my family anyway.

I wrapped my arm around her and tugged her onto my lap. "No," I assured her as I held her close. "More impressed than anything, I think."

"Then why are we leaving?" she whispered, turning in my arms so that her wide, lavender eyes could search mine.

"Because I love my family dearly but I also love my space. And my privacy."

The tension drained out of her shoulders, and I loosened my grip to release her, but she made no move to stand. "Oh," she responded, relief clear in her voice. "Where will they go?" she asked. "Your family," she clarified when I didn't understand her question. "You mentioned before that no one lives here."

I nodded and settled back against a pillow, reaching for a tendril of her hair that had escaped her braid and feeling the texture of it between my fingers. "They will rest here for a few days, and then go back to their tasks of collecting the dead," I told her. Careful arrangements were made to guarantee that the areas we were assigned to had plenty of coverage from other reapers who could watch over them when one of us was otherwise occupied. It was a duty we all shared, and it was important to ensure none of us had too large a population to watch over at any one time. My family would return to their jurisdictions and relieve the temporary guardians of their extra duties.

"Oh," she said again, but this time her voice seemed smaller. "Will you have to do that?"

"Eventually." I hadn't been told how long my respite would be, but it was common for our people to take a year off after a marriage or birth of a child. My grandmother had implied that it might be several years due to my need to protect Celeste while my magic finished taking hold, but it would probably depend on a multitude of factors.

"What happens if you just... didn't?" Celeste asked. "What if you just let people live, instead?"

I blinked at her, trying to mentally untangle her questions. "I don't cause mortals to die," I explained. At least... not in the way she was imagining. *Usually.*

She held very still in my arms. "You don't?"

I couldn't help but frown at her question. "Mortals have a great deal of misunderstandings about death. It's true that we are often *called* Death. We are a personification of it. But those we are called to guide are already dead. Their bodies are ruined... no longer fit to house a soul. *They* are in between and have nothing to return to."

She was silent for a long moment as she turned that over in her mind. "But what about the people who don't deserve to die?" she asked quietly, and I thought I might have detected a hitch in her voice.

That struck me as an odd thought, that death would somehow be deserved or not deserved. Like birth, it was simply a process that *was*. All things must have a beginning and an end. Mortals rise with the sun in the morning and fall into sleep as the sun descends into darkness to ready itself for a new day. Seeds sprout and bloom, then wither and fall, creating new seeds to sprout again. The young ewe is born in the spring, and the old ewe succumbs to the cold in the winter—and in doing so sustains the crow and coyote.

Whole galaxies are formed of ice and dust, their stars burning for eons while new life evolves within their warmth, before erupting into dust again and destroying everything they have created. This is the way of the universe that the Creator has formed.

"What about the ones who haven't even had a chance to live yet?" she continued, blinking away tears that had begun to well up in her eyes. "How... how do you reap a child?"

Unbidden, my mind's eye was flooded with the small forms I had collected over the years. The task of taking the flickering spirit from a still, silent body being held by their weeping mother was a devastating one. To leave them there—to fail to remove them—would not return their soul to their body. It would recklessly endanger them, leaving them vulnerable to the terrifying reality that is the spirit world without a guide. It would be a disaster. My duty, *my purpose*, was to bear them safely back to their Creator. And I did so, often gathering this precious cargo into my arms because it felt to me like the right thing to do. Always speaking a quiet blessing and comforting words to them as I carried them home to their ancestors. And I loved them, as deeply as one can love anything, in those moments.

I lowered my eyes to take in my wife's pained expression, and told her honestly, "With great difficulty."

She hugged me hard, and I held her in silence for a little while as she absorbed this information, before she finally nodded against my neck and sucked in a breath.

"I'm sorry you have to do that," she said quietly. I didn't know what to make of that. I had no more choice in doing so than she had in drawing her next breath. But even if I could choose not to, I couldn't imagine doing anything else. She turned to stare at me for a beat, studying my face, and then stretched up to kiss me on my cheekbone, before rising to stand. I pressed my fingers to the spot, confused by her response, and she smiled a small, crooked smile at me. "What should I bring?" she asked with a sigh, returning to her packing with her little box of trinkets. As she flipped open one of the trunks that my family had brought up for her, she pulled out a folded piece of paper and froze.

"What's the matter?" I asked, concerned at the change in her posture, feeling myself tense up just as she had.

"It's—" She didn't finish her sentence, opening the paper and quickly scanning the contents with her eyes.

Her expression was one of anxiety, and every impulsive fiber of my being urged me to stand and pluck the note from her hands so I could read it for myself, but I was not an impatient man. I restrained myself, staying seated and reminding myself that she would explain when she was ready. My fingers might have twitched a time or two.

She read the note a second and then a third time before folding it back in half and letting her gaze drift to mine. Her expression was one of sadness and perhaps a mild annoyance, but then her lips pressed together. "Apollo left me a note," she said, her voice unsteady again.

The urge to snatch it from her fingers rose in me again. I locked my muscles to prevent me from doing just that.

When she continued her voice was a little more even. "He said the same thing he told my mother, that he couldn't bear to see me marry someone else. But he says he loves me and he always will." She shook her head and tucked the note back into her belongings, and I watched her intently, trying to discern her response to this overture. Would he become a problem in our marriage? Or was this the closure that she needed from her former friend?

"What can I do?" I asked, setting my calling stones aside and standing to go to her.

She shook her head again, shutting the trunk and returning to her task of packing. "There's nothing to be done. He just is who he is."

I wasn't sure what that meant, and as much as I hoped his note would have made her feel better about his absence from our wedding, that didn't seem to be the case. She seemed more resigned about it than anything. "I'm sorry," I told her, and I meant it. Her hurt was my hurt, and I was sorry that this man continued to bring her tears.

She gave an odd little shrug like it wasn't important, but it was clear that it was. "Me too," she said. "But it doesn't change anything. What should I bring?" she repeated.

I wanted to know what that meant, but it was clear she didn't want to talk about it right now, so I let it go for the moment. I returned to my calling stones and tried to reorient myself to the matter at hand, pushing magic into them again to recall the maps. "Some changes of clothes and your little box is fine. Dress in layers," I added. "It's cold here, but we'll be in the desert before nightfall, and most of the cities in between have milder climates. Whatever we don't want to carry will be delivered by courier." I would only bring a few changes of clothes for myself, along with the gift I'd promised for Elara and Levi's son.

"Do you think..." She stopped and glanced away before continuing her question with a frown. "Will we be able to find more of that pudding that Helda makes us?"

It was the first time she'd shown deliberate interest in a food that she enjoyed, and my heart ached with something that might have been joy or pride. "I don't believe I've seen it outside of this region, but I bet she would be willing to share the recipe with us."

Celeste's cheeks pinked and her small smile was sheepish this time, but I noted that for once she didn't protest that it would be too much trouble. She was delightful, and her growing comfort with me warmed my soul more than I ever could have imagined. Had I thought her lovely when she walked down the aisle to meet me? Standing here with her wings out, wisps of hair escaping her braid, and a bruised but healing soul, was the most captivating person I'd ever known. Her form had begun to fill out nicely in the past few weeks, and she was getting stronger every day. She was no longer a broken flower, but a full, robust blossom just beginning to unfurl. A perfect, healthy bloom who was just coming to know herself and her value. "Do you think she has any extra we could take with us?" Her hesitant, tiny grin was so beautiful I couldn't respond immediately.

"I'll go ask," I murmured, thrilled to my core to do so.

As I figured she would, Helda supplied me with not only the recipe but several pounds of pudding to take with us, as well as a stack of tiny cakes and a bag of nuts that were nearly impossible to find outside of the Dragon's Teeth. *"Gifts for your friends and that lovely new wife of yours."* I'd never seen Helda so happy as she was when I told her Celeste liked her pudding.

I loaded it all onto the back of my wraith along with Celeste and climbed up behind her. "I would like for you to save your magic today. Let me deal with anything we encounter along the way," I murmured as I wrapped my arms around her and took hold of the reins. She'd expended more than she should have this morning when she blasted my cousin into the wall and had been slightly shaky for over an hour afterward. As we left the keep, I looked back to find Nikolai shaking a hanky for us from an upper window. His bandages had been removed. Probably by my sister.

We traveled the same path we'd taken before into Bhalden's Post, and when we passed the cliffs that the ghoul had been in the last time, her whole body tensed up. There were no ghouls there today, and I rubbed her arm as we rode to remind her that I was with her. Perhaps the number of reapers in the vicinity have driven them off, but our trek was uneventful and by the time we reached town Celeste seemed to be enjoying herself as she took in the snow-capped scenery.

I noticed the high fae riding an irin toward us first, causing Celeste to make a confused noise when I directed our wraith to halt. The man rode at a fast clip, coming up the road from Granite Cross where the Gate from Faery was, and his expression was one of determination as he barreled at us.

Celeste finally noticed him and stiffened between my arms, a quiet gasp leaving her lips.

"What is Apollo doing here?" she asked quietly.

Chapter 24

Grim

APOLLO WAS LEANLY MUSCLED, with sweat dampened ringlets of golden hair that hung about his ears and the same lavender high fae eyes my wife had. His skin shifted between being nearly as pale as mine and icy blue that I imagined probably tipped his wings when he allowed them to be seen. His mount was large, one of the bigger irin I'd seen, and the flowers that most of them sprouted from their antlers had mostly been rubbed off, a sign that it was territorial and liked to challenge other irin. Though it traveled on silent paws, as he pulled it to a stop in front of us, it blew heavily as if it had been running hard for a long time.

The man's eyes flicked to mine for the briefest second before focusing on Celeste and quickly scanning her from head to toe and back. "I found you," he panted, as short of breath as his mount was.

I expected Celeste to respond, but she didn't. She simply sat in front of me and watched him. I desperately wished I could have seen her expression to gauge her response.

He panted for several more seconds, trying to slow his breathing. "Celeste, we need to talk."

"I think you've said what you wanted to say," she finally replied, her voice sounding oddly empty in a way that made my lungs ache. She had been many things with me since we'd arrived at the keep—tearful, angry, upset, hurt, nervous, scared, comforted, happy, calm—but never empty, as if she was numb inside. Her body was still tense where she sat between my forearms, entirely motionless.

Dwarves were beginning to gather at the edge of town to stare at us where our mounts stood facing each other at the crossroads just outside of the market area. The older people at least pretended they were doing other things, but the younger ones openly stared at the irin, having never seen one before.

"I made a mistake," he said, and my heart instantly softened toward him.

He'd come to apologize for hurting her. Perhaps she would allow him to repair their damaged friendship. "Can we—" He paused to take in the small gathering of dwarves that was forming to gawk at him. "Can we go somewhere private to talk?" His gazed shifted to me and back. "Alone?"

I narrowed my eyes at him, my heart suddenly less soft. This man who'd declared his love for my wife wanted to speak to her alone.

Her voice was still emotionless and empty when she responded quietly with a simple, "No."

Relief washed through me.

Apollo gritted his teeth in frustration, glancing at me again before addressing her. "I thought about what your mom said, that you needed to marry him for his magic to save your life." He finally addressed me, saying, "Thank you for that," before shifting his gaze back to her. He set his jaw before continuing. "But now you don't need him anymore."

Every muscle in my body tensed. I briefly considered how many witnesses were gathered around that would notice a portal to the underworld opening beneath him, mount and all. Wrath poured through my veins like a toxic poison.

Celeste gasped, her emotion finally cracking through the mask she was creating. "Excuse me?"

"You don't have to stay with him! You already have his magic, so you can come home now, with me."

She flinched and reached down to set her palm on my knee, a reassuring gesture that stayed my baser impulses. It was true. She could walk away from me and return to her homeland if she wanted. But she didn't respond at all, simply sitting and staring at him. My heart felt like it was beating out of my chest. Anger, fear, a primal feeling of possessiveness, and malice toward this man, all warred with my innate knowledge that I did not own Celeste. She was, of course, free to walk away from me at any time.

But would she? She'd vowed to be my partner, and I'd promised the same. I'd become very attached to her, and he was trying to convince her to leave right in front of me. Every fiber of my being wanted to snuff this man out of existence right here, consequences be damned. But I'd given her my word that I wouldn't harm him, a fact that chafed now that I was presented with him. In another situation I might have rolled my eyes at myself. I couldn't just go around smiting someone I disliked, even if he was trying to run off with my wife. Not without censure from the elders, at least. But the dark thoughts rampaging inside my mind took an amount of control not to act on that I hadn't expected. It would be so easy.

"You don't want this," Apollo insisted angrily, flinging an arm out to gesture at me. "I'm here to save you."

This statement gave me pause. Was I a villain to be saved from?

She laughed, but it was mirthless and bitter-sounding. "You don't have any idea what I want." The anger I felt was not reflected in her words, only sadness and grief. "What I wanted was my friend—the person who I spent my childhood with, just me and him against the world. But you left me, Apollo. On purpose. Because I couldn't return your romantic feelings."

Now it was Apollo's turn to flinch. And in another life I might have pitied him—been able to see past my own desires to the core of who he was: to his wants, and needs, and hurts, and failures, and loved him as a person. But not this life.

I was too tied up in my feelings for Celeste and my anger with him for anything remotely kind toward him to exist in me, at least in this moment.

Celeste wasn't finished. She fought to keep her voice even as she spoke, but the tremor in it betrayed her. "That's not love,

Apollo."

He opened his mouth to argue but she cut him off, the sadness in her voice slowly making way for the anger that I'd been expecting.

"Did you only remain friends with me because you hoped I would change my mind?" she asked.

"Of course, n—"

"Because that's not friendship," she insisted. "And what you are suggesting is heartbreaking, both for him and for me. I do love him—"

"It's been days—" he started to argue, clearly outraged at her statement, but I could hardly hear him over my shock at her statement.

"Months, Apollo," she interjected, finally raising her voice. "We've been here for months. We are married in every sense of the word, and I will not be leaving him."

Though I'd made myself abundantly clear—at least I thought so—in my assertion that I belonged with her for eternity, other than our wedding ceremony, this was the first time she'd made such a declaration. Her words might as well have been enchanted for all the power they held over me. This strange alchemy that was love settled deep enough in my bones that even the wrath I felt toward this man began to be soothed away. He was nothing to me, but the woman seated in front of me on my wraith? She was everything.

Her voice was resigned as she finished speaking to the man in front of us. "Go home and be grateful my husband has shown the amount of restraint he has, to not repay your insult to him with something far more injurious."

He finally caught an inkling of the danger he had placed himself in, wild eyes flashing to mine before turning his irin and retreating back the way he'd come, but I felt no satisfaction in him leaving. Instead, I wrapped my wife in a tight hug and held her to my chest as she allowed her tears to freely fall. She grieved the friendship she thought she'd had.

"I'm sorry, Doveling," I whispered, and pressed my cheek to

the top of her head once he was out of sight, only then realizing that the dwarves had turned their gawking to me, because I'd unknowingly gathered enough of my magic to have my cloak whipping about my back. I flushed as deeply as I had when Madam Helda had caught us kissing in the library and instantly released my magic so that my shadow cloak hung still and respectable from my shoulders. The younger dwarves skittered away and the older ones were suddenly much more interested in the tasks they were pretending to be doing. I sighed and waited until she'd calmed and given me a nod confirming that she was ready to continue on our way, then directed the wraith toward the center of town. Drawing it to a stop at our first Gate, I held Celeste steady as I allowed the wraith to dissipate and deposit us neatly on the ground with our belongings.

"G'day, Master Reaper," greeted the dwarvish guard at the Gate, unaware of the turmoil he'd missed just outside of town. I shouldered our bags and nodded in response, impatient to be on our way. Celeste was more composed, but her face was still tear-stained as she took in our surroundings. This Gate was much smaller than the ones I'd seen in other places, but then, Bhalden's Post wasn't exactly a teaming city. The stone arch, barely taller than me but with the same shimmering haze that made up the one between Faery and the Boundlands, had a wooden sign with hand-painted letters posted beside it—*Amsterdam Gate: Enter at your own risk. No magic beyond this Gate!*

"I'm afraid your companion won't do well beyond the Gate, Master Reaper," the guard said formally, before continuing in a more casual tone. "Not unless she's part human, but I got an eye for that, I do." He frowned at my wife, concern etched on his features. And normally, he would have been absolutely correct. A high fae in the Void would perish within a few steps without the environmental magic they needed to survive.

"Thank you for your concern, but she's with me," I told him, taking her wrist gently in my hand and turning her arm so that he could see my magic etched into her skin. My mark. My claim. My promise. My power. Seeing it there bolstered me almost as much as hearing her declare that she would be staying with me. She was mine, and I was hers. Darkness and light. Two halves of one whole.

So with that, I led her into the Void.

Chapter 25

Grim

THE SUN WAS LOW in the sky when we stepped out into one of the southern suburbs of Amsterdam.

"Oh, that's weird. I don't like that."

I glanced down at Celeste to find her rubbing briskly at her skin before I quickly returned to scanning the park for anything concerning. "What's wrong?" I asked, ready to haul her back through the Gateway at the first hint of bodily harm.

She gave a full-body shudder and then placed her hand in mine. "That prickly feeling coming through there was intense. It was like I'd lost blood flow to my whole body for a moment. It's going away now." She shivered again. "Did you not feel it?"

I nodded once. "It happens every time." I probably should have thought to warn her. "What else do you feel?" I asked, trying to decide if this had been a bad idea or not.

"Just strange," she said, looking around with wide lavender eyes. "I can feel the missing magic, but it's hard to put into words. It's like being on a mountain when there's not enough oxygen. My body is missing something it needs even though I'm not doing anything different. It's uncomfortable, but I think I'll be okay." She didn't seem terribly concerned as she curiously scanned the brick buildings that lined the park. "I'd heard rumors or whispers of a place like the Void, but no one ever thought it was real. Why are they all square?" she asked, peering up at the apartment blocks. "The buildings are mostly rectangles and squares even when they're not made of brick or stone." We started walking down the street toward the closest Metro station with Celeste peppering me with questions about the city and cars and the humans we passed.

"We're just cutting through," I told her when she wanted to know more about the city than I could tell her, and I saw a little bit of the sparkle die in her eyes. "I don't know this city, but I live in one of the cities we'll pass through," I explained, hoping to make up for not knowing much about this one.

"Oh! Can I see your home?" That perked her up.

"We could stop there and pick up some of my things if you really want to. It's very humble," I warned her. I'd enjoyed my years living in my apartments, but I had no way of knowing what she would make of the simple style of lodging.

"I still want to see it," she said, her curiosity shining through.

Her questions continued as I led her into the station to buy our tickets— *"How did the humans survive without magic? Where did they keep the animals that pulled the parked cars? Was there someone inside the ticket machine? How did they get the glass windows so thin and clear?"*—until I had to coax her through the process of using the "moving stairs" to get to the upper platform. I continued to scan our surroundings, unable to shake the feeling of an eerie presence like something was lurking, but as far as I was aware, the only thing out of place was the craven desire that had been haunting my every breath since joining with her.

The train was loud when it arrived, making her cringe away from the sound, but she followed me onto the rail cars when the doors opened. We seated ourselves away from the doors, and Celeste kept her small bag in her lap with her hands laced over the top of it protectively while she stared at the inside of the metal car with visible apprehension.

"Will you tell me about your trinkets?" I asked, nodding to the bag. I was curious about the meaning behind the little items she'd chosen to bring with her from Faery, and I hoped that talking about something familiar to her would help to ease some of her anxiety in this new situation.

She blinked at me and seemed to only then remember that she was holding them. "Oh, yes." Opening the cloth bag that she cradled in her lap, she pulled out the small wooden box she'd brought and opened the latch. Inside were a handful of tiny, carved figurines made of stone. "They were my friends," she said with a self-deprecating smile. "They're just little animal carvings," she explained as she plucked one out, holding it up for me to take as the train began to move.

I plucked it from her fingers and assured her that all was well when she gripped the armrests of her seat and gave me a startled expression. "This is normal," I said to reassure her. "Tell me about this one," I said, holding up the carving. It was a shiny, pale-green stone with white threaded through it, similar to a piece of jade. The other pieces in her box were different pale colors of similar stone—pinks and blues and a few light browns. "That one is an irin," she said, referring to the mounts they rode, "and this one—" She paused to pick out a blue piece. "—is a bear. I've got a bird, and a mouse, and a cat, too." She passed them to me, each in turn, all of them about an inch tall and simply carved.

"How did you come to have them?" I asked, passing the last one back to her. I kept my focus split between her and the rail car, careful not to let myself become too distracted by this intriguing insight into something important to her.

She tucked them carefully back into their box and closed the lid and latch before returning the whole thing securely to her bag. "My uncle gave them to me one at a time when I was little. He would visit other kingdoms as an emissary, and when he returned, he always brought me a new one if he could find one. They're made from a really common gemstone found in Faery, but I loved them. I didn't have many friends growing up, mostly just Apollo and my brother and sister, so when they were busy, I would imagine that the little animals were my friends and come up with little adventures in my mind. I have jewels and gowns and fancy artworks, but there's something about these cute little carved animals that makes me happy to look at them."

An announcement from the speakers let us know that we were arriving at the next station, which was our stop.

"Which one is your favorite?" I asked as the train began to slow.

"The irin," she answered immediately. "I always thought they were the most enchanting creatures."

"Thank you for sharing them with me." *You're not alone anymore.*

Her answering smile as we rose and made our way off the train made my heart beat faster. Someday I would ask her more about them—what caused the color variations in them, which ones had been given to her first, what her imaginings had consisted of. But for now, we had a Gate to find.

The guard at this one was a man with obvious elvish ancestry who barely acknowledged us as we passed through. Gateways within the Void were much more spartan than the ones in the Boundlands, and generally sported the same metal signage found on highways—clear, concise, easily legible, but entirely lacking in any kind of character.

Snowgard was an elvish town in the far north that seemed to do brisk business with Amsterdam and was at least five times the size of Bhalden's Post. I hired a small wyvern drawn carriage from the bevy of coachmen lining the street at the Gate, hoping to spare Celeste the exertion of riding horseback any more than necessary.

"Would you like to stop at one of the restaurants here for lunch?" I asked as we passed through a business district. Our destination was on the far side of the city, and I was genuinely concerned about her energy levels. A break would probably be good for her. I was just about to ask the driver for a dining recommendation when she shook her head absently as she watched the shops and diners go by.

"No, I don't want to stop," she said lightly, surprising me.

I frowned at her. "It's lunch time." It was a little past lunch time here, but it was lunch time according to what our bodies were used to from our time at Sorrow's Keep. "Aren't you hungry?"

"A bit," she admitted, turning to me. "But I can just eat some of the snacks that Helda packed us." Her smile was earnest, but

I felt like I was missing something. I dug one of the miniature cakes out of my bag to hand to her, and as she politely accepted, I raised an eyebrow, waiting.

She bit her bottom lip, trying to keep her grin from widening. "The faster we leave the sooner I can... " Her words cut off, but her gaze dropped to my lap before returning to meet my eyes again with a knowing look.

I grabbed the corner of my cloak and stuffed it over my lap, feeling my face and ears grow hot. Evidently, I hadn't been doing as well as I thought hiding this new unrelenting need that vexed me to no end. She tossed me a flirty smile and took another bite out of her cake, which only made me grow harder. For a brief moment I considered asking our driver to divert and take us to the nearest hotel. We could stay the night and finish our journey tomorrow. Until I remembered that my friends were expecting us, and Levi had already told Lysander I was coming. I couldn't bear to disappoint that little face. I closed my eyes and groaned, letting my head thump against the back of the carriage, but I couldn't help but be smitten when Celeste giggled in response. This was torture.

The elvish guard at the São Paulo Gateway greeted me, but only managed to give Celeste a wary glance before we slipped through the Gate amongst the long line of people entering the city. It was startlingly warm once we stepped out into one of the parks near the city's center. Trees towered overhead, blocking out the view of the nearby buildings and providing ample shade for the moment. We moved off the wide footpath out of the way of the elvish commuters to remove her cloak and outer layers of our clothing, placing the extra garments into our bags before making our way to the edge of the park.

Celeste's mouth dropped open when we reached the street, clearly shocked at the abrupt change in our surroundings. "Where *are* we?" Her eyes were the biggest I'd ever seen them as she took in the masses of buildings that suddenly crowded the skyline.

"The largest city in the southern hemisphere," I explained as I fished my phone out of my bag, trying to pay attention to both her and our surroundings. The niggling thought that I shouldn't have her here in the Void still bothered me, but I was beginning to think that was just my mind reacting to the vulnerable nature of having Celeste in a place like this with prowling spirits and no sustaining magic.

"What is that?" Celeste asked, looking at my phone.

"It's like a calling stone, only with more cat videos," I explained. *And less useful.* A small prayer for a decent amount of battery formed on my lips as I powered it on, and I was relieved to see I had more than enough to order a ride-share to the next Gate. "I'm arranging our transportation." There was a cafe with outdoor seating farther down the block, so I led her to one of the covered tables while we waited for our ride.

"Why do people call you so many different things?" Celeste asked me as we took our seats, her attention seemingly focused on the architecture and masses of people around us. "The guard at the last Gate called you Reaper. Do you want me to call you something else? No one seems to call you Victor but me." The frisson I felt when her gaze momentarily touched mine made my skin prickle.

I watched the crowd, people meandering through street vendors and looking in storefront windows as I considered her question. "I feel like the names people give me relate more to who I am to them than who *I am* to myself. To my family I am Vitya, or occasionally Victor. To friends and acquaintances, I am Grim. To the souls I protect, I am Death. To strangers in the Boundlands, I am a Reaper, and to your people, I am *Veardur.* To my closest friends, I am something else entirely." I had no idea how I was going to explain the "Eeyore" moniker Levi—and, therefore, now also his son—bestowed upon me. I studied Celeste's face, wishing I were better with my words. "I like my name, Victor. Not many people actually call me that, so it feels special coming from you."

"You don't want me to call you Vitüshka?" she asked with a grin.

"It's kind of a mouthful," I muttered wryly.

It didn't take long before our ride arrived, and I opened the door to the back seat for Celeste and showed her how to use her seat belt. Once I was seated beside her and we were moving, she commented that she was still mystified that the vehicle "drove itself"—meaning it wasn't pulled by anything. I tried to convey internal combustion in the simplest terms, grateful that our driver didn't speak Common Tongue and was unaware of how badly I was mangling my descriptions of gasoline engines. Her attention split between the driver, the car itself, and the passing scenery as we rode, which was useful because it meant she didn't notice the swarm of spirits that began following us a few minutes into our journey. These weren't just ghouls, they were demons.

The truest scourge of the Void, they often traveled in packs, and while a living human didn't usually have much to fear from them, a dead one was another story. Without an angel to stand guard over their souls, they were entirely vulnerable to eternal destruction. Unfortunately for the magical races, they were *just* as vulnerable without a body in this land unless one of my people stood against the demons.

The ones following us were lower-level spirits, and I felt them before I saw them. Not especially intelligent and driven by hunger, they would continue to chase their prey until I drove them off. My kind weren't capable of killing demons, only the angels were capable of that. I peeked out the back window to find them floating along behind us about a half a block back as we moved through traffic. If we'd been faster, we could have just outrun them, but there wasn't going to be any chance of that in heavy traffic like this. Being stuck in a slow-moving car while trying to defend us and not draw attention was frustrating beyond measure.

I took hold of my magic, pulling from the very few shadows around us at this time of day, and cast a flock of shadow birds into the sky as discreetly as I could. As far as I was aware, crows didn't even exist on this continent, so I tried to shape them with more generic features and hoped no one would notice that they weren't simply local birds. Keeping an ear toward Celeste's absorbed murmuring about the enormous cemetery we passed, I directed my flock at the largest of the demons and attacked it with far more magic than necessary. I wanted to drive them off as quickly as possible.

The largest demon of the pack—the leader—dropped back to fend off my attacks, and the rest of them spread out when I directed my birds back to focus on them. As a focused effort they shot a volley of what looked like flaming arrows at us, entirely invisible to the humans surrounding us on the street and sidewalks. I tossed up a temporary wall of shadows that arced over the moving car to shield us, just long enough for the arrows to impact it and fizzle out, and then ripped it away to strike the rejoining leader with a bolt of magic as thick as my wrist. The shadow birds swarmed the weaker members of the pack, pecking and diving to force them away, and within minutes the whole group fell back and faded into the distance.

"They painted the bridge rainbow colors!" Celeste gasped happily, with her face nearly pressed to the car window.

I spent the rest of the ride on edge, searching the skies and the road around us, as we nudged through traffic. Celeste's occasional cheerful remarks about the passing buildings and the samba music playing over the tiny hatchback's radio made a surreal backdrop to my nerves. We made it to our destination—a Gateway in a large park that housed an odd white dome and circular footpath—without any more skirmishes. I grabbed all our bags, thanked the driver, and practically hauled Celeste bodily out of the car.

"What's going on?" she asked.

"Demons," I muttered, tucking her under my arm and wrapping us both in my cloak of shadows to hide her from sight.

We passed through the Gate into a town next to Oar's Rest, and an hour of traveling later stepped from a Gateway in Oar's Rest into Seattle, the city where I lived.

Chapter 26

Grim

It was hard to say for sure, but Seattle might have been my favorite city. There wasn't anything that truly stood out about it compared to any of the other cities in the Void or the Boundlands. And certainly not compared to Faery. It was a small city—especially compared to somewhere like São Paulo. It wasn't flashy like New York or opulent like Golden Laurel, back in the Boundlands. It was overcast and rainy nine months out of the year, and the other three months were plagued by heavy smoke coming up from the forest fires in California lately. But it was *green*, quiet, and had a fantastic library system. Most importantly, it felt like home. Especially the older neighborhoods here in North Seattle, with little postage stamp yards, the elderly neighbors chatting over their hedgerows, or a new family following a toddler on a tricycle down a sidewalk. I wondered what it looked like to Celeste. Quaint, probably. Perhaps even a little shabby. But that didn't mean it wasn't dangerous.

"I'm not sure that taking you to my apartment is a good idea."

"Because of the demons?" Celeste asked me. She'd had no knowledge of them until I'd explained that they were this world's version of ghouls... only worse.

"Yes." I pulled out her cloak and helped her into it before pulling the hood up to shield her face from the falling drizzle. "How are you feeling?" I asked her. I didn't want to be trapped in a car again if I needed to fight—I didn't like not being able to move and counter them myself if needed—but I wasn't sure if she felt up to riding the wraith again. I'd carry her myself if I had to.

"I'm certainly feeling the travel," she admitted, rubbing at the muscles in one of her legs. "But we don't have too much farther, right? I'd really love to see your home." Her shoulders dropped at the last part, and her disappointment hit me harder than I might have expected.

I frowned at her before glancing down the street. The Gate into Dry Gulch was only a little way from here, and my current apartment wasn't terribly far off the route. "Why do you want to see it so badly?" I asked.

She raised one shoulder in a half-hearted shrug. "Because it's yours."

I scanned the street again, my heart squeezing at the thought of denying her this simple request. Maybe if we hurried... "Do you feel like you can ride a horse again?"

She perked up considerably. "If it means getting to see where you live, I can ride for leagues."

I made myself release my clenched jaw, took a deep breath, and nodded. As long as we didn't see anything suspicious, I would take her. I tried to ignore the weird butterfly feelings that filled my chest when her happy smile spread from ear to ear. It might have been the most pleased I'd ever seen her. *Well... outside of physical relations...* I pushed that thought away and made myself focus on the task in front of us.

This would be okay.

I gathered my magic and created our mount, giving it strong legs and a sturdy frame. I wanted a war horse this time, not a racehorse. Celeste and our bags went on first, and then I hauled myself up, wrapping us both in shadows to hide us from view. We set off at a slow, plodding walk down the tree-lined sidewalk, in an effort to make as little noise as possible.

Cars rolled by and a pedestrian crossed the road in front of us and entered a hardware store we passed, but there wasn't much in the way of traffic here. Most people were at work or school and the area was largely quiet. The falling mist and the turning leaves gave the air a sweet, crisp scent that mingled with car exhaust and the smell of drying clothes from a nearby laundromat. I watched carefully as we rode, my eyes never stopping in my search for anything that could cause Celeste harm.

But as diligent as I was in my surveillance, it was already watching us before I spotted it. My adrenaline spiked almost painfully before my mind had even made the connection of what I was looking at—a powerful overlord demon staring me right in the face. It was at least a foot taller than I was on horseback. He leered at us from where he hovered near the corner of a dingy 7-Eleven on a main road in the middle of the day, staring me dead in the eyes with its gruesome, gaping eye holes.

My wraith halted without a conscious command on my part. Instinct took over, and I pulled magic into my body so forcefully that tendrils of darkness erupted from the ground around us, stretching upward and coiling over on themselves, searching for an outlet for release. The scythe that materialized in my hand was the heaviest I'd ever carried, and the handle stretched nearly to the ground from where I sat on horseback. I intended to drive it right through this monster's neck.

"Is there a demon?" Celeste breathed, fear rattling her whispered words.

"Yes."

"I can feel it," she whispered. But she couldn't see it. A small blessing.

The haggish looking spirit had grotesque skin that reminded me of maggots behind the other-worldly glow it cast. We were a contrast in color, its garment a ghostly white that matched its face and mine as black as night. It flexed its fingers as it watched us—macabre-looking, skeletal things on disturbingly long hands and arms that stretched down past the knees of its spindly, spider-like legs. Enormous, tattered, leathery wings stretched over its head—deformed structures that could never have carried it if it had a physical body. It was an angel whose outward form was now a reflection of his inner corruption, the way a tumor corrupts the healthy tissue it once was.

Strange laughter echoed off the buildings around us.

"What was that?" Celeste whispered, crouching down closer to the horse's neck. She could hear it, then. Unfortunate, that.

"Stay on the horse, Doveling." I vaulted off the horse and landed on my feet with my scythe held aloft. Without taking my eyes off of the demon in front of us, I spawned a pair of shadow hounds and placed them on both sides of her mount. I would only be able to sense them and the horse peripherally, but I wanted to make sure she was protected at all times, so I granted them as much autonomy as I was able.

The demon leaned backward a fraction, and that was the only warning I got before it hurled itself at me head-first at high speed, the long strips of its ghostly garment flapping wildly in a wind I couldn't feel. I ran toward it at a full sprint, determined to keep it as far away from Celeste as possible. Pitching my weapon forward, I slid my hands to the end and swung it as hard as I could with the goal of keeping myself away from its long claws. *It'd be nice if I could take a piece of it with me as well. Preferably its head.* It was a false hope.

The creature swooped up at the last second to avoid my strike, reaching out with a long arm to reach over my weapon at my face. I morphed my reaper's scythe mid-swing into a double-bladed war scythe, bringing the back end up to sink it into the demon's arm. A piercing shriek let me know I'd hit home, but I had less than the blink of an eye to step out of the way of its other arm. We were locked into our deadly dance—spinning, dodging, striking, deflecting. I put all the effort I could into injuring the demon badly enough that it would have no choice but to flee.

There was very little in the way of shadows for me to pull magic from, with the sun high and the overcast sky diffusing the light. I wanted to throw even more at him, to overwhelm him as quickly as possible, so after another swing of my scythe, I morphed the weapon into my staff and lantern, slamming the butt of it into the ground between us. Multiple portals to the underworld opened up in the ground around us, pulling larger tendrils of darkness like thick, black tentacles up from the depths. I used them to boost my own magic, but also to grab at the demon and hold him in place while I struck out at him. His cackling laughter turned into more shrieking when we were suddenly blasted from behind me by a pulse of magic so powerful it rocked me forward. I had to catch myself with my weapon to stay upright.

The demon released an ear-splitting scream as it collapsed in on itself, until abruptly, *shockingly*, it was *gone*. I was heaving for air, trying to make sense of the sudden silence, never before having seen a demon disappear like that unless an angel killed it. They always fled when I bested them, turning and flying away like cowards. They *never* disappeared. Not unless an angel intervened.

I turned and looked at Celeste, still perched upon my wraith with her head held high like a tiny queen, her wings out and spread wide again. The color was drained from her face and her eyes looked exhausted, but her mouth set in a grim line of determination.

"Did you just kill that demon?" I asked.

"I thought it was going to kill you with all those tentacle things."

I blinked at her before glancing around at the dark tendrils of shadow stretching into the sky around me, flailing wildly now that there was no focus from me. "Those are mine," I said, snuffing out the portals and all of my magical conjurations in an instant, so that only her horse was left.

She merely frowned at me.

The implications of her having the ability to *kill* a demon made my brain spin out in a dozen different directions. "Are you descended from the angels?" I asked, eyeing her feathered wings with new interest as she folded them up and they disappeared. I didn't know how that could even be possible, since angels were spiritual beings, not physical ones. They didn't reproduce.

Celeste simply shrugged, clearly flagging, and I jogged over to hold her steady when she swayed in her seat. "There are old legends that claim the royal lines have some kind of 'angelic' ancestry, but I've never believed any of it. That seems like just the kind of hubris royalty would claim about itself, you know?"

My mind flickered through the scraps of ancient texts I'd seen that hinted at angels having offspring, but it seemed like such an odd concept to me. I'd have to ask my grandmother if she knew anything.

"Come here, love," I murmured, pulling her down from the saddle along with our bags and allowing the wraith to dissipate. "You rescued me again," I told her with a small smile and watched her lavender eyes sparkle as they locked on to the curve of my mouth. "We're going to have to skip the apartment this time, but I'll find a way to show you my things if you would like." Her energy was completely spent.

Tucking her head under my chin, I held her against my chest and slung our bags over my other shoulder, and then carried her in my arms to the next Gate. She needed rest, and I knew just the place where she could do that.

Chapter 27

Grim

"Huck, you have to be gentle with her," I warned, speaking with a calmness I didn't feel. The adolescent dragon that lived near Levi was territorial and protective, and viewed the property and all its inhabitants as *his*. It had been an amusing quirk when he was the size of an average dog, but he had grown *incredibly* rapidly over the last few years and was currently the size of a small bus. Spikes had erupted through the black scales on his forehead and lined the back of his neck, and his jaw and throat had grown so thick and muscular that he made a fully grown alligator look like a dainty lizard. Teeth that had once been used for catching crickets and mice now brought down adult cattle. I didn't like how close he was to my wife as he loomed over the top of her, or the interest he was taking in sniffing her hair. His head was larger than her whole body, and when I reached out to take her wrist her hands were shaking. That upset me. She'd been through enough today. "Huck, *back up*," I told him firmly.

Unfortunately, there was only one person this dragon listened to, and it wasn't me. He cocked his enormous, horned head and narrowed an eye at me, before growling his response—a deep thrumming bass that could be felt more than heard. Celeste silently turned wide, panicked eyes on me, so I tucked her behind me. Huck had never given me a problem before, so I hadn't even thought to forewarn her, but then I usually entered the property via a portal and was with one of my friends—the inhabitants he trusted—before he ever noticed I was present. This time we were entering through the main gate and approaching the house the way a normal guest would, and he had landed in front of us with a ground shaking thud almost immediately, scaring the daylights out of Celeste.

While I was capable of defending her against Huck, I hoped it wouldn't come to that. Sidney loved this creature.

I took hold of my magic and formed my staff—half a second from either thumping him on the end of the nose with it or opening a portal between us—when I heard a door open and a gasped, "Oh, shit," come from up the hill. Huck flinched, just a hint of a crouch, but it gave the impression of a cat laying its ears back.

Sidney—Jordan's partner and Elara's best friend—stood on the front porch of the small stone house that she shared with Jordan on the back of Elara's property. I only caught sight of her for a fraction of a second before she collapsed in on herself and emerged from the neck hole of her shirt as a Eurasian magpie. Her clothing dropped to the front steps as her black and white feathered form shot up into the sky. She made a beeline straight for us, yelling about "oversized lizards with zero brain cells," in the reedy-sounding bird-version of her voice the whole way. She shifted again when she reached us, landing to my left in her "human" form, naked as the day she was born, her long fair hair hanging loose down her back. She hollered at her dragon and shoved his cowering bulk backward with all of her might. Sidney was muscular and fit, but it would take a lot more than her strength to physically move a dragon this size. "Humphrey Herbert Hucklebee, you listen to me right now! You are not allowed to menace our guests! You *know* Grim, you big overgrown goofball! Go *home* before he turns you into a ghost-dragon." She pushed on his face with both hands, and he cringed back from her with a sullen-looking posture, huffing and puffing in irritation but inching backward nonetheless.

"He's not going to eat her, Grim," Sidney shouted at me over her shoulder. "He's just making sure she smells safe. Don't hurt my baby."

"Your—" Celeste paused in confusion for a beat. "—baby?"

I glanced down to find her peeking around my arm, her face painted in bewildered awe.

"Well, sure." Sidney lowered her voice and leaned forward to wrap her arms around the dragon's enormous head, somehow ignoring the way the spikes across his forehead pressed into her naked flesh. "This is Huck, my dragon baby." A pigeon flew up at that moment and alighted on one of the dragon's horns, and she didn't even need to look up to know which bird it was. "And that's Pidgy, Huck's emotional support pigeon." Without looking she waved her hand at the completely standard looking city pigeon, who began to bow and coo at her repeatedly—something she'd referred to in the past as *flirting*—at her acknowledgement. She ignored him. "Together they make up the brainless duo."

Celeste blinked at Sidney with as much bafflement as I used to feel around the woman, but I'd become used to her over the years. Sidney released the dragon from her "hug" only to grab him firmly by the nostrils and shake his huge head back and forth with big, exaggerated motions, speaking to it in the same sing-song tones that people used for beloved dogs. "If dragon not baby, why dragon baby-shaped?" The dragon was shaped nothing like a baby. It was distinctly dragon-shaped.

Huck snorted and shook her hands off, lifting his head out of her reach when she grabbed for him again. She groused and made shooing motions at him. "Go home, you big goober. Grim is always welcome here," she said, pointing at me, "and he's *fully capable* of turning you into a lizard-colored smear on the ground. Take the silly pigeon with you."

One time, Levi had asked her how she had acquired the pigeon, as it seemed like an odd animal to have made itself at home with a dragon, a shifter woman, and a vampire that didn't particularly like animals. Her response had been a casual, "Oh, don't worry, pigeons are free. You can just take them from any park." We still didn't know the real story. Levi suspected she was amassing a pigeon army, but she didn't actually seem to want the bird around, only tolerating it because Huck did.

She turned to us, hands on her hips. "Pidgy's been back on his bullshit all day," she grumbled as the pair turned away and slowly made their way up the path toward the caves where Huck was living now that he'd grown too big to fit inside Sidney's home any longer. Pidgy rode on Huck's head the whole way.

I wondered how long pigeons normally lived, and how long it would take for Sidney to realize this one had come to bear the same Dragon's Mark she did—a slight shimmer at the edge of its aura that set it apart from all the other pigeons. Even my wife's aura didn't have a shimmer as strong as this... "Pidgy," and she'd had my magic placed directly into her veins. Sidney seemed perpetually annoyed by the bird, and some long-buried childish part of me delighted in the knowledge that he was going to be around for a very, very long time and she had no idea.

Suddenly remembering herself, Sidney greeted Celeste with a bright, "Hello there!" She held out her hand to my wife, who—*bless her*—shook the crazy woman's hand. "I'm Sidney. I normally wear clothes." She crossed her arms in front of her chest, trying to hide her breasts while acting as if she was not, and glanced at me, daring me to contradict her. And I could have. As far as I knew, Sidney spent at least as much time nude as she did clothed. Every time she shifted forms, her clothing stayed behind. She usually planned for such situations in advance, but there had been plenty of occasions where she'd been startled into shifting or otherwise felt the need to shift spontaneously. Sometimes she took her sudden nudity in stride, and other times she was mad about it. I had no idea what caused the various emotional reactions, but then... dead people didn't care about being seen without clothing—I knew very little about living people's motivations.

"Sidney, this is my new wife, Princess Celeste of House Morningstar," I said, introducing them formally. It might not seem like it to most people, but I knew already that Sidney would make a good friend to my wife. She was chaotic and wild, but she loved fiercely and was responsible and protective in her own way. I trusted her almost as much as I trusted Elara, which was saying a lot. But most of all, Sidney had a way of seeing past a person's exterior, and I knew that she would look beyond Celeste's meek appearance to the fierce heart she kept closeted within.

My wife lowered her head and sketched a shallow curtsy. "I'm glad to meet you," she replied. Her tone wasn't necessarily shy, but she was certainly overwhelmed.

"Oh, my goodness, a real princess!" Sidney exclaimed. She forgot about covering her chest and dropped her breasts to clap her hands over her cheeks in delight. "Oh, whoops. Listen, I've got clothes at Elara's place. Let's head up there. I know Lysander is waiting for you, anyway," she said to me as an aside. "Ugh, this is going to hurt. Three times in a row now," she grumbled, before shifting forms with a soft cracking sound. Once again a black and white bird, she beat her wings until she was high enough to land on my shoulder. She turned around, shook out her feathers, and settled in to get comfortable. "Onward, noble steed!" she croaked out.

I glanced down at Celeste and found her staring up at me with wide eyes, as if she didn't know how to respond to the situation and was looking to me for guidance. I'd known Sidney almost as long as I'd known Elara, and... in this, I had no guidance. I shrugged the shoulder that Sidney wasn't perched on to let her know that this was normal. Apparently, that only served to confuse her further, because her expression grew even more baffled. I took her hand and led her toward the house.

"Just go in," Sidney said once we reached the front door of Elara and Levi's home. Since Jordan was a vampire and he slept most of the day, Sidney often made herself at home at Elara's house while she waited for him to wake. As soon as I opened the door, she dove from my shoulder and flew into the house, winging her way toward a room in the back. "Elara! The eldritch horror is here, and he wants his woobie!"

The patter of little feet hitting the stone floor announced Levi and Elara's son, Lysander, before he ran into the living room. "Uncle Eeyore!" He launched himself at me, and I caught him in my arms and hoisted him up. He was five years old and small for his age, with his father's blond waves and his mother's brown eyes. He was usually quite shy with strangers, so he probably hadn't noticed Celeste standing with me yet. It didn't help that he had inherited Levi's siren lure, and everyone who heard him speak was literally enchanted by him. He had his mother's timid disposition paired with his father's charisma, as well as magic from both of them. It was a lot for a little boy his age to handle.

I adored him.

"Eeyore's back!" Levi said as he entered the room, using the nickname he'd given me in middle school. He'd been grumpy about the fact that I poured a cup of water on him—I'd wanted to see if he'd shift forms like a "real merman"—and had decided to poke fun at my moroseness. *I wasn't morose, I was reserved.* He knew that, but the man still lived for giving people odd nicknames.

He approached us with a grin and didn't speak again until reaching into a bowl on the credenza near the doorway and withdrawing a thick bracelet set with large purple stones. He tried to hand it to my wife, but she wasn't capable of comprehension.

I wasn't personally affected by enchantments like Levi's or Lysander's, but I recognized the signs when I saw them—the glassy eyes and enamored expression. Shooting Levi a wry look, I took the bracelet from him—a ward against enchantments that Elara provided for their guests to wear—and placed it on Celeste's wrist to break the thrall.

With an apologetic grimace that he didn't entirely mean, Levi took Celeste's hand and welcomed her graciously to his home. "Elara is just finishing up in the guest room and then she'll be right out. She's looking forward to meeting you." Reaching out to take Lysander from my arms, he set the boy on his feet and then wrapped his own arms *and legs* around me, so that he was clinging to me like a baby koala with a goofy grin on his face. "It's my turn. Get your own reaper, kiddo," he told his son, who pulled on his leg, trying to dislodge him.

"What's a *woobie*?" Celeste asked quietly as she blinked off the effects of the enchantment, before pausing to stare at the spectacle of Levi wrapped around me, octopus-style.

"A blankie!" Sidney responded brightly as she re-entered the room, fully clothed and working an intricate plait into her hair. "You know. Cause you 'would be' cold without it?"

"What are you talking about?" Levi asked.

"Case in point," she said, gesturing at the two of us as she flopped onto one of Elara's cream-colored couches. "You're basically the man's Linus blanket. Or maybe he's yours, I can't even tell anymore. You two have an epic bromance." She tied off her braid and made a face at us. "Come sit down. Why is everyone standing around the door? Levi, this poor woman looks like she's about to keel over and you're dicking around with Grim. Have some manners," she groused. He pouted as he removed himself from my person, mumbled an apology to Celeste, and gestured for us to move to the seating area.

Elara padded into the room and greeted us happily. "Oh, you're here!"

Though she was even more introverted than I am, I knew her enthusiasm to meet my new wife was genuine and heartfelt. Her eyes flickered over Celeste's form in a clinical way, cataloging her health, her demeanor, and most likely how her magic had changed since she'd visited us while Celeste was unconscious. I would have to ask her later what she was able to feel had changed in the last few weeks, but for now I was just grateful for her warmth and her welcome.

Chapter 28

Grim

"THIS IS MY CELESTE," I told Elara as she joined us. *She has the most enchanting spirit I've ever known. She carries hurts from her raising and her friendships, and sometimes she feels alone. She would make a dear friend for you. I can't wait for you to see her spirit the way I do.*

"It's so wonderful to see you with your eyes open," Elara told my wife. "May I hug you? I came to check on you when Grim was worried after you first arrived in the Boundlands. It's good to see you awake and looking so well."

I'd never really thought of Elara as terribly small—most people were shorter than me—but now that I saw them together, I noticed Celeste had several inches on her. Both had a similar build, but where Celeste had golden skin and blonde hair, Elara had darker skin and dark hair, with the same chestnut-colored eyes that were peeking out from behind her now that Lysander had migrated over to hide behind his mom. She wore a plethora of jewelry as usual, various pieces she'd made herself that contained bits of her magic for different uses—a wrist cuff, necklaces, rings, thin chains in her hair. Everything held stones with a magical purpose of some kind or another.

Elara offered to show Celeste to the guest room so she could rest, but Celeste declined, determined to stay and get to know my friends since she hadn't been able to see my apartment. Elara shepherded us toward the seating area and Levi went to retrieve the refreshments with Sidney following behind to help. Lysander curled up on the sofa next to me, pressed against my side like a child-sized barnacle, peering across me with owlish eyes at Celeste. I tucked him under my arm and dug out my gifts, passing off the pudding and nuts to Elara and handing a tiny tree to Lysander.

"This is a Prometheus Pine seedling," I told him. "One of the great conifers that grow in the arid regions of the Dragon's Teeth mountains. It can live for thousands of years, and I think it would create good shade for the little hidden oasis you're making with Rafe." Rafe, a dryad, was a childhood friend of Elara's who came to visit regularly. Being a forest-dwelling race, he and his family had taken to starting a little garden in the back of the desert property. Lysander *loved* helping Rafe with the plants.

Lysander gasped as he took the seedling in careful fingers. "Momma, do you think Rafe could help it grow here?" he asked in a whisper, as if too much noise might disturb the baby tree.

She grinned at him. "I bet he could. Why don't you go put it in a little pot for now. Then when he comes again, he can tell us the perfect place for it."

He cautiously climbed from the couch, balancing the little cloth-bound root ball in his cupped hands, and left the room with determined steps.

"He's going to plant it and then re-pot it in every empty pot he can find just for fun," she said, shaking her head, making the chains in her hair sway with the movement. "Luckily, Rafe can repair the root damage."

"Elara, Sidney's talking in code again," Levi said when they returned. "I have no idea what a Linus blanket is."

Sidney huffed at him. "I am not! You lived in the Void for years and you don't know who Linus from the Peanuts cartoon is? I know my references are lost on most Boundlanders, but you guys spent even more time in the Void than I have."

"Sorry, we weren't really spending our time sitting around watching kids' cartoons."

"Oh, right, my bad, you just sat around playing kid's video games. That's totally different and less strange for a siren and his vampire and reaper besties." She smirked at him. "We should marathon a bunch of shows before Grim ends his lease on his apartment. Add Scrubs to the list. I need to be able to make Turk and JD references, and you guys are ruining my vibe." They were still bickering when Sidney flopped back onto the couch and Levi started to pass out drinks.

Elara—knowing better than to feed the conversation—asked about our travels and frowned in thought as Celeste explained the encounters we'd had with banshees and demons.

"Uh, I don't know anything about demons, but banshees are an easy fix," Sidney mumbled around a mouthful of the nuts that we'd brought.

Elara turned her frown on her. "Banshees are easy?" she asked in disbelief. "Even exterminators have problems getting them out." Levi settled onto a seat next to her.

Sidney waved her off as she swallowed her food. "Solandis's whole study in college was on those little mushroom sentinels she keeps. You know the ones that Alistair is always ranting about taking over his plant pots? They keep all kinds of bad spirits away." She turned to Celeste. "I have friends with an abundance of magical mushrooms. They're a little bitey some-times, but you could keep some in your house and they'd keep the banshees away. No problem."

Celeste's magic was returning quickly, and I knew she would soon be able to defend herself even if I weren't around, but if we were going to be staying here for a while, it would be good to have a defense in the home to protect the other inhabitants as well. The last thing I wanted was for our presence to attract something that could harm my friends. My wife glanced at me, her mouth silently moving as her lips formed the word "bitey?" but Sidney was already discussing the logistics of how to travel with the mushrooms to get them here from Golden Laurel, where her friend Solandis lived.

The conversation began to drift, and I could tell Celeste's attention was waning as she melted against my side. She was having a hard time keeping her eyes open, and I was about to excuse us to the guest room when I heard Elara mention the

Phantoms in an offhand manner. I was immediately on high alert. It was a group of people who had tried to harm her in the past, and she had relocated her home out here in the desert partially because of the privacy it afforded.

"No, don't worry, Grim," she reassured me, noticing my shift in focus. "I was just saying that this is a good place for Celeste to be, since my home is so defensible. Once we get the mushrooms established in the area, anyway."

I narrowed my eyes at her. "Have you had more problems with the Phantoms?" I asked.

Sidney shook her head and swallowed her food this time before answering. "She's fine. Do you think Huck *or I* or Jordan would let anyone onto this property without her permission?" She had a point. "Anyway, Jordan's team mostly wiped them out," she said, referring to the group of enforcement officers that he—and occasionally Sidney—worked for, "but we've brought in what we think are the last of the stragglers. It's been really quiet around here. Huck hasn't even had to eat anyone lately."

Levi choked on his drink.

"I've warned you about drinking when she's talking," Elara told him, patting him on the back as he coughed.

"I never learn."

Elara shook her head. "I am safe here, and Celeste will be too," she told me confidently. "Why don't you two go take a nap now? We're not going anywhere," she said kindly to Celeste. "We've got loads of time to get to know each other." Her smile and words were genuine and warm, and they made my heart ache in a wistful way that my mortal friends' words always did when they talked about time, but I resolved to exist in the moments I was allotted with them and stop looking forward into eternity.

Lysander burst into the room with a happy grin before re-membering there was a "stranger" with us and skidding to a halt at the door. My wife cast him a shy smile of her own.

Sidney tutted at him. "Aw, buddy, you don't have to be shy with Celeste. She's a de facto member of your godparents' club now."

"I don't know what that means," he whispered.

"It means she married in. You've got a new auntie," Sidney explained, straightening from the couch. "Elara, you and Levi should take a nap too," she told her friend with a suggestive eyebrow waggle. "I've got some Official Auntie Business of my own with this one." She reached for Lysander and scooped him up, tossing him over her shoulder and making him squeal with delight, completely unconcerned about the fact that he was streaked in potting soil up to his elbows. She carried him from the room, and I heard their conversation as they exited through the kitchen. "You know what I found outside? There's a *huge* boulder at the top of the hill. I bet we could dig it out and roll it down the cliffs for Huck to fetch. I'm going to need your super strong muscles to help me push it, though. Wanna help?"

"*Yeah!*"

Elara already had Celeste on her feet, leading her down the hall to the guest rooms, but Levi caught me by the elbow.

"Hey, congratulations, Grim. We want to have some kind of celebration for you and Celeste once she's rested, okay?"

I nodded as I watched the two women walk away, chatting amiably with their heads bent together. It was a measure of my trust in Elara that I only fretted a little bit about Celeste going on ahead of me. Would they get along? Did Celeste feel safe? Should I have said something different? Is this what love feels like? What strange alchemy had she caused in me? My heart felt like it had been turned upside down and spun around a few times. My emotions had somehow become entirely foreign to me.

"It doesn't get better," Levi said with a low chuckle.

I turned to look at him.

"That bewildered lovesick feeling you've already got written all over your face," he said, motioning at me. "It doesn't get any better. I still feel that way whenever I look at Elara." He slapped me affectionately on the shoulder, and from him, I didn't mind it. "I'm glad you're back, man. Stay as long as you like. Move in here permanently, for all we care," he said with a laugh. "You know she had that whole guest wing built for you."

I hadn't known that, but it did seem like something Elara would do.

"Go on, Eeyore," he said, giving me a gentle nudge. "We'll come get you two for dinner."

I glanced down at my closest friend, grateful for his steady, cheerful, welcoming presence in my life. "I missed you, too," I told him quietly, and set my hand on his shoulder before following after my wife so I could hold her while she rested.

I couldn't ask for better friends, and I knew they were exactly what Celeste needed to mend the hole in her heart left by her former friend.

This *was* love, I knew it in my soul.

As soon as the door clicked shut, Celeste was on me, practically climbing my body so she could kiss my mouth and unbutton the neck of my shirt.

I tutted at her as I supported her squirming body and mumbled against her lips as she kissed me. "What are you doing? You're supposed to be resting."

She deepened our kiss, pressing my mouth open and twisting her hands in my shirt, and I forgot what my protest was for a moment as I lost myself in her. The slide of her lips, the caress of her tongue, the smell of her in my nose. But then I came back to myself enough to realize what she was doing.

"Doveling, you need to rest. Come, let me hold you while you sleep. Today's travel was a lot." Not to mention her use of her magic to such an extent. My new wife was sweet and empathetic and generous with her body. She had already spent too much time and physical effort slaking this need for her that had plagued me since our first time together, taking me into her own body to stem this raging desire I'd suddenly developed.

It wasn't that I didn't understand physical desire or the sexual nature of romantic relationships. I'd just never seen the point of it. I'd been more or less unaffected by those needs myself. Somehow my own body had become a stranger to me, frustrating and unrelenting in its ability to haunt me within hours of finding completion with her.

She *growled* in response and popped a thread in my shirt before her fingers managed to release the next button. As much as I wanted to insist she lie down and sleep, my body was already responding to her overtures. "This *is* restful," she argued, her panting breaths belying her words. "You've been walking around with an erection all day, and the way you looked fighting that demon made me so hot. And then you were so adorable with your friends and that sweet little boy. If I don't have you right now, I'm going to be very grumpy."

I very nearly laughed at her ferocity, but I kept it inside, concerned I might cause offense. If she had her own needs, then this was a different story.

She dropped back to the floor and used the leverage to try to push me toward the bed. It was with no small amusement that I acquiesced, allowing myself to be directed to her desired location at the edge of the mattress. The triumph in her eyes as I lowered myself to the bed made every second of waiting for this moment with her worth it. I delighted in her newfound ability to declare what she wanted, and the fact that *I* was what she wanted, even more so.

She was more graceful with her own clothing, stripping off her blouse and leggings until she stood bare, and releasing her wings and antlers to stand before me in all her majestic glory. No longer did she feel the need to keep her wings close to her body, instead flaring them seductively at me with a flicker of interest so obvious it stirred the air in the room. Golden hair twisted back from her face and antlers, falling over golden-skinned shoulders that were rounded with a healthier weight than they'd been when I met her. Lavender eyes surveyed my bare chest from a head held high with more confidence and ease than I ever could have imagined from the tearful darling I'd pledged myself to. I loved her.

Her beauty shone through from the inside out. As gentle and meek as a mourning dove and as fierce and protective as an angel of war, she'd adapted multiple times to difficult changes in her life. She'd shown strength and tenacity I couldn't even dream of in persevering through multiple kinds of suffering. She was generous and kind, passionate and powerful. She was mine. I let my eyes drift past her beautiful breasts to trace the mark above her wrist that was slowly forming the tree of life, roots stretching toward her hand and branches up her arm and toward her heart. *Mine.*

"Lovely," I told her in a whisper. "So lovely."

I helped her rid my body of the rest of my clothing and lay back to watch her as she put a knee on the bed and climbed on top of me, allowing her to take whatever she wanted and basking in the radiance of her poise and spirit. The intensity of her eyes did something to my insides.

But not as much as the feeling of her taking my aching hardness in her hand and then into her own body, sinking down over me with a flare of ecstasy that I know was reflected in my own expression. I was lost to her. I was *hers.*

The slick, hot grip of her body clenching around my length nearly sent me over the edge immediately, so I gritted my teeth and shut my eyes against the rise and fall of her breasts before me. But I could still hear her quiet moans, her panted breaths. I dug my fingers into the sheets below me, trying to anchor myself in something. Anything. Whatever I could focus on to not let this end yet.

"Victor," she whispered, her voice colored with her own amusement. "You can touch me." Her body stilled on my hips, but her fingertips brushed the back of my hands.

I slowly opened my eyes to take her in, like a starved man at a banquet feast, and then brushed the pads of my fingers up her thighs to her hips, up her sides to the swell of her breasts, across her shoulders and down the insides of her wings. Her reaction to each touch was fascinating. I could dwell on each area of her body for hours. But the insides of her wings made her eyes flutter closed in the most delicious way. Her tiny gasp made me lose control. I gripped her hips in both hands and pulled her down against me in a rolling motion as I drove up into her, making her mouth open in a silent scream as her muscles began to tense and flutter around my cock.

I'm yours.

I let my desperate hunger for her take control and began to thrust into her mindlessly. That insanity-causing sensation of her body clenching and tugging as she climaxed around me made me chase the feeling even harder until my lungs were burning and all I could hear was our gasping breath as I filled her again and again. This feverish intimacy served to draw out her climax, and though I hadn't realized I'd moved, I found myself sitting upright, clutching her tightly in my arms as I drove into her as deeply as I could. The stifled cry of pleasure she made against my chest triggered my own groan as I clutched her tighter and the intensity of my orgasm overtook me like a tidal wave.

I'm forever yours.

Epilogue

Grim

Several Weeks Later

"She is safe with these friends of yours?" my grandmother asks, trying to keep her doubt from her voice.

"She is." Safe is a relative term, but Celeste has nothing to fear from my friends, other than perhaps becoming overwhelmed by their tomfoolery. However, she seems to be more comfortable with them every day. And since we've been with them, they've shown themselves to be just as protective of her as I am. Even Lysander has taken to tucking little sentinel mushrooms into pots around the house "to keep Celeste safe," despite his mother's warnings not to touch the tiny fungal guardians and the nips he's received from them. My friends would never allow harm to come to her—even if she wasn't capable of defending herself, though I'm coming to trust that she is, now that she's growing stronger and her magic is returning.

Sidney declared that tonight is "girl's night," and male presence isn't welcome. Celeste was intrigued by the mentions of "a belated bachelorette party" and "giant margaritas," even though she had no concept of what those things are. So while I still had to fight my discomfort at leaving her without my personal protection for the evening, I trust her to know what she is comfortable with and I'm only a portal away if they need me. I decided to take advantage of the opportunity to catch up with Grandmother Zdenka over tea.

She scans me with a critical eye as she blows gently across her steaming cup before relenting. "I trust your judgment, dear one." She tries a sip and presses her lips together—still too hot. "You know... It will be a few years yet before you receive your next jurisdiction assignment, but once you do, I can ensure you receive Dry Gulch, if you desire."

She waits for my response, but I give her none, choosing to listen instead of imposing my own will. If it were up to me, I would still be assigned to northern Seattle and would simply open a portal there whenever I was needed, but that isn't allowed. The Elders dictate that we reside in the area we are assigned to so that we know the community we serve, and Grandmother has no say in that. She is an elder but not an *Elder*. And while I firmly believe that our preferences have value, sometimes we need to compromise for our family units or the greater good of everyone. This is one of those times. I will do whatever she requests.

She sighs. "Though I don't understand it myself, I know you must be put out about being unable to stay in your beloved Void city any longer, and I feel that your deference in the matter deserves to be rewarded. I would like to give you your choice of whatever Boundlands assignment would please you when it comes time. If you feel some affinity toward this Dry Gulch..." She taps her finger against her cup in thought, a shrewd expression overtaking her features. "We do have a holding out that way, but it's higher up in the Ardac Mountains, and the population centers have shifted away from its location over the last few thousand years. If you can find land close enough to the city to be useful, but far enough to not be living on top of the mortals day in and day out, I will provide you with the funds needed for an estate there."

I lower my gaze to my own tea to keep her from seeing how much this interests me. She probably already knows. She always knows.

If I were to have my choice of anywhere in the Boundlands, living near my friends would certainly be preferable. I have the rest of my life to explore various cities and new places, but I only have so much time with the mortal people I love. I press my fingers to the sides of my teacup, focusing on the warmth of the porcelain as I think.

When Elara bought the property to build their house in the desert, it came as a parcel much larger than she needed. The seller refused to divide the plot, so she bought all of it. I know she would allow me to purchase several hundred acres from her if I wanted, no questions asked. I could see if I can find my own parcel nearby, but if not, there are multiple areas of her holding that could accommodate a small estate of an acre or two, easily. I give my grandmother a single nod to show I agree.

She blows on her tea one last time before taking another sip. "An estate," she reiterates. "Please don't put the princess up in one of those dreadful apartments, Victor."

I quirk my lips to smile at her. "I rather enjoyed my apartment."

"You've already scandalized the royal family enough, I think," she tells me dryly. "Housing the *princess* in an *apartment* in inner Dry Gulch would surely do them in. Please be good."

My lips twitch again, but I have no desire to scandalize anyone simply for the sake of it. "Yes, Grandmother."

THE STARS ARE TWINKLING in the evening sky when I step through the portal to return to Levi and Elara's home. I give a nod to Huck as I pass him on the path to the back of the house. He huffs a kerosene-scented breath at me from where he lies with his head poking out from behind Elara's potting shed. He's no longer small enough to effectively hide behind it, but he doesn't seem to realize that. He returns his focus to what the girls are doing in the garden, and as I round the shed to see for myself, I have to stop in my tracks to take it in.

For starters, all three girls are on the ground in various states of disarray, and Elara is the only one wearing any clothes. I approach Celeste, who is lying under the trees a short distance from the other two, drunk in the moss—antlers, wings, and breasts out—giggling to herself as she stares up at the leaves and sky.

Elara, though fully dressed, is sitting in the dirt, dressing some of the little mushroom sentinels in tiny outfits and trying not to get bitten. Her hair is a veritable rat's nest of tangles, the tiny chains she always wears in it hanging helter-skelter as she works to get a tiny piece of clothing to stay on a mushroom creature that has no shoulders or arms. It's just a stem with some black, beady-looking eyes and a red and white mushroom cap. But then she snatches her hand away from it and shakes it out as if she's been bitten, so it truly must also have a mouth.

Sidney is naked and also sitting in the dirt, but this isn't unusual for her. There are several empty bottles of ready-to-drink margaritas from the Void laying next to her on the ground, all plastered with black and white stickers that state in bold letters, "FOR ANAL USE ONLY"—also not necessarily unusual. Jordan and Levi have been placing them on each other's things for years, but I've always suspected Sidney was the instigator there. This only deepens my suspicion. Sidney and Elara are debating the profitability of selling lingerie versus costumes, but Elara is paying more attention to the mushroom outfits than to the debate.

"Hey, Grim's here." Sidney's speech is slurred enough to make me do a double take. She can drink an orc under the table, and I've seen her do it. I start counting bottles, not coming up with enough to account for how much she would have needed to drink to actually get drunk. Unless the other two girls are lightweights... which... they are.

"I need the name of that tailor lady who made the spicy lingerie for Celeste," Sidney says. I do a triple take, feeling my cheeks heat. Celeste told them about that? "I bet we could sell that shit like hotcakes down here!" Sidney continues, turning to

Elara to return to their conversation. "I could set up shop with the desert people and sell lingerie to goblins." She picks up a half-empty bottle of watermelon-flavored booze and holds it toward me. "Come sit with us, Grim. My brothers smuggled in my favorite margarita mix for us. It's so good."

I blink at her. "Uh, one moment please," I tell her before walking over to lift my wife into my arms first. I brush the dirt and moss from her shoulders and back as I carry her toward the other girls. Her wings are as much of a mess as Elara's hair, and I don't dare try to sort those out on my own. I'm surprised to see them out in front of the other girls, but then I'm surprised to find her naked too.

"Doveling, why are you naked?" I ask as I work to clean her off.

Celeste ignores my question, beaming at me beatifically before giggling and telling me how handsome she thinks I am. She reaches out to pet my cheek with gentle pats.

"Oh! That's—*hic*—that's my fault," Sidney says, still with a hint of a slur to her words. "I got in a fight with this guy who was digging through Elara's trash."

Immediately on high alert, I hold my wife closer, pulling the darkness of the night to me and scanning the yard with my magic to feel for anyone who could be a danger to Celeste or my friends.

"It wasn't a *guy*. It was just a regular old raccoon," Elara puts in, clearly exasperated but still not concerned enough to look up from her work.

Finding no one in the yard but us, I release my magic and stare at the two of them, completely lost.

Sidney is undeterred. "Well, I could have sworn it was a shifter—"

"I told you it was a regular raccoon. I can *feel* people's magic, Sidney. You *know* this," Elara interjects huffily.

Sidney continues cheerfully without missing a beat, "—but it really was just a regular raccoon! *Anyway*, it got a hold of my leg and wouldn't let go, so I shifted forms to get away from it, right? And then, obviously, I was naked when I shifted back," she says, gesturing to her entirely nude body. "But then the raccoon ran off with my clothes, and it was too much trouble to chase him down."

I narrow my eyes at Sidney. How much has she had to drink that she was unable to catch a raccoon carrying clothes? Or fight one off, for that matter? I've heard stories from Jordan of her taking down grown male trolls. And what does this have to do with *my wife's* nakedness? "And Celeste...?" I prompt when it becomes clear she isn't planning on further explaining.

She finally remembers the point of her story, saying, "Right, so Celeste didn't want me to feel bad about being the only one who was naked, and so she took off her clothes, too."

Elara gives a sleepy yawn before having mercy on me and filling in more of the gaps. "I tried to tell her Sid is always naked, but she was convinced Sidney was sad about it."

"Sad about... what?" I'm having trouble following this story as I scan the ground around them for Celeste's clothing, especially since Celeste is beginning to press kisses to my face and tangle her fingers in my hair. "Where are her clothes?"

"I told you, *the raccoon took them*," Sidney responds, as if I'm the stupid one. And perhaps I am. Everyone else seems entirely unconcerned about the situation.

"I like margaritas," Celeste tells me with a happy grin.

"I—I'm glad," I tell her, surprised enough by her statement to smile back at her.

"Oh, my god," Sidney breathes. "I didn't know he could do that."

I shake off my distraction, returning my attention to Sidney. "Where are Jordan and Levi?" I ask. Celeste's clothes are nowhere to be found, so I shift gears to try to get all the girls inside. This is chaos. Just *talking* to them feels like herding cats.

"Levi's on kid duty," Elara mutters. She appears to be *sewing* the strange mushroom creature into its outfit.

"Pretty sure my brothers kidnapped Jordan," Sidney states, holding the bottle of booze up to her eye and peering down into the spout to see how much is left inside. The bottle is clear.

"But he would have had to go willingly, because even the three of them combined would have trouble carrying off a vampire, I think."

I release a long sigh and do my best to ignore Celeste's giggles as she nuzzles her nose against my neck. "Sidney, I'm going to help you up," I tell her, shifting Celeste's weight to one arm and reaching out to pinch Sidney gingerly by the elbow.

"Why?" she asks, suddenly suspicious for no reason I can discern.

"I think it's time everyone heads inside." They all need water, maybe some aspirin. Definitely a bath, but they'll have to figure that part out on their own—at least in Elara and Sidney's case.

"I don't need help. I'm like a ninja," Sidney announces, rocketing to her feet with only a slight wobble.

"Don't step on the mushrooms!" Elara shouts at her. "I've only got five more stitches left, hold on," she says. I glance down to find her concentrating on her task with the tip of her tongue pressed between her teeth.

"Grim, listen," Sidney says, pointing a vaguely accusing finger at me and listing forward alarmingly. "Celeste told me about this former friend of hers. Apollo or whatever. Sounds like a douche." She over-corrects her stance and sways backward, stumbling where she stands. "And this is *totally* unrelated, but next time you go to Faery to visit with her family, I want to come with you."

I'm not sure how to make that happen, or if it's even allowed, but I will consider it.

Elara finally places the newly outfitted mushroom back on the ground and pats some loose soil around its tiny, hair-like roots. "Okay, I'm ready," she says as she stands. At least she has the presence of mind to dust the dirt from her behind, but I don't want to be *anywhere* in the vicinity when she catches a glimpse of her hair in a mirror. I start to direct the two of them back toward Elara's house while I carry Celeste, though I have to take Sidney by the elbow again to help guide her around a clump of mushrooms they've planted when she gets too close.

"Also unrelated," Sidney continues, holding one finger up at me again. "How many of those plastic pink flamingos from the Void do you think we could fit into a wraith-drawn carriage? Like ten? Maybe more? Do the guards check the contents of a princess's carriage at the Gate into Faery? Also, Jordan wants to know if he has to give up playing Peach whenever you guys play SmashBros or if Celeste gets automatic dibs now. I told him that just because she's a real princess doesn't mean she gets to call dibs on Princess Peach, but he said to ask you."

Something strange bubbles up inside of me, and the sound that comes out is unmistakably a bark of laughter. These women are chaos, but they're a lovely sort of chaos. Celeste is drowsing against my chest, but she's startled awake by my laugh and gives me a dazed kind of smile. Elara and Sidney both stumble to a stop, turning bewildered smiles on me as well.

I tell Sidney with mock solemnity, "I'm sure if he asks nicely, she'll be willing to share Peach with him." I open the door and hold it as I wait for them to enter the house, and then carry Celeste inside and, happily, into the rest of our eternity.

*

Want more of the Boundlands crew? Keep reading for more stories set in this world!

Green-Eyed Monster

He's an orc studying for his accounting exam. She's a forest faerie trying to salvage her botany project. There's a magically animated stone sentry crashing through campus like a two-story tall wrecking ball.

The first time Hyrak lays eyes on Solandis, he's too immersed in the chaos around them to notice her soft beauty, but once she's in his arms, he's enchanted by the opinionated little fae's passion. Can gentle Hyrak control the fiery possession scorching through his veins? Does Solandis really want him to?

GREEN-EYED MONSTER is a short (10K word), fun Fantasy Romance with a guaranteed HEA. Content warnings include adult language and consenting adult romantic scenes.

Get a free copy when you sign up for my newsletter at elsiewinters.com!

Leviathan's Song

When Elara races to save a dying city, her best hope lies with a seductive siren... but brooding Levi has his own reasons for keeping her at arm's length.

As an elven weapon smith, Elara is an expert in crafting beautiful, deadly things. When an underwater city known as the Deep sends for her help, she's determined to answer the call... but between murderous gangsters and razor-sharp foreign politics, Elara is ill-equipped to handle the situation on her own.

Levi Navarre is half-merman and all brooding, sardonic wit. Landlocked, jaded, and rejected by his people, the last thing Levi wants to do is get involved in underwater affairs. But soft-hearted, strong-willed Elara is a temptation he just can't resist... even if she is several miles out of his league. Levi has good reason to avoid the obvious magical bond forming between him and Elara—but if he isn't careful, playing bodyguard could soon turn into something more...

LEVIATHAN'S SONG is a slow-burn paranormal romance about a girl caught between multiple magical factions and the mysterious merman she longs for.

Available Now

Magpies & Mayhem

What happens when you stumble upon your childhood crush, only to discover that he's been turned into a vampire?

I feel like I spend my whole life putting out fires. That's probably just part of the territory with being a magpie-shifter from such a chaotic family. All I want is to keep my loved ones safe and have some fun. I've never been cut out to be the responsible one.

And Jordan Houjin is still everything I remember ... hot, sexy arrogance and smoldering smart mouth. Except now he's angry at the world and disappears every time I run into him. But that's fine because I want nothing to do with a vampire my family would never accept anyway. Don't I?

Unfortunately, he's the only one I know who can help me keep this dragon egg alive.

Available Now

Also By Elsie Winters

Green-Eyed Monster

Leviathan's Song

Magpies & Mayhem

Seduction of a Psychopomp

Acknowledgements

I'm eternally grateful to everyone who helps me bring my books to life. I want to thank Susan R, SL Prater, Erin Vere, Colleen Cowley, Lisette Marshall, and Vela Roth for all of their time, logistical help, and emotional support with each book I write.

Amira Naval painted my lovely cover. Leigha Wolffe-Stoirm provided invaluable edits and kindly hid all my grammar sins.

About the Author

Elsie Winters writes sweet, cozy comfort reads with a dash of spice and a dollop of fantasy. Her favorite pastimes are feeding the birds who knock on her window for snacks and spending way too much money on plants. She also reads paranormal romance books like they're going out of style and collects monster art that she has to hide from her kids.

Never miss a story! Check out my website to sign up for my newsletter or follow me on social media!

Contact info:
www.elsiewinters.com
elsie@elsiewinters.com